Styles of Political Action
in America

Styles of Political Action in America

Edited with
Introductions by

Robert Paul Wolff

University of Massachusetts, Amherst

Random House · New York

ISBN: 0-394-31648-7
Library of Congress Catalog Card Number: 77-156339
Manufactured in the United States of America.
Composed by Cherry Hill Composition, Pennsauken, New Jersey.
Printed and bound by Halliday Lithograph, Inc.,
West Hanover, Mass.

First Edition
987654321

Photo Credits:
Part 1: Shelly Rusten
Parts 2 & 4: George Gardner
Part 3: Black Star (Franklynn Peterson)
Part 5: Magnum (Charles Harbutt)

Typography: Andrea Clark
Cover Design: Charles Schmalz
Cover Photo: Steve Wasserman

Acknowledgments

I should like to thank Miss Kathleen Merryman, whose energetic and imaginative assistance in the search for selections contributed greatly to the preparation of this book.

R.P.W.

Contents

Styles of Political Action
in America

Introduction

There is an old joke that goes something like this:

Grammar Problem: Decline the noun "politician."
        Answer: I am a statesman.
                You are a politician.
                He is a low-down crook.

Many of us, when we hear the word "politician," think of a fat man smoking a big cigar, wearing a derby, and making backroom deals with the mayor or the governor. In the movies of the 1930s, Edward Arnold used to play the part to perfection, complete with oily charm and a heart of pure stone. Even today, when we want to praise a man in public life, we say that he is "above politics."

Now, if "politics" means the wheeling and dealing of a big-city machine, then perhaps this low opinion of politicians is understandable, although there is actually something to be said in favor of the old machine bosses. But as soon as we broaden our notion of politics to include all the activities connected with electing, pressuring, influencing, advising, and running our local, state, and federal governments, we realize that the cigar-smoking Edward Arnold image won't do.

Who are the politicians in America today? Big-city bosses are politicians, but so are Southern senators, farm-belt congressmen, labor leaders, drug company lobbyists, and civil rights lawyers. Fat-cat campaign contributors are politicians, but so too are welfare protesters, striking auto workers, fundamentalist anticommunist crusaders, and ghetto mothers demanding quality schooling for their children.

The fact of the matter is that it is very hard to find an American who has not been a politician in *some* way or other at *some* time in his life! For young Americans, particularly, the important question is not whether to participate in the political life of our country but rather how to participate and in pursuit of what ends or goals.

The primary purpose of this book of readings is to give you some idea of the variety of ways in which you can become political in America today. Each selection presents a vivid portrait of a real, contemporary man or woman who has taken a particular road into the American political world. You will find accounts of revolutionaries and public officials, self-made men and Establishment figures, leaders and followers. The cast of characters is as diverse as the American scene itself, although it represents only a fraction of the entire repertory of political roles that our society offers. Indeed, for every style of political action illustrated here, you should be able to think of two that have been omitted. I will feel that the book has been a success if you put it down with a clearer idea of how and why you want to be political in America of the 1970s.

Why does a man or woman get into politics, anyway? The obvious answer is, to accomplish some goal—to get cleaner air or a subsidy for wheat, to increase Social Security benefits or change the pornography laws, to reduce property taxes or integrate the elementary schools.

There is much truth in this explanation, but it cannot be the whole truth, for it leaves too much unexplained. If I want to improve housing in the black ghetto of South Side Chicago, I can work for the election of a reform city government, apply for a job with the Department of Housing and Urban Development, get a law degree and donate my services to needy tenants, or start a rent strike. What determines which of these alternatives I will select?

To some extent, of course, a style of political action is chosen to fit the goal. Oilmen working for continuation of the depletion allowance in the tax law are hardly likely to organize street demonstrations! Nevertheless, most political goals can be pursued in a variety of ways, and so we must look to the subjective motives and personality of the individual if we are to develop a complete explanation for men's choices of political style.

These introductory remarks are hardly the place for a full-scale theory of political motivation (besides, I don't *have* a full-scale theory!), but I would like to offer a few suggestions that may help you to understand the subjective side of politics a bit better as you read this book.

Let me begin by laying to rest a very common misconception that turns up again and again in discussions of American politics. All of us use the metaphor of a left-center-right spectrum in our thinking about politics, and the almost universal tendency, at least in the United States, is to suppose that wisdom, truth, goodness, or virtue on any issue lies somewhere between the two extremes. As a result, we are always offering psychological explanations for the behavior of extremists while assuming that no particular explanation is required for the actions of moderates. A bomb-throwing member of the Weatherman faction of S.D.S. or an official of the John Birch Society is seen by many political commentators as some sort of queer duck who must have deep emotional problems underneath his political exterior. But a farm-belt congressman or an American Medical Association lobbyist is taken at face value, as a man simply doing a job.

The major thesis of this book is that every man and woman who participates in the American political process is motivated by subjective emotional needs, whether he aligns himself on the left, on the right, or in the middle of the political spectrum. Motives differ from individual to individual; they are shaped by upbringing, religion, geography, economic need, education, and a hundred other factors. But we cannot understand the political behavior of any man until we see the way his subjective needs interact with the objective social and political opportunities available to him.

To clarify this thesis a bit, let us ask ourselves what moves a man to run for public office. Certainly there are policies he wishes to implement, goals he hopes to achieve through the power of the office he seeks. But most candidates seem to enjoy the political process itself, regardless of the success of their program. Men like Richard Nixon, Edmund Muskie, John Lindsay, and Ronald Reagan *like* the endless round of speeches, handshaking, press conferences, and meetings. So too, at a less exalted level, do the men and women who run for mayor, state senator, or city councilman. Not all of us would get much pleasure from night after night of party conferences, committee meetings, talks to the local Kiwanis Club or League of Women Voters, but politicians do. Just as some people like working with their hands and others prefer the paper work of an office, so some Americans find elective politics personally rewarding.

Many of us have plunged for a brief time into electoral politics, moved by anger or fear or a deep belief in some political goal: the students who worked for Eugene McCarthy in 1968, the parents who have organized in many communities to fight sex education in the public schools, the antiwar protesters, the antipollution campaigners. Over and over again the same pattern is repeated. Many turn out, but few remain. When the excitement has died down, only the regulars are left to answer the telephones, run the Mimeograph machines, and carry on the daily work of politics. The fact is that under normal conditions, when we are not driven by economic suffering or severe injustice to seek redress in the political arena, most of us simply don't enjoy the bread-and-butter activities of organized politics.

An old French proverb says, "To understand all is to forgive all." In these days of psychological debunking, we appear to have turned the proverb upside down: "To understand all is to condemn all." When we point to the emotional roots of a man's behavior, it may seem as though we are trivializing him, making him look smaller or less serious. But this is a complete misunderstanding of the purpose of psychological explanation. We do not diminish the greatness of Dr. Martin Luther King, Jr., by pointing out that his espousal of nonviolence was in part an attempt to deal with the powerful anger and hostility which he felt. Nor do we take so much as an inch from Robert Kennedy's stature if we recognize the connection between his remarkable ability to sympathize with the downtrodden and outcast of American society, on the one hand, and his position in the Kennedy family, overshadowed by his two older brothers, on the other. Every person who accomplishes great things in the world must draw strength and solace from some inner source; it can only heighten our appreciation of political achievements to understand their emotional roots.

From the endless variety of motivational patterns that underlie political behavior, I should like to single out two—or, more precisely, two *pairs*—for special attention in this introduction. Let me label these "the rebellious son versus the dutiful son" and "the professional versus the amateur."

The elemental patterns of family relationships are the most deeply rooted in us all, for we learn them as infants and make them a part of our innermost selves. Mother, father, son, daughter, sister, brother, grandfather, grandmother—these are the roles we enact and reenact throughout our lives. We constantly think of political and institutional relationships in familial terms. A king or president is the "father" of his people. An administrator who protects his subordinates is a "mother hen." A close-knit fighting group thinks of itself as a "band of brothers." Wise old public figures are "grandfatherly." We even extend this to nations, as when we speak of "Mother Russia" or "the Fatherland."

In the repertory of political roles modeled on familial relationships, the roles of the dutiful son and rebellious son crop up repeatedly. We are all familiar with the roles in private life. There are some young men who seem to fall in naturally and comfortably with the desires, plans, standards, and expectations of their elders. They go into their fathers' businesses or run the family farm. They become the doctors or lawyers or professors that their parents always dreamed they would be. They marry eminently acceptable wives and live in the right part of town. They tend to look and dress older than they are; they listen respectfully to the opinions of older men; they are said to be "good boys," "sound," "promising." They remember family anniversaries and come home to visit regularly. Mothers fortunate enough to have such sons are secretly envied by those who do not.

Young men of this type identify themselves with the authority and position of their fathers. More generally, they identify with the authority of their fathers' generation. They see the older, established men in charge as a group to be joined, not as an enemy to be challenged. In politics these dutiful sons tend to adopt moderate, "sound," acceptable positions on public issues (whether on the Democratic or the Republican side). They enter politics by submitting to the authority of their elders, not by attacking it. Typically, such men may start as assistants to men already established or as junior functionaries in a large political machine. In this book the essay on Senator Charles Percy of Illinois describes him in precisely these terms. Percy was, in fact, the hand-picked heir of a man already established as the president of the Bell & Howell Company.

A dutiful son may sincerely believe in the policies and principles of the older men with whom he associates himself, needless to say. After all, the older men (and institutions) in the public world represent a wide diversity of political orientations, and a young man can pick and choose among them. But it should be clear that a young man will not choose this particular path into the political world unless some inner need is satisfied by the chance to play the role of dutiful son.

Sharply contrasting with the dutiful son is the rebellious son, and we hardly need to spend much time characterizing *him* in this Age of Aquarius! The rebellious son is an irritation to his father and a torment to his mother. He rejects the dress, the manners, and the style of his parents. He pursues an idiosyncratic career (or no career at all), he dates "unacceptable" girls, and he openly defies the wishes—indeed the commands—of his father.

The rebellious son sees the power of the old men as an outrage; he sees their authority as a challenge, a gauntlet thrown down which must be picked up. He dreams not of being welcomed into the board room or executive suite but of storming it with a band of brothers. Whereas his dutiful brother hurries to look "mature" before his time, the rebellious son prolongs his youth, fearing the day when age, parenthood, and even (alas!) success will turn him into that most hated of all figures, a father.

American politics is alive with rebellious sons who reenact in the public arena the drama of the challenge to the father: rebel priests in the Catholic Church, dissident GIs running coffee houses, reform candidates challenging the machine, crusading lawyers out to cut the big corporations down to size, students who seize campus buildings and seat themselves ceremoniously in the president's chair. Over and over, the pattern reappears. An established institution, run by a group of men in

their fifties or sixties, is attacked by rebellious sons as tyrannical, unjust, repressive, stagnant, unresponsive to the needs and
desires of those it rules. A challenge is mounted and the
demand is issued that the young men be given the reins of
power. Sometimes the challenge is met head-on and beaten
down; sometimes the challenge succeeds, and the rebels
become the Establishment. Most often, the old men yield a bit
in an attempt to maintain their authority while accommodating ⌐
the demands of the rebels. One of the most striking features of
this familiar pattern is its inward-looking, or family, character.
The rebellious sons always challenge their own institutional
fathers—students challenge deans, young priests challenge
bishops, interns challenge senior doctors.

I have been arguing that subjective, personal factors relating
to family roles and patterns affect a young man's choice of
political style, but you mustn't suppose that a person's *actual
politics* are simply a reflection of childhood experiences. In this
book the selections on the Berrigan brothers and Roger Baldwin
provide an effective contrast. Daniel and Philip Berrigan are
probably the two greatest thorns in the side of the American
Catholic Church today. They are rebellious sons in the classic
mold (even though, as priests, they are both called "father"!).
Roger Baldwin is the grand old man of the civil liberties movement—founder of the American Civil Liberties Union, lifelong
champion of unpopular causes—at one and the same time a
dutiful son, an Establishment figure, and a great dissenter.
Baldwin and the Berrigans show us that very similar policies
can be pursued in utterly divergent styles.

It should also be noted that a rebellious son need not remain
a rebellious son (especially if he finally accedes to power himself). In addition, a rebellious son may serve as a father figure.
Many great revolutionary leaders have been essentially father
figures to their followers. Lenin and Mao are obvious examples.
In our own society the socialist leader Norman Thomas, the
migrant workers' organizer Cesar Chavez, and of course George
Washington have played father roles while attacking established
authority.

An even more fundamental contrast in styles of political
action (as opposed to political goals or principles) than the

contrast between left and right or between dutiful sons and rebellious sons is the contrast between the professional and the amateur. Now, in sports, a pro is someone who plays the game for money; an amateur (theoretically) plays for glory, or fun, or some other nonmaterial reward. The same distinction can, of course, be drawn in public life, for some men and women make their living from politics while others engage in political action as an avocation. But I have in mind a slightly different distinction from that one. When I speak of a professional in politics, I mean a man or woman whose primary commitment is to the political process itself rather than to some particular issue. Let me try to clarify the distinction with an analogy. All of us travel (by car or plane or boat) when we want to get to a particular place, but some people travel just because they like traveling. Give them a vacation and off they go, to Europe or the Rockies or the Orient. We might call them professional travelers, not in the sense that they make their living that way (as a traveling salesman does), but in the sense that traveling itself is for them an exciting, worthwhile activity.

Politics is to the professional politician what travel is to the professional traveler. A political pro has goals, of course, but if he achieves them, he doesn't drop out of politics (any more than the professional traveler quits traveling once he arrives at his destination). Instead, he sets new goals, finds new issues, takes up new causes. By contrast, the political amateur gets into politics the way the amateur traveler gets into travel—for the specific purpose of achieving a particular end. Once he succeeds (or decisively fails), he retires from the political arena, leaving it to the other amateurs still pursuing their goals and, of course, to the pros.

The obvious place to look for political pros is in the halls of government and in the ranks of the political machines. Most senators and congressmen are professional politicians who remain active in the political process as much out of a liking for politics as out of a devotion to some cause. When new issues arise, such as race relations or disarmament or pollution, the pros adopt a position and go right on running for office. If strong antipollution legislation is enacted, the environmentalists will retire from the arena; their battle will be won. But a senator who runs on an antipollution platform won't resign his seat after the bill is passed. He will look around for another issue—gun controls or textile tariffs, say—and run again.

The same thing is true of the thousands of party regulars who staff the organization headquarters. They work for the party's candidate, and if he is defeated, they work for next year's candidate. For them, politics is a way of life, not merely a means for achieving specific goals. Like the professional traveler, they set out on a new journey as soon as the old one is completed.

Now it goes without saying that most professional politicians have commitments to issues and principles that limit the sorts of political activity they will undertake. A liberal senator may take up pollution when disarmament slips into the background as a subject of public concern, but he will not merely adopt whatever position he thinks will win votes. So, too, a political speech writer may go to work for Spiro Agnew after Barry Goldwater disbands his campaign staff, but he isn't very likely to turn up on Ted Kennedy's team after he leaves Agnew's employ. What marks a man as a political pro is not a lack of principle but a commitment to the activity of politics itself as an ongoing succession of struggles over many issues and principles.

American politics is, by and large, a politics of coalition and compromise. Each of the major parties reaches out to embrace the widest possible spectrum of opinions in its attempt to put together a majority coalition in Congress and a victorious presidential ticket. Each candidate for office is under great pressure to achieve the same breadth, for if he defines his position too narrowly, his opponent is liable to gather up a winning combination of voting blocs. In order to be a successful political pro—in order, that is, to stay in the political process, win elections, and rise to a position of importance—a man must be temperamentally capable of the flexibility, accommodation, and compromise required to forge many diverse and even antagonistic groups into a majority combination. This generalization is true throughout American political life, not merely in electoral politics. If we look at those who run labor unions, universities, professional associations, or fraternal organizations, we see the same pattern. The men at the top are the political pros who have worked their way up, adjusting to the competing pressures, seizing on issues as they become popular and dropping them when there is no more mileage to be got from them.

Now it is a fundamental law of psychology, as it is of zoology, that the leopard cannot change his spots. There is no point in demanding that a dutiful son act rebelliously or that a wheeler-dealer suddenly become a dramatic charismatic leader. By the same token, there is no reason to hope that men who have risen to the top of the American political system by their ability to adjust to the shifting winds of opinion will suddenly "get religion" and become single-issue, do-or-die political amateurs, ready to sacrifice their careers for one great victory.

Students in America frequently feel betrayed by the political leader on whom they pin their hopes. The McCarthy supporters were let down by their hero's unleaderlike behavior after the 1968 primary campaign. Young conservatives, who pinned their hopes for a time on Barry Goldwater, finally grew disgruntled with what they felt to be his temporizing with the moderate Republican Establishment. Richard Nixon, Adlai Stevenson, John Kennedy, and Robert Kennedy all disappointed their political-amateur followers. So, too, did Martin Luther King, Jr., Walter Reuther, and Roy Wilkins. An understanding of the difference between professional and amateur politicians together with a grasp of the workings of the American political system would have saved the followers from being disappointed.

These brief remarks on dutiful and rebellious sons and political pros and amateurs merely suggest the complexity of styles of political action in America today. As you read the selections in this book, you will encounter many other patterns and styles. Naturally, I hope that your theoretical understanding of politics will be increased thereby, but that is not my principal concern. It is far more important that you clarify your own goals, purposes, and subjective motivation so that you can select a style of political action that suits you.

Revolutionaries

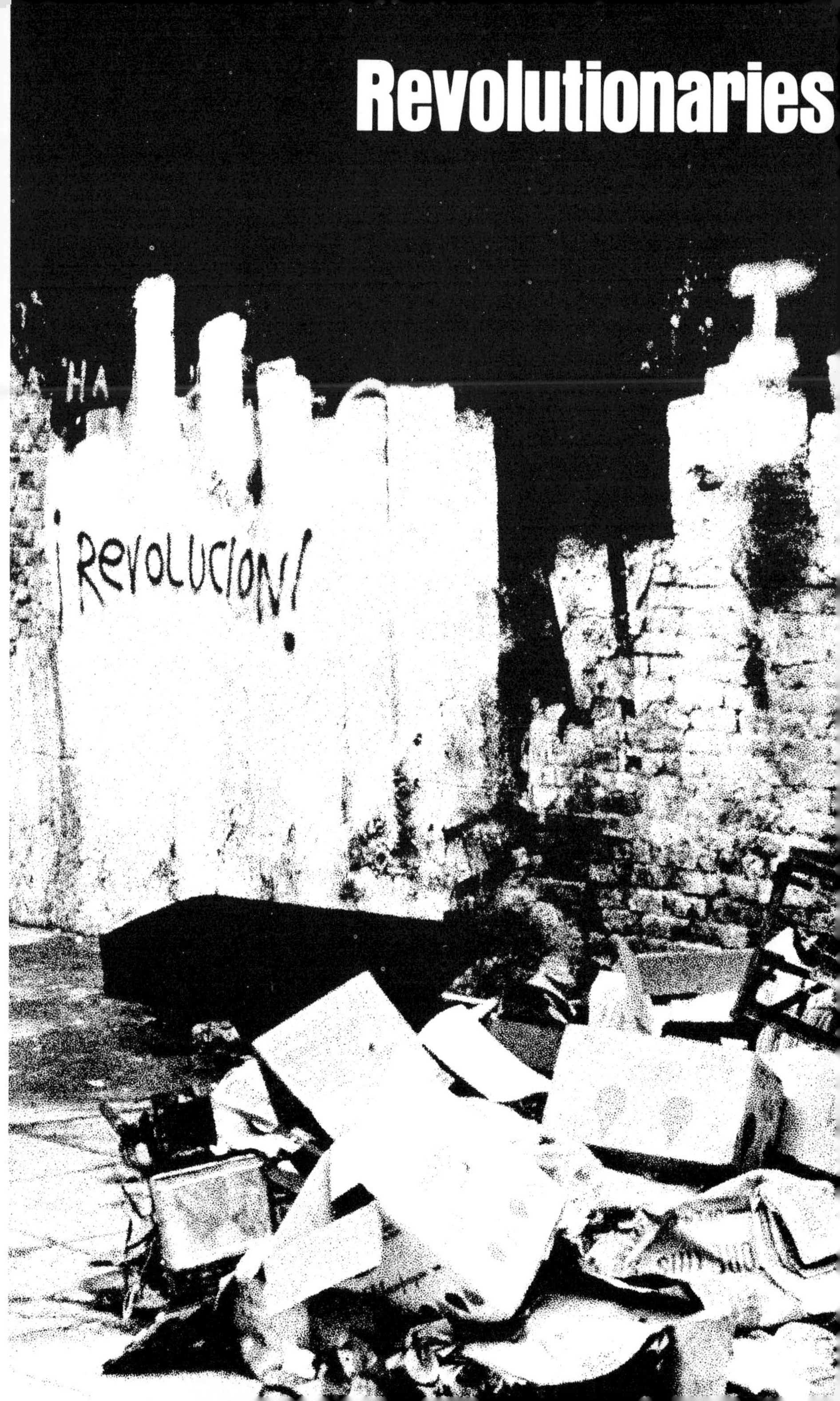

We begin with portraits of four American revolutionaries: men who seek radical change in America's political, social, and economic institutions and who are ready to break the law to achieve their ends. The four men portrayed in these selections come from backgrounds as diverse as American society itself. Ted Gold was a white, middle-class Jewish student; the Berrigan brothers are white, working-class Catholic priests; Eldridge Cleaver is a product of the black ghetto. As I write this introduction, the first is dead of a bomb explosion, the second and third are under indictment for an alleged plot to kidnap a presidential advisor, and the fourth is in exile in Algeria. Yet, despite the diversity of their origins and their fates, these four men represent a single, coherent view of American society. All four agree that our country (and theirs) is racist, imperialist, exploitative, and repressive. All four agree that modest adjustments, reforms, and institutional revisions are utterly inadequate as solutions to America's social ills. All four speak to the poor, the outcast, the powerless in American society, although of the four, only Eldridge Cleaver can claim to have come from the American underclass.

What makes a man take arms against his own government and society? Why have these four and growing numbers like them rejected the established political and legal processes of the United States, opting instead for action outside the law? Political observers offer two opposite explanations, neither of which seems to me to fit the facts adequately.

One school of political analysis tells us that revolutionaries are emotionally disturbed people who act out their violent and rebellious fantasies in the public world. Bomb throwers, assassins, draft-card burners, and campus rebels are psychologically deranged according to this view, and we must look to the details of their personal lives for an understanding of their behavior.

An opposed school of thought argues that revolutionaries are made by objective social conditions, not by the accidents of subjective psychological factors. It is racist institutions, economic exploitation, a bloody and unjust war that provoke men to fight against their government. And it is the unresponsiveness of the political system that drives decent men to violent and extralegal courses of action.

Neither of these explanations is satisfactory as it stands because neither can account completely for the obvious facts of revolutionary activity. Consider first the subjective, or psychological, theory. If it is correct, then there ought to be a fairly constant level of terrorist and revolutionary violence in all industrial societies, since they all have emotionally disturbed segments of their populations. But the facts are exactly contrary. England has little or no such political violence now, even though Ireland is experiencing a great deal. France is relatively stable today (1970), but several years ago she was wracked by massive student uprisings, and fifteen years ago she almost succumbed to a military insurrection on the right. In America bombings and assassinations are a phenomenon of the 1960s and early 1970s, not of the 1940s and 1950s.

It seems obvious that objective social, economic, and political conditions play a major role in determining the existence and intensity of revolutionary activity. But the objective explanation by itself is not sufficient either, for it fails to account for the fact that under any circumstances whatsoever, only *some* men and women become revolutionaries. Even if we grant that Ted Gold, Daniel and Philip Berrigan, and Eldridge Cleaver were driven to violent or extralegal struggle by the injustice of American society and the intransigence of the established political order, we still want to know why these four men took the course they did while so many others like them remained politically orthodox or even politically inactive. There are students like Ted Gold, priests like the Berrigans, convicts like Eldridge Cleaver. What differences in their experiences, in their family backgrounds, indeed even in their genes, set them on their revolutionary paths?

I don't know. Nor does anyone know, although psychiatrists, historians, and novelists have given us considerable insight into the emotional roots of revolutionary politics. As you read about these four men, try to imagine yourself inside each of them. Would you react as they did to the experiences in their lives? What would it take to turn you against American society? Could anything persuade you to set a bomb or attempt an assassination?

1. Ted Gold:
A White, Middle-Class Bomb Thrower

"Ted Gold: Education for Violence"

by J. KIRK SALE

A sign in a store on 8th Street in Greenwich Village says: "Ted Gold died for our sins." On the wall of a building near Columbia University someone has scrawled: "Ted Gold Lives." And at the base of a flagpole on the Columbia campus, students who tried to lower the flag to half-staff wrote, in crayon: "In Memory of Ted Gold. Fight Like Him."

Ted Gold's death, in a Greenwich Village town house explosion on March 6 [1970] was heavy with symbolism. He was suffocated in the fancy paneled walls of an incredibly luxurious building worth, in these inflated times, some $250,000. Its owner was a man who made much of his fortune as an advertising executive for Young & Rubicam, who was a frequent defender of the role of advertising in the American system, and who put his money into commercial radio systems in the American heartland.

The explosion was probably caused by dynamite, that roman-

Reprinted from J. Kirk Sale, "Ted Gold: Education for Violence," *The Nation*, April 13, 1970, pp. 423–429, by permission of author and publisher.

tic 19th-century revolutionary weapon. And at the time of his death Ted Gold may have been seated at a desk, working on a history of Students for a Democratic Society that he was reputed to have been researching, probing the roots of the New Left, and determining how it had come so far in such a few years.

The details of what happened in this tragic explosion are still murky. But it does seem clear that those in the house were Weathermen, a splinter group so far down the road of violence from the rest of the old SDS that it no longer even thinks of itself by those initials, and is indeed composed mostly of people who are not students and scorn the notion of a "democratic" society. They had a sizable stockpile of explosives in the house— probably 100 sticks of dynamite, some packed into 12-inch lead-pipe bombs, and others into tape-wrapped packages; plus detonating caps, wires and cheap alarm clocks for timers—and were probably planning their imminent use. At least three people died: Gold; a Weatherwoman, Diana Oughton; and a second man as yet unidentified.

.   .   .

To understand this rage-turned-to-revolution it may help to focus on Ted Gold, who believed in it. There are hazards, of course. Gold was only one man, and such concentration can make more of him than we should. He was not, by the usual yardsticks, a major leader of the Weathermen, nor in any sense a "typical" member. There is no special pattern to his life that sets him apart from his comrades, and even his death was an accident of the sort that can exaggerate a humble man into a hero. The lens too narrowly focused on Ted Gold causes the edges to blur, making unclear the larger issues. . . . [Nevertheless,] by the vagaries of history, even instant history, Ted Gold has become a signal figure.

Theodore Gold was born in New York City on December 13, 1947, into a milieu that is by now almost predictable for contemporary activists. He was an only child. His parents were liberals of the upper West Side Jewish variety, living in a pleasant apartment on tree-lined 93rd Street, comfortably well-off if not exactly rich. His father, Dr. Hyman Gold, an internist in a Health Insurance Plan clinic and a volunteer emergency doctor for an East Side day-care center, is regarded as having an evident concern for bringing medicine to the poor. His mother, Dr. Ruth Gold, is an associate professor of education at Columbia University's Teachers College. Most sociological studies suggest that activist youth come from just this kind of background, where both parents work and the dinner table ideas are likely to be at least liberal. What they don't go on to say is that when both parents are away all day and the child is raised by a black maid, as in Ted Gold's case, the resulting psychological dislocations may be as great an impetus to radicalism. In fact one might even imagine that part of the attraction of a close-knit, intimate group—as were those formed during the Columbia confrontation of 1968 and as are the Weathermen collectives and "affinity groups"—stems from family deprivation in early life.

At high school, Gold was so ordinary as to make him almost invisible. He was very bright and very normal. His teachers, if they remember anything, recall a "bright-eyed" or "attentive" or "very smart" boy, but for the most part they agree with his high school biology teacher, Mrs. Elektra Demas, that "there was nothing really to distinguish him from the other boys." At Manhattan's top-level Stuyvesant High, he did well in all his courses (graduating 212th in a class of 699, with an 89 average), was a member of the Stamp Club and the History and Folklore Society, and ran on the track and cross-country teams. "All in all," says Stuyvesant Principal Leonard Fliedner, "he was the kind of boy you like to have around a school, the kind you'd want your own son to be like."

There are some suggestions of a burgeoning political sense even in these days. He was involved in civil rights work, largely through the Friends of SNCC, a Northern group composed mostly of students, which raised money and food for civil rights workers in the South, and whose Stuyvesant chapter Gold helped organize. And he went, for a couple of years at least, to Camp Webatuck, in Wingdale, N.Y., one of those "leftist" camps that serve Left-liberal New York: labor songs, unstructured hours, muted Marxist rhetoric, involved kids. During the summer of 1963, one old friend remembers, Gold was "already very pro-Cuba—and therefore somewhat, you know, bitter about Kennedy—and already upset about American involvement in Vietnam"—plus being "an outasight third baseman."

Still all this was within what another friend calls "acceptable student activism." In his first two years at Columbia, Gold was quiet, intellectual and unobtrusive; his concern took the form of work with CORE and a summertime slum-tutorial group. He spoke vaguely about going to law school to become a poor people's lawyer, or about concentrating in urban studies. One of his freshman teachers noted at the time that he was "quiet but had convictions."

Gradually Gold gravitated to a few like-minded students who in the spring of 1966 were restarting an intermittent SDS chapter, and early in 1967, his junior year, he became vice-chairman of the chapter. That fall he had his first taste of activism when New York SDS demonstrated in the streets against Dean Rusk —the first time, on the East Coast at least, that students had initiated violence rather than waiting to be clubbed. Gold was arrested and charged with rioting, a misdemeanor for which he was not even fingerprinted—so that, when his body was found in the town house, New York police were unable to make an identification and had to send to the FBI in Washington for his prints. (The FBI had a set, taken when Gold was arrested along with seven other Weathermen, for vandalizing a Philadelphia television station last January 10, after it broadcast what they called a "slanderous" TV documentary on the Black Panthers.)

Gold's politics began the turn toward revolution during the Columbia uprising in the spring of 1968, an affair that, in retrospect, illuminates some of his major characteristics.

First, he was a bright, intellectual, behind-the-scenes man ("quiet and reserved," says a friend) who, when possible, left the stage to more excitable grandstanders like Mark Rudd. He was, according to a student at the time, "one of the few people who really had *read* all that Marx and Lenin that they all quoted," and was one of a small group whose researches in 1967 had originally exposed Columbia's ties to the Institute for Defense Analysis. He was also a member of a moderate wing of Columbia SDS called the "praxis axis," which emphasized research and winning adherents by education and persuasion, as opposed to the "action faction," which emphasized confrontation and overt demonstrations as the best way to win follow-ers. This latter wing, led by Rudd, Nick Freudenberg and John Jacobs, won out in the March 1968 chapter elections and dominated much of the subsequent action.

Gold, however, never tried to bolt the organization or work outside it. For a second characteristic was that, though schol-arly, he never felt wholly comfortable with that role alone. He was one of the first on campus to affect proletarian blue shirts, and was obviously attracted to action-minded types. At times he tried to join them on the platform, and on several occasions during the uprising gave speeches to hold crowds together or encourage bystanders to join, though without noticeable suc-cess. (Once, before addressing a crowd, he turned to a friend and confessed, "I don't know what's happening," not realizing his bull horn amplifier was turned on.)

Originally in separate wings, Gold and Rudd nonetheless worked together throughout the Columbia battle, spent the next year in fairly close association around the New York SDS office, and finally went together into the Weathermen. But Gold never really liked Rudd, it would seem, or at least resented his style. Dotson Rader, one of the Columbia strikers and author of a very revealing account of New Left activism, *I Ain't Marchin' Any-more,* remembers that during the take-overs Gold "felt that Rudd was trying to establish a personality cult. He said one night he thought Rudd was grandstanding too much and wasn't directly involved with the building communes and what people were thinking." Still, Gold—short, bespectacled, quiet, intel-lectual, controlled—must have found something enormously appealing in Rudd—tall, loose, attractive, outgoing, reckless. It is easy to imagine that Rudd and the other actionists were very important to Gold. At Columbia (and after) they were contin-ually talking about the need for courage, for "putting your body on the line," for shaking off "bourgeois hangups" about violence and death, for ceasing to be "wimps." During the confrontations (and after) Gold, the quiet intellectual, moved steadily toward their camp.

Gold made what may have been a last break with standard liberalism during the Columbia fracas. He was apparently ter-ribly embittered by what he regarded as a liberal sellout by the

Ad Hoc Faculty Committee, with whom he was one of the chief student negotiators. As he later put it to the authors of *Up Against the Ivy Wall,* a history of the Columbia crisis:

> They were demanding complete abdication of our position, and we were talking in terms of their joining us. We were miles apart. But we didn't want to break off discussion. We were told that they were a more "liberal" group. We said, "All right, if you're on our side, then take a position in favor of amnesty and the other six demands." Those s.o.b.'s said that we should be more reasonable.

It is characteristic of student radicals that they feel betrayed and angered when they are confronted at first hand with the shoddiness and failure of those liberal institutions which they had once regarded as sacrosanct. Hence their particular dislike of Kennedy, Stevenson, Goldberg, Humphrey and the like.

Finally, the Columbia affair showed that Ted Gold had come to some understanding of the place of violence in society and its use as a political weapon. As early as April, in a letter to President Grayson Kirk that Gold helped draft, the SDS leaders said: "Until Columbia ends all affiliation with the IDA, we must disrupt the functioning of all those involved in the daily disruption of people's lives around the world." (Or, as the Weathermen were to put it eighteen months later in their Chicago action: "Bring the War Home.") Later, Gold recalled, "We didn't want a police bust, but we would rather have had that than give in to the administration." And the feeling of the eleven-man strike committee, of which Gold was a member, seemed to be that a bust, if it came, would be advantageous to the striking students, would lead to the kind of radicalization it indeed produced. In the heat of battle, in short, Gold accepted the need for violence.

The entire Columbia experience, in fact, was a test of personal courage in the face of violence, or threatened violence, and that must have left a mark. Perhaps even without so planning, the SDS students put themselves into situation after situation in which their courage would be on the line—taking buildings, refusing to leave after warnings, locking arms in the face of moving policemen. At first so unaccustomed to all this as to be terrified of the guns that the blacks were reported to have brought with them into a seized building, the SDSers by the end were steeled to it.

Ted Gold was suspended for a year by Columbia for his role in the occupations, though he had completed all his course work, and with a solid B average. That summer he began to organize a Teachers for a Democratic Society, part of a loose Movement for a Democratic Society that was forming in New York of SDSers who had graduated from college and wanted to continue their activism. . . .

TDS was Gold's last organized attempt to work through education and (however militant) persuasion. He was "an incredibly hard worker" and ran "the neatest office I've ever seen in the movement," says one who worked with him for a while that year. Not surprisingly he was one of the half dozen leaders of the organization. The thrust was toward organizing high school youth, an effort that seemed to have some success, especially in an atmosphere made electric by the teachers' strike that fall. . . .

But ultimately the TDS effort failed. The high school kids in effect resented the attempt by "outside agitators" to radicalize them, and once the strike was settled the air began to cool. Gold, according to some who were around him then, became more and more rigid, less and less inclined to trying to "change heads." "He had no patience for anyone not at the same level of consciousness," says one young man. "If you said something he didn't agree with, he'd say 'Bullshit' and walk away. He became terribly autocratic—he was *hell* to deal with." Rudd, who was also in New York directing the SDS regional office, took an I-told-you-so line—he had never been convinced that there was any way to radicalize students other than direct action—and for a while the two were somewhat estranged. Gradually, however, Gold seems to have been won around to the actionists' conviction that winning hearts and minds is perhaps best done by twisting arms.

By the end of the school year Gold had apparently made the break . . . . and though Columbia allowed him to get his degree after wresting from him a promise to behave, he apparently went through with it largely to please his mother. The stage was set for the SDS June convention.

At that convention, everyone knew that SDS was going to split. The Progressive Labor Party, an outgrowth of the left wing of the Communist Party, had successfully infiltrated SDS ranks and now planned to take over its national office. The national office people, with whom the ex-Columbia radicals were aligned, hoped to beat them down or force them out. When the test came, the PLers were in the majority, the national office followers split off into their own convention, and there the action wing, the Weathermen, was born.

The Weatherman line is complicated and has shifted over this past year to take account of different actions—and reactions. But basically the group is made up of those who feel that the only way to change this country is through violent confrontation: "The primary purpose, and the stance, of our organizing," writes Shin'ya Ono, "could not possibly be to 'turn people on,' or to have them like us, or to make them think that we are nice, but to compel them to confront the antagonistic aspects of their own life experience and consciousness by bringing the war home, and to help them make the right choice over a period of time, after initially shaking up and breaking through the thick layers of chauvinism-racism-defeatism." In other words, if you put people up against the wall, force them to choose, sooner or later they'll have to be either for the revolution or for the system.

Gold was a Weatherman from the start, though, characteristically, on its more moderate flank. ("If Gold was a member of some nihilist group, the farthest Left thing you could be," comments Dotson Rader, "he'd find some way of being on the moderate side of it: that was his nature.") And, as at Columbia, he seems to have been continually pressed—as indeed the whole group was, and deliberately—to prove himself. One young observer recalls: "Rudd continually accused people of cowardice, that was his big word then, and said how you had to get a gun, and stop being afraid, and be a man, and all that."

There is in all of this what seems to be an abiding sense of guilt, and it was probably as true for Gold as for other Weathermen and those like them. To oversimplify, they tend to feel guilty about the comfortable, privileged, often very rich homes from which they come, especially when they try to take their message into the mangled, oppressed and very desperate homes of the poor. They feel guilty about what they regard as their own inescapable middle-class racism and that of the society that has showered its benefits on their parents. They feel guilty that they are, at least at the start, frightened of violence, and envy those, like the blacks and the working-class youths, who have confronted violence from infancy. They feel guilty that their brains, money or pull has kept them safe on university campuses while others are sent to Vietnam. And they feel guilty that the society which has given them and their families so much, and which they have spent the better part of their adolescence trying to change, is obdurate in its basic inequities.

Out of all this, not surprisingly, grows an immense rage. Each day that rage is fed—with a My Lai or neighborhood police brutality, with a Moynihan memo or a black friend forced onto welfare, with a Chicago conspiracy trial or a local pot bust, with an ABM system, a Hampton murder, an illegal Laos bombing. The rage solidifies into something that contains all the elements of a religion: asceticism (no drugs, liquor or pets were allowed in the Weather collectives), intolerance, a conviction of one's own rightness, and the abiding need to demonstrate that rightness. And thus the last weapon of a religious minority, martyrdom. "So now also the revolution shall be magnified in my body, whether it be by life or by death. For me to live is revolution, to die is gain."

After the formation of the Weathermen at the SDS convention, a trip to Cuba in late summer began for Gold the solidification of his ideas. The Cuba trip provided not only an attractive, energetic, functioning Communist society that he could, for a time at least, identify with, but also a meeting with the Vietnamese Provisional Revolutionary Government and some of its shrewdest cadre. The message of the PRG people seems to have been that they needed allies within the United States to bring an end to the war, and Gold returned with the conviction, as he wrote it for Liberation News Service, that:

As people who are located inside the monster, revolutionary Americans are in a position to do decisive damage to the U.S. ruling class's plans to continue and expand its world rule. The upcoming U.S. defeat in Vietnam will be a vital blow to those plans: we must aim to do everything we can to speed up that defeat.

Next came October 8–11 in Chicago, what the Weathermen called, appropriately enough, the "Days of Rage," when they went up against the cops and found their courage not wanting. But not sufficient, either—the action was too weak, too many people were arrested, too much money ($1 million) was required for bail. The Weathermen retired to their collectives, to rethink their strategy, and for the next three months went through serious soul-searching. Gold apparently stayed at the Chicago collective, where most of the national leaders—Rudd, Jacobs, Bernardine Dohrn—also spent most of their time, and was an intimate part of those who planned the next strategic steps.

Those steps were more or less danced out at the Weathermen "war council" in Flint, Mich., December 27–30. The council's temper was suggested, though not wholly seriously, by its gimmicks: the slogans were such as "Piece Now," "Sirhan Sirhan Power" and "Red Army Power"; the greetings were four fingers slightly spread (symbolizing the fork which Charlie Manson's gang plunged into one of its victims), and forefinger pointed out with thumb cocked.

Violence, in short—though paid homage to in rhetoric rather than in fact—was the abiding theme. Gold made a speech in which he tried to show its immediacy. The American revolution, he said, would come about as part of a large worldwide revolution and as part of a revolt by the black colony within the nation. Once the country is brought to its knees, "an agency of the people of the world" would be established to run things here.

A critic in the audience objected: "In short, if the people of the world succeed in liberating themselves before American radicals have made the American revolution, then the Vietnamese and Africans and the Chinese are gonna move in and run things for white America. It sounds like a John Bircher's worst dream. There will have to be more repression than ever against white people."

"Well," replied Gold, "if it will take fascism, we'll have to have fascism."

Sometime after the Flint war council, the Weathermen decided to break up their collectives—the largest of which were in Chicago, New York, Boston and Philadelphia—into smaller four- and five-person affinity groups. They hoped in this way to ferret out the FBI informers who they were certain had infiltrated their ranks, and to plan guerrilla actions that could be carried out better by smaller bands. Some time early in the year Gold met Dotson Rader in the West End Bar, Columbia's watering hole, where he vigorously defended the Days of Rage and the actions of Weathermen at Harvard who broke into the Kennedy International Affairs Center and roughed up workers and professors. "He told me," Rader recalls, and with sympathy, "that we have to teach people that violence is not an abstraction. We have to confront them with it so that they can see what they're doing. You see, Gold was always an existentialist, not really a Marxist for all his talk. He really felt that man has got to be responsible for his actions, that the people who deal in abstract violence like the Harvard teachers or Herman Kahn, say, have to be *shown* what they're doing, what real bodies are like, what violence really is. You see, our lives aren't really threatened by the Vietnam war now, and the liberals can continue along their comfortable ways. I still remember Ted saying, 'We've got to turn New York into Saigon.' "

Perhaps that is what the 11th Street town house was to be used for; or perhaps the ultimate idea was simply to create the terror that would bring fascism.

How must it have felt to be living in a house full of explosives and to be preparing for actions which were certain to be dangerous? "I think the Weathermen were all prepared to die," one former Columbia student says. "They were in a way like disobedient children who wanted to be punished, and on a larger scale that's a death wish." A friend who saw Gold two weeks before the explosion reports his having said, "I've been doing a lot of exciting underground things, and I know I'm not afraid to die."

Another who knew Gold thinks it was more than just the absence of fear. "I think a desire for recognition was motivating him, I really do. He wanted to be in history—he wanted to be like Che, a tragic figure. And for tragedy you need a stage, like this historical point in time, and you need violence." And an adult around Columbia who knew Gold less well speculates: "I always felt that Ted, perhaps because of his size, or maybe his bookishness, had a kind of drive to get people to know who he was. I don't mean he wanted the limelight, not like that. But he wanted everyone to know who he was, what he was doing."

2. The Berrigan Brothers:
Activist Priests

"The Berrigans: I/Catonsville"

by FRANCINE DU PLESSIX GRAY

Shortly after the hour of noon on May 17, 1968, seven men and
two women walked into the Knights of Columbus Hall of
Catonsville, Maryland, a suburb of Baltimore. They climbed
the stairs to the second-floor room which houses the town's
Selective Service office and proceeded to empty the contents
of several filing cabinets into large wire trash baskets. The
head clerk screamed. "My draft files! You get away from my
draft files!" After a brief scuffle the clerk and her two aides
stood still, helpless and astonished. It was startling, as were
many other details of that afternoon, that several of the raiders
wore Roman Catholic clerical attire. They stuffed the draft
records into their wire baskets, exhorting each other with
terse, teamlike exclamations. "You're doing great, kid . . ."
"Don't pack them too tightly or they won't burn . . ." "Okay,
we've got enough, let's go." Toward the end of the raid, which

lasted ninety seconds, the youngest of the three clerks, with a desperation accentuated by her extreme surprise, threw a telephone clear through a closed window to attract the attention of passersby in the street below. The raiders walked swiftly down the stairway and into the parking lot outside. They emptied their haul of papers into a single pile, doused it with home-made napalm, and ignited it with matches. As the fire blazed savagely, devouring the draft records of 378 young Catonsville residents, the nine men and women awaited arrest by joining hands and saying the Lord's Prayer.

A small crowd of onlookers had gathered at the scene. "They're burning draft records!" exclaimed a young woman who had wheeled a baby carriage into the parking lot. "No, they're praying," someone else said. "They're burning draft records, they should be shot," another spectator said. Meanwhile the nine Catholics, their heads still bowed, began to talk gravely among themselves, as worshippers talk before the Eucharist in one of the spontaneous liturgies of the modern Church. "We burn these draft records," said a tall, massive man in clerical garb, "in the name of that God whose name is decency, humanity and love." "We do this because everything else has failed," another man in black softly spoke. "May this make clear that napalm is immorally and illegally destroying human lives in Vietnam." "Our Church has been silent," said a jowly man in a business suit, "we speak out in the name of Catholicism and Christianity."

.   .   .

Five policemen ran into the parking lot, and a brief interrogation ensued.

"Did you burn these draft records?"

"Yes, I wanted to make it more difficult for men to kill each other."

"Your name, please?"

"David Darst, Christian Brother."

"Did you burn these draft records?"

"Yes, I wanted to say 'yes' to the possibility of a human future."

"Your name, please?"

"Father Daniel Berrigan, S.J."

"Thank you, Father . . ."

The policemen, shaken and courteous, awed by the sight of Roman collars, as are most members of the law-and-order professions, questioned and identified the other seven offenders: Thomas Melville, a former priest of the Maryknoll order; his wife Marjorie Melville, a former Maryknoll nun; George Mische, a former State Department employee; Mary Moylan, a registered nurse; John Hogan, a former Maryknoll brother; Thomas Lewis, a Catholic civil rights activist, artist and art teacher; and Reverend Philip Berrigan of the Society of Saint Joseph, curate of Baltimore's largest Negro parish. The last two men needed little identification to residents of the Baltimore area. The preceding fall, in an equally extravagant and notorious protest against the Vietnam war, they had poured blood on several hundred draft records in a Selective Service office in downtown Baltimore.

As the files still smoldered at Catonsville's Draft Board, the doors of the white paddy wagon opened. The Nine entered— cheerfully smiling, embracing, and congratulating each other, extending their fingers in the V of protest. It was a handsome, photogenic group. But a photograph of the Catonsville Nine, as they were henceforth called, remains a collector's item. For the cameramen had focused their lenses throughout on Fathers Philip and Daniel Berrigan, long-publicized shock troops of the Peace Movement, idols of the Catholic New Left, the Church's most militant and prolific writers on pacifism and on civil rights. And so the Catonsville incident was publicized, on the front page of the evening's newspapers, by a picture of the Berrigan brothers praying over the burning remains of government property. At left, Philip Berrigan, tall and silver-haired, stands with hands folded and head bowed, his massive body coiled in prayer like a paratrooper curled for the shock of space. By his side is Daniel Berrigan, a mysterious smile on his delicate and puckish face, his arm spread out before him as if he were casting a libation into the flames.

That afternoon the Catonsville Nine were arraigned on charges of conspiracy and of destroying government property. They

were taken to the Baltimore County Jail in the western out-
skirts of the city. The two women were placed in the women's
detention wing. The seven men were housed in a large cell
block, with four cubicles at one end, an open area and a large
table at the other. Their only request upon arrest was that
flowers and an apologetic note be sent, through the intermediary
of the prison warden, to the head clerk of the Catonsville
Draft Board.

The scholarly prison schedule of the Catonsville raiders
reflected the composure of men who had deliberately chosen
jail as a new way of life. The mornings were dedicated to
reading, the afternoons to writing, the evenings to seminars:
Catholic Conscience and the Vietnam War; American Imperial-
ism in Guatemala; How to Move the Catholic Bishops on the
War Issue. Every hour, on the strike of the clock, a few minutes
of deep breathing and calisthenics were in order. A ten-foot
collage on the theme of peace, assembled from pages of
various periodicals, soon decorated a wall of the room. In the
evening, between the writing period and the seminar, the
prisoners read their articles and letters to each other. Daniel
Berrigan, poet laureate of the Jesuit order, had been awarded
a cell of his own so as to concentrate better on his writing.
And before the week was over, a variety of anti-war publications were already putting into print the articles that were
written in the Baltimore County Jail and smuggled out via the
vast underground of contemporary Catholicism.

The prisoners had begun a voluntary fast the evening they
entered jail. Six of the men fasted on liquids: coffee, tea, milk,
fruit juices. Brother David Darst, the youngest of the group,
insisted on the purer Gandhian practice of fasting on water.
Their fast was broken once, the Sunday after the Catonsville
raid, with Communion bread and wine. The jail warden, a
Roman Catholic who was particularly fond of Philip Berrigan,
brought bread and wine into the cell block and shared with his
wife and his five children in Father Berrigan's Mass. Later in
the week the Catonsville Nine were visited by a group of
Jesuits from Loyola University who presented them with a
package of books. The visit was brief. The Jesuits were choked
with tears. "We're embarrassed," one of them said. "We feel

we should be right in there with you . . ." He turned away, sobbing, and led the group out. The package was opened. It contained the latest volumes of Che Guevara, Herbert Marcuse, Régis Debray: all books on revolution.

Precisely a week after the Catonsville incident, on May 24, the Nine were arraigned again, this time in a Federal District Court. Daniel Berrigan, George Mische, Mary Moylan, Thomas Melville, Marjorie Melville, John Hogan, and David Darst were released on bail. But Philip Berrigan and Thomas Lewis were held captive, because two hours earlier, in another chamber of the same courthouse, they had been sentenced to six years' imprisonment for their attack on the Baltimore Draft Board the previous fall. They were denied bail pending appeal. It was an unusually severe legal move, but they had broken the self-recognisance bond placed upon them for their first protest. Thomas Lewis and Philip Berrigan were returned that same day to Baltimore County Jail. . . .

.   .   .

A biographical questionnaire returned by Daniel Berrigan to the Macmillan Company, which has published eight volumes of his verse and prose in the past decade, contains the following exchanges:

1. *Birthplace? Date?*
   Virginia, Minnesota, May 9th, 1921.

2. *Immediate family: Parents, brothers, sisters?*
   Mother and father; five brothers. A fairly heterogeneous double troika moving at present in several directions with interesting stress and balance.

3. *Education? Degrees?*
   Two equivalent M.A.'s, one in theology, one in philosophy. Continuing education, courtesy of the American Correction System. According to the first, I might be considered incorrigible; to the second, perhaps, educable.

4. *List of awards and honors?*
   Lamont Poetry Award, 1957.
   Indictment, 4 felonies, U.S. Government, May 1968: Conspiracy, Entering Government property, etc. etc.

5. *Why did you become a Jesuit?*
   They had a revolutionary history. I only suspected it at the time; now I am more certain, and more proud.

The Berrigan brothers' rebelliousness has myriad sources;
each Berrigan picks a different one. Jerome, fourth of the six
sons, oldest member of the younger "troika" of brothers,
attributes it to the spirit of the Irish Revolution. Daniel, at the
center of the triad, blames it on a wicked, witchlike aunt who
tortured him during a year of his childhood. Philip, the youngest, says he was made a rebel by his father, Tom Berrigan, "a
tyrannical, brutal man who made me bristle against authority."

Tom Berrigan was born in Syracuse, New York, a few years
after his own parents—poor Tipperary farmers—had fled the
Irish potato famine. The suffering of the Irish at the hands of
the English overlords had obsessed centuries of Berrigans.
Tom's generation conquered hard times by unusual brilliance.
Many of his brothers and cousins, by 1900, were college-
educated: they were teachers, nuns, priests, labor leaders,
founders of hospitals and of interracial councils. The Berrigans
never remained in the conservative mainstream of Irish immigrants. They were that maverick brand of Irish progressives
which continues to produce, in our day, a Eugene McCarthy
and a Paul O'Dwyer. "Dado was a Walt Whitman type, a final
model of nineteenth-century man," Daniel says about his father,
"well-versed in classics, poetry, theology, knowledgeable in all
realms . . . and if he wasn't, he thought he was, which comes
to the same thing."

Labor movements and poetry were the loves of Tom Berrigan's life. He had drifted away from the Catholic Church in his
teens because of its failure to support trade unionism. Impatient, enamored of physical exertion, he also left college after
two years to go to work as a railroad engineer, and immediately
rose in the ranks of labor boards. "At the age of thirty-three,"
he says, "I puffed through Minnesota, and met my bride."
Frieda Fromhart was a devout, infinitely gentle German girl,
whom Daniel describes as "a woman of marmoreal patience."
She swiftly brought Tom back to the Church, and bore him six
sons. To live with Tom Berrigan, as Philip says, was rough. A
tall, powerful, belligerent man given to terrible tantrums, he
made huge demands upon his family. He lost his job in Minnesota because of his militant participation in the Socialist party.
When he moved his family back to Syracuse, at the start of the

Depression, to a brick house by Onondaga Lake, Tom decided
to live off his land and save. With his sons' help, he farmed
the reluctant clay earth on evenings and weekends off from
his new job at the Niagara-Mohawk electric plant. The farm
work was laid out on a daily basis. Tom cuffed and buffeted
his boys when the assigned tasks were not done. The three
oldest children, Tom Jr., John, and Jim, frequently and angrily
fought back. Brawls seemed to soothe Tom Berrigan. Philip
recalls seeing his father strangely becalmed some mornings
at the breakfast table, his face full of cuts and bruises. "One
of your brothers and I had a good, good fight," Tom would say
with satisfaction.

.   .   .

Daniel, at an early age, had singled himself out as the most
sensitive and studious, the frailest and most devout of the six
children. "From the age of six," his mother says, "Daniel was
obsessed by the suffering in the world." He was the readiest for
tears, the top of his class, the tender mother's helper who
cleaned up the kitchen while his brothers struggled with the
farmwork. He spent much time by the family bookshelf, which
held the Bible, back issues of *Commonweal* and the *Catholic
Worker,* a few books of poetry, a five-volume work by a Jesuit
entitled *Pioneer Priests of North America.* Daniel had inherited
his father's passion for writing poetry. His weak ankles required
special shoes, and exempted him from farm work. He was indifferent to sports. Philip, two years younger, the sibling who has
remained Daniel's closest friend from earliest childhood, was
the mirror opposite: a brawny outgoing all-American boy, a
baseball and basketball star, an enormously gifted athlete who
was constantly anxious to test his physical prowess. But Daniel,
the ephemeral poet and dreamer, would lead and inspire, as
poets often do, the men of action. Of the three Berrigan boys
destined for the seminary, Daniel led the way. He had felt the
call of the priesthood since childhood. At the age of seventeen,
he applied for the Jesuit order because, he says, "it ran such
a cool scene."

"When I was sixteen a friend and I wrote in for literature
from all the orders in the United States we could think of—

Benedictines, Augustinians, Dominicans—about forty of them. What impressed us about the Jesuits was that they didn't seem to want us. All the other orders were trying to rope us in by showing us photographs of jazzy swimming pools in their prospectus. But the Jebbies just had a couple of tight little quotes from St. Ignatius in a very stark pamphlet. We thought that cool scene was revolutionary. We applied immediately." The Society of Jesus accepted the application, and in 1939, aged eighteen, Daniel left Syracuse for the Jesuit seminary near Poughkeepsie, New York, to begin the arduous thirteen-year training which the order imposes on its men before ordination. The loving ties of the younger Berrigan brothers were severed for a long time.

One forgets, in our age of worldly, picketing priests, how strict seminarians' rules were in the past. Short of a death in the immediate family a Jesuit was not allowed to leave the house of his order for the first two years of his novitiate. He could only be visited by his family four times a year. Daniel Berrigan, shy, studious, obsessed by the suffering of the poor, a model seminarian, did not come home for seven years.

. . .

On June 21, 1952, Daniel Berrigan lay prostrate before the altar of a church near Boston, Massachusetts, and was ordained a priest.

On a June morning, I lay in the chapel of Weston, while the voice of Cardinal Cushing shook the house like a great war horse. His hands lay on my head like a stone. I remember a kind of desolation, the cold of the floor on which I stretched like a corpse, while the invocation of the saints went over me like a tide, a death. Would these bones live? I arose to my feet and went out into the sunshine and gave my blessing to those who had borne with me, who had waited for me. A most unfinished man! What would it mean to be a Catholic? Who would be my teacher? It was, finally, the world. It was the world we breathe in, the only stage of redemption, the men and women who toil in it, sin in it, suffer and die in it. Apart from them, as I came to know, the priesthood was a pallid, vacuumatic enclosure, a sheepfold for sheep.

The paragraph comes from a long essay written by Daniel Berrigan in 1961. The Society of Jesus took a dim view of it because of its condemnation of the Catholic Church's lack of social consciousness. And it had become a favorite pamphlet of the Jesuit seminarians' underground. Five years later, after Pope John's liberalizing influence had opened the gates of the Catholic sheepfold, Daniel's essay became a Jesuit classic. It was printed by the thousands, distributed to numerous Catholic bookshops, assigned to novices' reading lists. From the start of their vocations, the Berrigans have been uncomfortably ahead of their time.

Docile seminarians though they were in their youth, Daniel and Philip were soon affected by the progressive theology that poured out of Europe after World War II. The French, Belgian, and Dutch churches had been radicalized by Catholics' participation in the Resistance Movement, by priests' and laymen's militant political involvements under the Nazi occupation. Even liturgy had been renewed by the improvised Masses which were often said, during wartime, in private homes, factories, or open fields. The Berrigans' vocations were deeply affected by the ideology of the French Resistance. In the late 1940's, when Daniel Berrigan was studying at Weston and Philip was at Holy Cross College nearby, the French avant-garde was a favorite theme of their Sunday afternoon conversations. Their heroes were men like Cardinal Suhard, a guiding spirit of the Missions de France and of the worker-priest movement, whom Philip regards as the greatest single influence on his life; the Jesuit Father Henri Perrin, who became a factory worker after his return from German concentration camps; Abbé Pierre, the Resistance leader and MRP deputy who ministered to thousands of homeless families in the Paris suburbs, and needled the French government into starting a massive new housing program for the poor. These men had preached, in Cardinal Suhard's words, "a fearless involvement in the temporal and social spheres." The classical missionary tactic of Saint Paul ("With the Jews I live like a Jew, to win the Jews") had been put into reverse gear by the worker-priests. The Berrigans had learned from them that their task was not to convert the world to the Church, but, rather, the Church to the world.

·   ·   ·

Philip Berrigan, S.S.J., a very tall, massive, handsome man with piercing blue eyes, has been described as "a compulsive leader of men," "a street-fighter with a paratrooper's daring," "a desperado obsessed by the Gospel," "the Gary Cooper of the Church." His teutonic, terribly respectable good looks conjure up the image of the affluent suburban in the Coca-Cola poster, the aspiring chairman of the board in the Wall Street Journal ads, the American Dream Man as depicted by the capitalist society which all Berrigans profoundly disdain. He exudes a terrifying energy, a terrifying impatience, and a maddening freedom. He is devoid of all the fears, the cautions, the proprieties that motivate normal men. His smile, like his brother's, is radiant and irresistible. The spell he casts over other humans is as great as Daniel's and more alarming. Daniel might be content to have his disciples rattle and needle at the world. Philip wants them to transform society as totally and as soon as possible. His revolutionary zeal is like the cold blue center of a flame. His eyes are merry, affectionate, and yet fiercely impatient. One recalls Camus' phrase: "The revolutionary loves a man who does not yet exist."

"The Berrigans are very traditional, conservative men," says Reverend William Sloane Coffin, the Yale chaplain who has also risked a jail sentence for defending the rights of draft resisters. "They are conserving the fire of the Holy Spirit, they are conserving the pure message of the Gospel. They are radical Christians, which is a redundancy. Radical means root; it doesn't mean being way out, but going deep down."

Although his semantics are personal, Coffin understands the Berrigans well. The Berrigans' radicalism did not grow out of any philosophical theorizing, but out of a disturbingly literal reading of the Gospels. "They remained faithful to the teaching of the apostles, to the brotherhood, to the breaking of bread and to the prayers . . . the faithful all lived together and shared out the proceeds among themselves according to what each one needed." There is a moral fundamentalism in the Berrigans which makes them follow this passage from the Book of Acts with total fidelity. It is a torment, for many Christians, to decide how literally to interpret the socialism of the Gospels. The Berrigans are untroubled. They are men sworn to poverty by their religious orders, and a conversion to poverty is perhaps the only conversion which they desire to impose on mankind. With a simplism that is sometimes maddening, they view the problems of racism, of war, and of most human suffering as created by a system of unequally distributed wealth, by human beings' greed for private property. "The next car," Philip says, "is every man's *Dolce Vita.*" "Read the Gospel, get poor, get with it," Daniel blithely told a student who had asked him how to live the Christian life. "It's just that simple."

Philip Berrigan had dedicated the first ten years of his priesthood to the plight of the black man. He realized with sorrow, after joining the only Catholic order dedicated to that task, that his Society of Joseph was as much of an Uncle Tom as any timid white liberal. And Uncle Tomism goes harshly against Philip's grain. For in his view the blacks are not children to be guided by the whites. They are rather the race of superior wisdom, gentleness, and maturity, the prophetic people purified and matured by suffering who could bring adulthood to the white man. "The Negro stands in perplexity and chagrin," he wrote in his book *No More Strangers,* a formidably documented work on the psychological roots of racism, "at the inconsistency of the white man-child who rules his world . . . freedom for the Negro and maturity for us are reciprocal endowments." Philip dedicated his study "To my brother, Father Dan, S.J., without whom neither my priesthood nor this book would be possible."

Philip's profound reverence for the black race, his fierce anti-paternalism, made him capable of communicating—as few white priests can—with the most militant blacks in the United States. He inspired virility and confidence in black men, and in their women he inspired a blind and total trust. "He never made a fuss with us because we were black," one of his parishioners says. "He was just more at ease with us than any white man we'd ever met." "If Father Phil said to me 'Come on, I'll take you to the moon,'" said another of his parishioners, "and all I'd see there was a little contraption to get into, I'd get into that little contraption because I know with Father Phil I could get to the moon in any contraption . . ." Even Stokely Carmichael is reported to have made the ultimate compliment.

"Phil Berrigan," he has said, "is the only white man who knows where it's at."

Philip had won the black's confidence with years of rash gestures which sometimes put the welfare of his order at stake. In 1963, he had boarded a plane for Jackson, Mississippi, to join in a mass sit-in protesting the segregation of bus terminals. Even then, Philip wished to be the first Catholic priest to be arrested in a civil rights demonstration. He wanted to make his point by going to jail. But his plans were snafued. A news leak occurred, causing one of the first civil rights crises that have agitated the American Church in our decade. A few hours after Philip had left New York, the Bishop of Jackson is said to have phoned the Josephite superior, and warned him that he would make a direct complaint to Rome if Father Berrigan arrived at his destination. Philip was paged to the phone as his plane stopped in Atlanta, and ordered by his superior to return to New York. He obeyed. But thanks to his talent for public relations, the incident hit the front pages. It was Philip's first confrontation, his first glory. For the greatest joy of this modest man's life is to flaunt his rigorous conscience, with as much publicity as possible, in the face of all institutions.

"Phil had been weaned in the Catholic Worker ideology," one of his friends says, "but there is a grimness about the Worker which he dislikes. He's a joyful man. Whether he's praying, eating, drinking, protesting or going to jail, he absolutely insists that everything be done with joy."

Gregarious and proverbially generous, Philip was known wherever he worked for his radiant good nature, his Falstaffian capacity for downing half a bottle of rye without showing it, his enormous tenderness. His lecture fees have helped to support several families through years of trouble. He was notorious, in every parish he worked, for being the first priest to arrive at any scene of accident and the first to empty his pockets for men in need. The power of his handshake, even upon a first meeting, is excruciating. He is devoid of Anglo-Saxon reserves. His greetings to friends, men and women alike, are accompanied by powerful, back-breaking embraces. "Thank God for womenkind he's not married," says the wife of one of his close friends. "He puts my spine out of joint each time he just kisses me." Everything about Philip Berrigan is magnanimous, obsessed, a little extreme. And his religious vocation dominates it all. "Christ's love, and this kid's," he signs his letters, "—Phil, S.S.J." "Carry on ole sport; Yours in Christ—Phil, S.S.J." "Great work buddy; God's love—Phil, S.S.J." "God's increase to you. Love ya, man—Phil, S.S.J." "Cool it man, we must all learn to live with Brother Ass. In Christ—Phil, S.S.J." The "S.S.J." always keeps its place, even in his letters to his family. The Berrigans long ago made a pact with each other that they would never leave the priesthood. Their attitude toward the Church is one of cynical but dogged loyalty. "The Church is a sinner," says Daniel, "But She's my mother." "The guys who leave," Philip says, "just don't have enough guts. It's our society that's evil, and the Church reflects the society. Staying in the Church gives you a chance to use the institution against itself."

It is a political attitude, for politics is to Philip's life what poetry is to his brother—a passionate second vocation. The brothers' reading tastes are explicit. Daniel reads *Partisan Review, Hudson Review,* and various obscure journals of theology and poetry. Philip ·subscribes to *The Nation, The New Republic, U.S. News and World Report, Dissent, The Progressive, The Guardian, Liberation, The Civil Liberties Quarterly, Ramparts.* He studies *The Wall Street Journal* and *Business Week* to keep abreast of the American economy. He looks upon progressive news analysts as the prophets of a society which the Churches have failed to reform. *I. F. Stone's Weekly* is the periodical which he prizes most highly for its advanced opinions, and which he sometimes sends in gift subscriptions to the congressmen and friends whom he judges to be in need of enlightenment. ("Read your *I. F. Stone,*" he signs off a letter to a friend. "Best love, and the Lord's keen peace.")

.   .   .

With Philip's first Vietnam confrontation, the Berrigans became the high priests of the Catholic peace movement, the commandoes of the new Guerrilla Christianity which, two years later, would invade the draft boards of Baltimore and Catonsville. The Berrigans' belligerence, and the actions of the Catonsville Nine, are a strictly Catholic phenomenon. They are not only a protest against the Vietnam war; they are also a defiance of the heavy-handed authoritarianism, the blind nationalism that makes the American Catholic community the most war-mongering segment of the nation. Goaded by the silence of his Church's hierarchy and of its hawkish flocks, the Catholic radical can become a desperado.

"What do you think of our policy in Vietnam?" a reporter asked Cardinal Spellman during his trip to Saigon in 1966. "Right or wrong, my country," the Cardinal staunchly answered. Catholics have always tended to give to the commands of the state a sacred and unchallengeable character. Spellman's flag-waving was a holdover from the medieval Catholic idea that the power of the state is God-given, a notion which the Reformation, in theory, tried to dispel. It has even deeper theological roots. The Catholic dogma that bishops speak with the voice of God, a distinction not offered to the Presbyterian or the Methodist hierarchy, has an intimidating effect upon independent political pronouncements. ("If I thought that God was likely to offer his views on the Vietnam war through me," says Lutheran Pastor Richard Neuhaus, one of the most militant peace organizers in the United States, "I too would be reluctant to speak.")

There are other causes. The moral absolutism of the Catholic Church tends to satanize Communism more readily than other religious traditions, and the American Catholic community has been steeped in a visceral fear of monolithic Communism, of which Joseph McCarthy was but an average exponent. It had as its spiritual leader, for three decades, a cardinal who was a patron of Diem, an architect of our intervention in Vietnam, and an enthusiastic supporter of the domino theory. There is also an immigrant nervousness in the American Church not evident in other countries. The Irish, Italian, and Polish who compose its rank and file resort to a simplistic flag-waving patriotism in their yearning for acceptance and quick assimilation. Finally, the enormous vested interests of the American Church makes it scandalously timid about dissenting from any aspect of government policy.

The Catholic pacifist, therefore, found himself infinitely more embattled and more controversial than the Protestant pacifist when the Vietnam protest began. The Protestant's hierarchy is more secularized and better geared to social action; his churches have smaller fortunes to protect; his religion is more steeped in a tradition of dissent against secular power. . . .

.   .   .

[In February 1968] three thousand Clergy and Laymen Concerned About Vietnam converged on Washington, D.C., for their yearly rally. "We live in a nation which is the greatest purveyor of violence in the world today," said Martin Luther King in one of his last speeches. Father Robert Drinan, dean of the Jesuits' Boston College Law School, thundered about "the pattern of lawlessness adapted by our government." "Fighting Communism, we are the Communists' most formidable allies in that unhappy country," said Rabbi Maurice Eisendrath, president of the Union of American Hebrew Congregations. Every religious leader in the peace movement was there—except Philip and Daniel Berrigan. Clergy and Laymen Concerned had become splendidly establishment. Therefore, for the Berrigans, it had turned into "another liberal bag." As soon as it had become fashionable for progressive clergymen to march, picket, and lecture against the war, the Berrigans had bowed out of the movement which they had pioneered. They had created a new fringe of radical dissent, a new community of risk. Once again, they had refused to be respectable. The arrogance of their commitment estranged many of their friends. "You can't criticize the Berrigans this year. They look down on anyone who hasn't risked as much as they have. They'll barely break bread with you if you haven't burned your draft card. Talk about ghettos! That ghetto of martyrs is the most exclusive club of all."

Philip, during that winter, was also estranged from two of his fellow martyrs, Jim Mengel and David Eberhardt.* He was annoyed by their frequent bouts of self-pity. They complained about the suffering which their pending jail sentences would

---

*Ed. note: Two of the Baltimore Four, a group of war protesters led by Father Philip Berrigan, who on October 27, 1967, poured blood on Selective Service records in Baltimore, Maryland, and then submitted to arrest.

bring to their families. Philip's reply to them was tough: "You've got another family—mankind." Up to then Philip had championed, like most liberal priests, a reform of the Church's laws on celibacy. The emotional consequences of the Baltimore protest made him change his mind. He suddenly realized that celibacy was an essential tool for revolution. If priests were to take their proper role as non-violent revolutionaries, they had better remain celibates. Acts such as his were still prophetic and unique, to be undertaken by men of great austerity who had nothing to lose, no property or emotions at stake . . . Determined to make a second prophetic act before being jailed for the first, Philip spent the winter in search of such men. He found the nucleus of his new cadre in two Roman Catholics: Tom Lewis, who had emerged from the October event as unscathed and austerely dedicated as Philip; and George Mische, a thirty-two-year-old professional peace organizer who, like Philip and Tom Lewis, was quite devoid of any fear of prison life.

.   .   .

As the winter wore on, Philip and George Mische traveled around the country looking for men to join them in the next assault. . . .

.   .   .

Participation in the forthcoming raid, to the surprise and delight of the protesters, restricted itself to Catholics. "We were inviting Protestants and Jews all over the place," Mische says, "but it only seemed to attract the Catholics. A few Episcopal clergymen promised to go along but at the last minute they copped out because of their big hangups with their families. But this was healthy because the Catholic community had been the most silent on the war. Jews and Protestants had been the backbone of the religious peace movement on all levels. Since you can't talk to the Catholic bishops, we wanted to force a stand from the Church, we wanted to make it either support or condemn us, but take a stand . . ."

The site of the protest had to be decided upon. The month of May was spent scanning the Baltimore area for the right draft board. The little town of Catonsville, eight miles north of down-town Baltimore, was chosen because it was a sitting duck, and highly symbolic. Catonsville was a lily-white, middle-class sub-urban town of smug brick houses and pleasant oak-lined streets, a Maryland version of Larchmont or Purchase. "We loved the idea of hitting that kind of conservative, racist community," Mische says. "We loved to hit them with an action not per-formed by hippies but by college graduates, three of them clerics, all nicely dressed in white collars or in suits and ties . . ."

.   .   .

But a most important ingredient of the new action was still lacking, and that was Daniel Berrigan. During the winter, he had been absent on a mission to Hanoi, sponsored by pacifist groups, to receive three American prisoners of war from the North Vietnamese government. After his return he was re-peatedly invited, by persons other than his brother, to partic-ipate in the next raid. He acted mysterious, guarded, unhappy, unsure. A week before the scheduled foray Daniel and Philip Berrigan sat up alone, over a bottle, until four o'clock in the morning. A few hours later Philip telephoned Mische: "Dan's in." And that very day, according to his friends, Daniel came out of the gloom which he had been in ever since October. He seemed relieved of an enormous burden of guilt. He was his luminous and joyous self again. ("I was threatened with being the golden boy of the Movement," he wrote, "I was too old to burn a draft card. Suddenly I saw that my sweet skin was hiding out behind others.")

The night before Catonsville, after the definitive batch of napalm had been made and tested, the Nine met for a last brief-ing, each holding a copy of Lewis's exquisitely detailed plan of the Knights of Columbus Hall. Daniel, noted for his poetic vagueness, his inability to read any maps, train or plane sched-ules, studied the plan silently, with a quizzical expression, dur-ing the three-hour session. At one a.m., as the group was about to disband, Daniel looked up to his brother and said "I didn't understand anything, Philly . . . never could read a map. I'll follow you, Philly, okay? I'll just follow you."

The Catonsville Nine slept at a friend's house in the suburbs of Baltimore. They waited for one of their aides, who had assembled the press at a nearby motel, to phone the go-ahead signal. A Washington reporter was a half hour late. Philip was beside himself with impatience. When the phone call finally came he shouted "Let's go, let's go," threw himself into the nearest car and almost drove off alone. His friends spent a few minutes reorganizing him.

The Nine went to Catonsville in three cars, each driven by a non-participating member of the peace group. On the way to Catonsville, Daniel, smiling, jesting, was more joyous than his friends had seen him in years. "This is like going on a picnic," he exclaimed. "What a beautiful day for a picnic, what a beautiful day . . ." He turned to the man at the wheel and said: "After the long yawn of history, I've finally found something good."

The reporters, guided to Catonsville's Selective Service Office by members of the Baltimore peace group, had parked at the edge of the oak-lined street. It was a very hot, sunny May day. Three cars passed them and parked across the street. Seven men and two women got out—three of them dressed in clerical attire, two of them carrying large wire trash baskets. The group walked quietly into the Knights of Columbus Hall. The Nine's helpmates, drivers of cars, soothers of nerves, distributors of press statements, brewers of newsmen's coffee, quickly dispersed from the scene. Several of them had studied for the Catholic priesthood. ("Five years in a seminary and you want *us* to go to jail?") After a minute and a half had elapsed the Nine ran out of the building, baskets filled with papers. The reporters, as instructed, tore open the sealed envelopes that they had been handed earlier that morning, and read:

Today, May 17th, we enter Local Board No. 33 at Catonsville, Maryland, to seize Selective Service records . . . We, American citizens, have worked with the poor in the ghetto and abroad . . . All of us identify with the victims of American oppression all over the world . . . We submit voluntarily to their involuntary fate . . .

3. Eldridge Cleaver:
Black Panther Leader

"On Becoming"

by ELDRIDGE CLEAVER

Folsom Prison, June 25, 1965

Nineteen fifty-four, when I was eighteen years old, is held to be a crucial turning point in the history of the Afro-American—for the U.S.A. as a whole—the year segregation was outlawed by the U.S. Supreme Court. It was also a crucial year for me because on June 18, 1954, I began serving a sentence in state prison for possession of marijuana.

The Supreme Court decision was only one month old when I entered prison, and I do not believe that I had even the vaguest idea of its importance or historical significance. But later, the acrimonious controversy ignited by the end of the separate-but-equal doctrine was to have a profound effect on me. This controversy awakened me to my position in America and I began to form a concept of what it meant to be black in white America.

Of course I'd always known that I was black, but I'd never really stopped to take stock of what I was involved in. I met life as an individual and took my chances. Prior to 1954, we lived in an atmosphere of novocain. Negroes found it necessary, in order to maintain whatever sanity they could, to remain somewhat aloof and detached from "the problem." We accepted indignities and the mechanics of the apparatus of oppression without reacting by sitting-in or holding mass demonstrations. Nurtured by the fires of the controversy over segregation, I was soon aflame with indignation over my newly discovered social status, and inwardly I turned away from America with horror, disgust and outrage.

In Soledad state prison, I fell in with a group of young blacks who, like myself, were in vociferous rebellion against what we perceived as a continuation of slavery on a higher plane. We cursed everything American—including baseball and hot dogs. All respect we may have had for politicians, preachers, lawyers, governors, Presidents, senators, congressmen was utterly destroyed as we watched them temporizing and compromising over right and wrong, over legality and illegality, over constitutionality and unconstitutionality. We knew that in the end what they were clashing over was us, what to do with the blacks, and whether or not to start treating us as human beings. I despised all of them.

The segregationists were condemned out of hand, without even listening to their lofty, finely woven arguments. The others I despised for wasting time in debates with the segregationists: why not just crush them, put them in prison—they were defying the law, weren't they? I defied the law and they put me in prison. So why not put those dirty mothers in prison too? I had gotten caught with a shopping bag full of marijuana, a shopping bag full of love—I was in love with the weed and I did not for one minute think that anything was wrong with getting high. I had been getting high for four or five years and was convinced, with the zeal of a crusader, that marijuana was superior to lush—yet the rulers of the land seemed all to be lushes. I could not see how they were more justified in drinking than I was in blowing the gage. I was a grasshopper, and it was natural that I felt myself to be unjustly imprisoned.

While all this was going on, our group was espousing atheism. Unsophisticated and not based on any philosophical ration-
ale, our atheism was pragmatic. I had come to believe that
there is no God; if there is, men do not know anything about
him. Therefore, all religions were phony—which made all
preachers and priests, in our eyes, fakers, including the ones
scurrying around the prison who, curiously, could put in a good
word for you with the Almighty Creator of the universe but
could not get anything down with the warden or parole board—
they could usher you through the Pearly Gates *after you were
dead,* but not through the prison gate *while you were still alive
and kicking.* Besides, men of the cloth who work in prison have
an ineradicable stigma attached to them in the eyes of convicts
because they escort condemned men into the gas chamber.
Such men of God are powerful arguments in favor of atheism.
Our atheism was a source of enormous pride to me. Later on,
I bolstered our arguments by reading Thomas Paine and his
devastating critique of Christianity in particular and organized
religion in general.

Through reading I was amazed to discover how confused people were. I had thought that, out there beyond the horizon of
my own ignorance, unanimity existed, that even though I myself
didn't know what was happening in the universe, other people
certainly did. Yet here I was discovering that the whole U.S.A.
was in a chaos of disagreement over segregation/integration.
In these circumstances I decided that the only safe thing for
me to do was go for myself. It became clear that it was possible
for me to take the initiative: instead of simply *reacting* I could
act. I could unilaterally—whether anyone agreed with me or
not—repudiate all allegiances, morals, values—even while continuing to exist within this society. My mind would be free and
no power in the universe could force me to accept something
if I didn't want to. But I would take my own sweet time. That,
too, was a part of my new freedom. I would accept nothing until
it was proved that it was good—for me. I became an extreme
iconoclast. Any affirmative assertion made by anyone around
me became a target for tirades of criticism and denunciation.

This little game got good to me and I got good at it. I attacked
all forms of piety, loyalty, and sentiment: marriage, love, God,

patriotism, the Constitution, the founding fathers, law, concepts of right-wrong-good-evil, all forms of ritualized and conventional behavior. As I pranced about, club in hand, seeking new idols to smash, I encountered really for the first time in my life, with any seriousness, The Ogre, rising up before me in a mist. I discovered, with alarm, that The Ogre possessed a tremendous and dreadful power over me, and I didn't understand this power or why I was at its mercy. I tried to repudiate The Ogre, root it out of my heart as I had done God, Constitution, principles, morals, and values—but The Ogre had its claws buried in the core of my being and refused to let go. I fought frantically to be free, but The Ogre only mocked me and sank its claws deeper into my soul. I knew then that I had found an important key, that if I conquered The Ogre and broke its power over me I would be free. But I also knew that it was a race against time and that if I did not win I would certainly be broken and destroyed. I, a black man, confronted The Ogre—the white woman.

In prison, those things withheld from and denied to the prisoner become precisely what he wants most of all, of course. Because we were locked up in our cells before darkness fell, I used to lie awake at night racked by painful craving to take a leisurely stroll under the stars, or to go to the beach, to drive a car on a freeway, to grow a beard, or to make love to a woman.

Since I was not married conjugal visits would not have solved my problem. I therefore denounced the idea of conjugal visits as inherently unfair; single prisoners needed and deserved *action* just as married prisoners did. I advocated establishing a system under Civil Service whereby salaried women would minister to the needs of those prisoners who maintained a record of good behavior. If a married prisoner preferred his own wife, that would be his right. Since California was not about to inaugurate either conjugal visits or the Civil Service, one could advocate either with equal enthusiasm and with the same result: nothing.

This may appear ridiculous to some people. But it was very real to me and as urgent as the need to breathe, because I was in my bull stage and lack of access to females was absolutely a form of torture. I suffered. My mistress at the time of my arrest, the beautiful and lonely wife of a serviceman stationed overseas, died unexpectedly three weeks after I entered prison; and the rigid, dehumanized rules governing correspondence between prisoners and free people prevented me from corresponding with other young ladies I knew. It left me without any contact with females except those in my family.

In the process of enduring my confinement, I decided to get myself a pin-up girl to paste on the wall of my cell. I would fall in love with her and lavish my affections upon her. She, a symbolic representative of the forbidden tribe of women, would sustain me until I was free. Out of the center of *Esquire*, I married a voluptuous bride. Our marriage went along swell for a time: no quarrels, no complaints. And then, one evening when I came in from school, I was shocked and enraged to find that the guard had entered my cell, ripped my sugar from the wall, torn her into little pieces, and left the pieces floating in the commode: it was like seeing a dead body floating in a lake. Giving her a proper burial, I flushed the commode. As the saying goes, I sent her to Long Beach. But I was genuinely beside myself with anger: almost every cell, excepting those of the homosexuals, had a pin-up girl on the wall and the guards didn't bother them. Why, I asked the guard the next day, had he singled me out for special treatment?

"Don't you know we have a rule against pasting up pictures on the walls?" he asked me.

"Later for the rules," I said. "You know as well as I do that that rule is not enforced."

"Tell you what," he said, smiling at me (the smile put me on my guard). "I'll compromise with you: get yourself a colored girl for a pinup—no white women—and I'll let it stay up. Is that a deal?"

I was more embarrassed than shocked. He was laughing in my face. I called him two or three dirty names and walked away. I can still recall his big moon-face, grinning at me over yellow teeth. The disturbing part about the whole incident was that a terrible feeling of guilt came over me as I realized that I had chosen the picture of the white girl over the available pictures of black girls. I tried to rationalize it away, but I was fascinated by the truth involved. Why hadn't I thought about it in this light before? So I took hold of the question and began to inquire into my feelings. Was it true, did I really prefer white girls over black? The conclusion was clear and inescapable: I did. I decided to check out my friends on this point and it was easy to determine, from listening to their general conversation, that the white woman occupied a peculiarly prominent place in all of our frames of reference. With what I have learned since then, this all seems terribly elementary now. But at the time, it was a tremendously intriguing adventure of discovery.

One afternoon, when a large group of Negroes was on the prison yard shooting the breeze, I grabbed the floor and posed the question: which did they prefer, white women or black? Some said Japanese women were their favorite, others said Chinese, some said European women, others said Mexican women—they all stated a preference, and they generally freely admitted their dislike for black women.

"I don't want nothing black but a Cadillac," said one.

"If money was black I wouldn't want none of it," put in another.

A short little stud, who was a very good lightweight boxer with a little man's complex that made him love to box heavyweights, jumped to his feet. He had a yellowish complexion and we called him Butterfly.

"All you niggers are sick!" Butterfly spat out. "I don't like no stinking white woman. My grandma is a white woman and I don't even like her!"

But it just so happened that Butterfly's crime partner was in the crowd, and after Butterfly had his say, his crime partner said, "Aw, sit on down and quit that lying, lil o' chump. What about that gray girl in San Jose who had your nose wide open? Did you like her, or were you just running after her with your tongue hanging out of your head because you hated her?"

Partly because he was embarrassed and partly because his crime partner was a heavyweight, Butterfly flew into him. And before we could separate them and disperse, so the guard would not know who had been fighting, Butterfly bloodied his crime partner's nose. Butterfly got away but, because of the blood, his crime partner got caught. I ate dinner with Butterfly that evening and questioned him sharply about his attitude toward white women. And after an initial evasiveness he admitted that the white woman bugged him too. "It's a sickness," he said. "All our lives we've had the white woman dangled before our eyes like a carrot on a stick before a donkey: look but don't touch." (In 1958, after I had gone out on parole and was returned to San Quentin as a parole violator with a new charge, Butterfly was still there. He had become a Black Muslim and was chiefly responsible for teaching me the Black Muslim philosophy. Upon his release from San Quentin, Butterfly joined the Los Angeles Mosque, advanced rapidly through the ranks, and is now a full-fledged minister of one of Elijah Muhammad's mosques in another city. He successfully completed his parole, got married—to a very black girl—and is doing fine.)

From our discussion, which began that evening and has never yet ended, we went on to notice how thoroughly, as a matter of course, a black growing up in America is indoctrinated with the white race's standard of beauty. Not that the whites made a conscious, calculated effort to do this, we thought, but since they constituted the majority the whites brainwashed the blacks by the very processes the whites employed to indoctrinate themselves with their own group standards. It intensified my frustrations to know that I was indoctrinated to see the white woman as more beautiful and desirable than my own black woman. It drove me into books seeking light on the subject. In Richard Wright's *Native Son,* I found Bigger Thomas and a keen insight into the problem.

My interest in this area persisted undiminished and then, in 1955, an event took place in Mississippi which turned me inside out: Emmett Till, a young Negro down from Chicago on a visit, was murdered, allegedly for flirting with a white woman. He had been shot, his head crushed from repeated blows with a blunt instrument, and his badly decomposed body was recovered from the river with a heavy weight on it. I was, of course, angry over the whole bit, but one day I saw in a magazine a picture of the white woman with whom Emmett Till was said to have flirted. While looking at the picture, I felt that little tension in the center of my chest I experience when a woman appeals to me. I was disgusted and angry with myself. Here was a woman who had caused the death of a black, possibly because, when he looked at her, he also felt the same tensions of lust and desire in his chest—and probably for the same general reasons that I felt them. It was all unacceptable to me. I looked at the picture again and again, and in spite of everything and against my will and the hate I felt for the woman and all that she represented, she appealed to me. I flew into a rage at myself, at America, at white women, at the history that had placed those tensions of lust and desire in my chest.

Two days later, I had a "nervous breakdown." For several days I ranted and raved against the white race, against white women in particular, against white America in general. When I came to myself, I was locked in a padded cell with not even the vaguest memory of how I got there. All I could recall was an eternity of pacing back and forth in the cell, preaching to the unhearing walls.

I had several sessions with a psychiatrist. His conclusion was that I hated my mother. How he arrived at this conclusion I'll never know, because he knew nothing about my mother; and when he'd ask me questions I would answer him with absurd lies. What revolted me about him was that he had heard me denouncing the whites, yet each time he interviewed me he deliberately guided the conversation back to my family life, to my childhood. That in itself was all right, but he deliberately blocked all my attempts to bring out the racial question, and he made it clear that he was not interested in my attitude toward whites. This was a Pandora's box he did not care to open. After I ceased my diatribes against the whites, I was let out of the hospital, back into the general inmate population just as if nothing had happened. I continued to brood over these events and over the dynamics of race relations in America.

During this period I was concentrating my reading in the field of economics. Having previously dabbled in the theories and writings of Rousseau, Thomas Paine, and Voltaire, I had added a little polish to my iconoclastic stance, without, however, bothering too much to understand their affirmative positions. In economics, because everybody seemed to find it necessary to attack and condemn Karl Marx in their writings, I sought out his books, and although he kept me with a headache, I took him for my authority. I was not prepared to understand him, but I was able to see in him a thoroughgoing critique and condemnation of capitalism. It was like taking medicine for me to find that, indeed, American capitalism deserved all the hatred and contempt that I felt for it in my heart. This had a positive, stabilizing effect upon me—to an extent because I was not about to become stable—and it diverted me from my previous preoccupation: morbid broodings on the black man and the white woman. Pursuing my readings into the history of socialism, I read, with very little understanding, some of the passionate, exhortatory writings of Lenin; and I fell in love with Bakunin and Nechayev's *Catechism of the Revolutionist*—the principles of which, along with some of Machiavelli's advice, I sought to incorporate into my own behavior. I took the *Catechism* for my bible and, standing on a one-man platform that had nothing to do with the reconstruction of society, I began consciously incorporating these principles into my daily life, to employ tactics of ruthlessness in my dealings with everyone with whom I came into contact. And I began to look at white America through these new eyes.

Somehow I arrived at the conclusion that, as a matter of principle, it was of paramount importance for me to have an antagonistic, ruthless attitude toward white women. The term *outlaw* appealed to me and at the time my parole date was drawing near, I considered myself to be mentally free—I was an "outlaw." I had stepped outside of the white man's law, which I repudiated with scorn and self-satisfaction. I became a law unto myself—my own legislature, my own supreme court, my own executive. At the moment I walked out of the prison gate, my feelings toward white women in general could be summed up in the following lines:

TO A WHITE GIRL

I love you
Because you're white,
Not because you're charming
Or bright.
Your whiteness

Is a silky thread
Snaking through my thoughts
In redhot patterns
Of lust and desire.

I hate you
Because you're white.
Your white meat
Is nightmare food.
White is
The skin of Evil.
You're my Moby Dick,
White Witch,
Symbol of the rope and hanging tree,
Of the burning cross.

Loving you thus
And hating you so,
My heart is torn in two.
Crucified.

I became a rapist. To refine my technique and *modus operandi,*
I started out by practicing on black girls in the ghetto—in the
black ghetto where dark and vicious deeds appear not as aber-
rations or deviations from the norm, but as part of the suffi-
ciency of the Evil of a day—and when I considered myself
smooth enough, I crossed the tracks and sought out white prey.
I did this consciously, deliberately, willfully, methodically—
though looking back I see that I was in a frantic, wild, and
completely abandoned frame of mind.

Rape was an insurrectionary act. It delighted me that I was
defying and trampling upon the white man's law, upon his system of values, and that I was defiling his women—and this
point, I believe, was the most satisfying to me because I was
very resentful over the historical fact of how the white man has
used the black woman. I felt I was getting revenge. From the
site of the act of rape, consternation spreads outwardly in
concentric circles. I wanted to send waves of consternation
throughout the white race. Recently, I came upon a quotation
from one of LeRoi Jones' poems taken from his book *The Dead
Lecturer:*

A cult of death need of the simple striking arm under the street
lamp. The cutters from under their rented earth. Come up, black

dada nihilismus. Rape the white girls. Rape their fathers. Cut the mothers' throats.

I have lived those lines and I know that if I had not been apprehended I would have slit some white throats. There are, of course, many young blacks out there right now who are slitting white throats and raping the white girl. They are not doing this because they read LeRoi Jones' poetry, as some of his critics seem to believe. Rather, LeRoi is expressing the funky facts of life.

After I returned to prison, I took a long look at myself and, for the first time in my life, admitted that I was wrong, that I had gone astray—astray not so much from the white man's law as from being human, civilized—for I could not approve the act of rape. Even though I had some insight into my own motivations, I did not feel justified. I lost my self-respect. My pride as a man dissolved and my whole fragile moral structure seemed to collapse, completely shattered.

That is why I started to write. To save myself.

I realized that no one could save me but myself. The prison authorities were both uninterested and unable to help me. I had to seek out the truth and unravel the snarled web of my motivations. I had to find out who I am and what I want to be, what type of man I should be, and what I could do to become the best of which I was capable. I understood that what had happened to me had also happened to countless other blacks and it would happen to many, many more.

I learned that I had been taking the easy way out, running away from problems. I also learned that it is easier to do evil than it is to do good. And I have been terribly impressed by the youth of America, black and white. I am proud of them because they have reaffirmed my faith in humanity. I have come to feel what must be love for the young people of America and I want to be part of the good and greatness that they want for all people. From my prison cell, I have watched America slowly coming awake. It is not fully awake yet, but there is soul in the air and everywhere I see beauty. I have watched the sit-ins, the freedom raids, the Mississippi Blood Summers, demonstrations all over the country, the FSM movement, the teach-ins, and the mounting protest over Lyndon Strangelove's foreign policy—all of this, the thousands of little details, show me it is time to straighten up and fly right. That is why I decided to concentrate on my writings and efforts in this area. We are a very sick country—I, perhaps, am sicker than most. But I accept that. I told you in the beginning that I am extremist by nature—so it is only right that I should be extremely sick.

I was very familiar with the Eldridge who came to prison, but that Eldridge no longer exists. And the one I am now is in some ways a stranger to me. You may find this difficult to understand but it is very easy for one in prison to lose his sense of self. And if he has been undergoing all kinds of extreme, involved, and unregulated changes, then he ends up not knowing who he is. Take the point of being attractive to women. You can easily see how a man can lose his arrogance or certainty on that point while in prison! When he's in the free world, he gets constant feedback on how he looks from the number of female heads he turns when he walks down the street. In prison he gets only hate-stares and sour frowns. Years and years of bitter looks. Individuality is not nourished in prison, neither by the officials nor by the convicts. It is a deep hole out of which to climb.

What must be done, I believe, is that all these problems— particularly the sickness between the white woman and the black man—must be brought out into the open, dealt with and resolved. I know that the black man's sick attitude toward the white woman is a revolutionary sickness: it keeps him perpetually out of harmony with the system that is oppressing him. Many whites flatter themselves with the idea that the Negro male's lust and desire for the white dream girl is purely an esthetic attraction, but nothing could be farther from the truth. His motivation is often of such a bloody, hateful, bitter, and malignant nature that whites would really be hard pressed to find it flattering. I have discussed these points with prisoners who were convicted of rape, and their motivations are very plain. But they are very reluctant to discuss these things with white men who, by and large, make up the prison staffs. I believe that in the experience of these men lies the knowledge and wisdom that must be utilized to help other youngsters who are heading in the same direction. I think all of us, the entire nation, will be better off if we bring it all out front. A lot of people's feelings will be hurt, but that is the price that must be paid.

It may be that I can harm myself by speaking frankly and directly, but I do not care about that at all. Of course I want to get out of prison, badly, but I shall get out some day. I am more concerned with what I am going to be after I get out. I know that by following the course which I have charted I will find my salvation. If I had followed the path laid down for me by the officials, I'd undoubtedly have long since been out of prison— but I'd be less of a man. I'd be weaker and less certain of where I want to go, what I want to do, and how to go about it.

The price of hating other human beings is loving oneself less.

"Affidavit #1
I Am 33 Years Old"

by ELDRIDGE CLEAVER

In the aftermath of the Oakland shoot-out Cleaver's parole was revoked and he was sent to Vacaville Prison. While there, he prepared the following affidavit as a document to be used in his legal defense.

[—Robert Scheer, Editor]

I am thirty-three years old. My first fifteen years were given to learning how to cope with the world and developing my approach to life. I blundered in my choices and set off down a road that was a dead end. Long years of incarceration is what I found on that road, from Juvenile Hall at the beginning to San Quentin, Folsom, and Soledad State Prisons at the end. From my sixteenth year, I spent the next fifteen years in and out of prison, the last time being an unbroken stay of nine years.

During my last stay in prison, I made the desperate decision to abandon completely the criminal path and to redirect my life. While in prison, I concentrated on developing the skills of a writer and I wrote a book which a publisher bought while I was still in prison and which was published after I was out on parole.

It looked like smooth sailing for me. I had fallen in love with a beautiful girl and got married; my book was soon to be published, and I had a good job as a staff writer with *Ramparts* magazine in San Francisco. I had broken completely with my old life. Having gone to jail each time out of Los Angeles, I had also put Los Angeles behind me, taking my parole to the Bay Area. I had a totally new set of friends, and, indeed, I had a brand new life.

The thought of indulging in any "criminal activity" was as absurd and irrelevant as the thought of sprouting wings and flying to the moon. Besides, I was too busy. I joined the Black Panther Party, and because of my writing skills and interest in communications, became the editor of the party's newspaper, *The Black Panther*. In this I found harmony with my wife, Kathleen, who had worked in the communications department of SNCC in Atlanta, Georgia, and who, after our marriage, moved to San Francisco, joined the Black Panther Party, and became our Communications Secretary. Also, she is our party's candidate for the 18th Assembly District seat in San Francisco, running on the Peace and Freedom Party ticket. With my job at *Ramparts,* my political activity, editing the newspaper, and work on a new book, I had more to do than I could handle. My life was an endless round of speeches, organizational meetings, and a few hours snatched here and there on my typewriter.

I thought that the parole authorities would be pleased with my new life because in terms of complying with the rules governing conduct on parole, I was a model parolee. But such was not the case. My case was designated a "Special Study Case," which required that I see my parole agent four times each month, once at home, once at my job, once "in the field," and once in his office. My parole agent, Mr. R. L. Bilideau, was white, but his boss, Mr. Isaac Rivers, was a black man. Together these two gentlemen were my contact with the parole authorities. On a personal level, we got along very well together, and we spent many moments talking about the world and its problems. However, I could never believe in them as sincere friends, because they were organization men and experience had taught me that, on receiving orders from above, they would snap into line and close ranks against me.

The first time this happened was when, on April 15, 1967, I made a speech at Kezar Stadium criticizing this country's role in the war in Vietnam. The speech was part of the program of the Spring Mobilization Against the War in Vietnam, during the International Days of Protest. There were demonstrations from coast to coast. Dr. Martin Luther King spoke at the rally in New York and his wife at our rally at Kezar. The crowd was estimated at about 65,000 and the speeches were shown on television. Members of the parole authority, who don't like me, I was told, saw excerpts of my speech on TV and launched their campaign to have my parole revoked, but failed. Even though I had a perfect right to free speech, Mr. Rivers and Mr. Bilideau said there were those in the State Capital who, for political purposes, were clamoring to have my parole revoked and me returned to prison. They advised me to cool it and forsake my rights in the interest of not antagonizing those in Sacramento who did not like my politics. From then on, I was under constant pressure through them to keep my mouth shut and my pen still on any subject that might arouse a negative reaction in certain circles in Sacramento. Because I was violating neither any law of the land nor any rule of parole, upon being assured by my attorney that I was strictly within my rights, I decided not to accept these warnings and continued exercising my right to free speech and to write what was on my mind.

The next crisis occurred two weeks later when I was arrested in Sacramento with a delegation of armed Black Panthers, who visited the Capitol in this manner as a shrewd political and publicity gesture. The news media, heavily concentrated in the Capitol, gave the Black Panthers a million dollars' worth of publicity and helped spread the Panther message to black people that they should arm themselves against a racist country that was becoming increasingly repressive. Although I was there as a reporter, with an assignment from my magazine, and with the advance permission of my parole agent, I was arrested by the Sacramento police; and then the parole authority slapped a "Hold" on me so that I could not get out on bail. To the surprise of both the cops and the parole authority, their investigations proved that my press credentials were in order, that I was indeed there on an assignment, and that I had permission from my parole agent—also, that I had been armed with nothing more lethal than a camera and a ball point pen. Still the Sacramento cops would not drop the charges and the parole authority would not lift its "Hold" until the judge, citing the obvious "mistake" on the part of the cops, released me on my own recognizance. Then, magnanimously, the parole authority lifted its "Hold."

When I returned to San Francisco, I was again told about the clamor in Sacramento to have my parole revoked. My enemies, I was told, had stayed up all night scanning TV film footage, trying to find a shot of me with a gun in my hands. No luck. But anyhow, severe new restrictions were to be imposed. 1) I was not to go outside a seven mile area; specifically, I was not to cross the Bay Bridge. 2) I was to keep my name out of the news for the next six months; specifically, my face was not to appear on any TV screen. 3) I was not to make any more speeches. 4) And I was not to write anything critical of the California Department of Corrections or any California politician. In short, I was to play dead, or I would be sent back to prison. "All that Governor Reagan has to do," I was told, "is sign his name on a dotted line and you are dead, with no appeal." Knowing that this was true and with my back thus to the wall, I decided to play it cool and go along with them, as I didn't see what else I could do. My attorneys said that we could challenge it in court, but that I would probably have to pound the Big Yard San Quentin for a couple of years, waiting for the court to hand down a decision. I was in a bad bag.

Things stayed like that, but after a couple of months the travel ban was lifted with all the other restrictions remaining in force.

Then, on October 28, 1967, Huey Newton, Minister of Defense and leader of our party, was shot down in the streets by an Oakland cop and was arrested and charged with the murder of one Oakland cop and the wounding of another. Bobby Seale, Chairman of our party, was serving a six months' jail sentence for the Sacramento incident, and I was the only effective public speaker that we had. A campaign to mobilize support in Huey's defense had to be launched immediately. So in November, 1967, I started making speeches again and writing in Huey's defense. The political nature of the case, and the fact that it involved a frame-up by the Oakland Police Department and the D.A.'s office, dictated that I had not only to criticize politicians but also the police. Well, helping Huey stay out of the gas chamber was more important than my staying out of San Quentin, so I went for broke. TV, radio, newspapers, magazines, the works. I missed no opportunity to speak out with Huey's side of the story. Mr. Rivers and Mr. Bilideau told me that the decision had already been made above to revoke my parole at the first pretext. Living thus on borrowed time, I tried to get as much done as I possibly could before time ran out.

In the latter part of December, 1967, Bobby Seale's sentence ran out and he was free to speak. Mass public support for Huey had developed. Our party had formed a coalition with the new Peace and Freedom Party, demanding that Huey be set free. In addition, we arranged to run Huey for Congress in the 7th Congressional District of Alameda County, to run Bobby Seale for the 17th Assembly District, and, as I have mentioned, to run my wife, Kathleen, for the 18th Assembly seat in San Francisco.

With such a forum and with the assurance that we had already stimulated overwhelming support for Huey, I decided to back up a little. Maybe it was possible to stay the hand of the parole authority. I cut back drastically on my public speaking.

In January, the Police departments of Oakland, Berkeley and San Francisco unleashed a terror and arrest campaign against the Black Panther Party. Members of the party were being arrested and harassed constantly. On January 15, 1968, at 3 a.m. the Special Tactical Squad of San Francisco's Police Department kicked down the door of my home, terrorizing my wife, myself, and our party's Revolutionary Artist, Emory Douglass, who was our guest that night.

On February 17, which was Huey Newton's twenty-sixth birthday, we staged a huge rally at the Oakland Auditorium, featuring Stokely Carmichael and his first public speech following his triumphal tour of the revolutionary countries of the world, and also featuring, as a surprise guest, H. Rap Brown, along with the venerable James Foreman, who took the occasion to announce the merger of SNCC and the Black Panther Party. Held in the shadow of the Alameda County jail wherein Huey is confined, the theme of the rally was "Come See About Huey." Over five thousand people showed up, a shattering and unequivocal demonstration of the broad support built up for the Minister of Defense. A similar rally was held in Los Angeles the next day, and altogether Stokely spent nine days in California beating the drums for Huey.

Every time we turned around Bobby Seale was getting arrested on frivolous, trumped-up charges. On February 22, 1968, a posse of Berkeley police kicked down Bobby's door, dragging him and his wife, Artie, from bed and arresting them on a sensational charge of conspiracy to commit murder. The same night, six other members of the party were arrested on the same charge. The ridiculous charge of conspiracy to commit murder was quickly dropped, but all arrested were held to answer on various gun law violations, all of which were unfounded. All in all, during that hectic week, sixteen members of our party were arrested gratuitously and charged with offenses that had never been committed. Although we know that we will ultimately beat all of these cases in court, they constitute a serious drain on our time, energy, and financial resources, the last of which have always been virtually non-existent.

During these hectic days, public sentiment throughout the Bay Area swung heavily in our favor because it was obvious to a blind man that we were being openly persecuted by the police.

In the midst of all this, McGraw-Hill Publishing Co., on February 28, 1968, published my book, *Soul On Ice,* and a lot of publicity was focused on me as a result. By this time, my parole agent had virtually given up coming to see me, sending for me, or even calling me on the phone, a development that kept my nerves on edge. Was this the calm before the storm?

I was out of the state most of the month of March, filling TV appearances with my book, mostly in New York.

On April 3, 1968, the Oakland Police Department invaded the regular meeting of our party at St. Augustine's Church at 27th and West Street. Led by a captain, brandishing shotguns, and accompanied by a white monsignor and a black preacher, about a dozen of them burst through the door. Neither Bobby Seale nor myself was at that particular meeting (Bobby was in L.A. and I had left minutes before the raid in response to an urgent call). Our National Captain, David Hilliard, was in charge. David said that the cops came in with their shotguns leveled, but that when they saw him in charge they looked confused and disappointed. Mumbling incoherently, they lowered their weapons and stalked out.

Father Neil, whose church it is, happened to be present to witness the entire event. Theretofore, criticism of the police had been just that, and although he was inclined to believe that there was some validity to all the complaints, it was all still pretty abstract to him because he had never witnessed anything with his own eyes. Well, he had witnessed it now, and in his own church—with ugly shotguns thrown down on innocent, unarmed people who were holding a quiet peaceful assembly. Father Neil was outraged. He called a press conference next day at which he denounced the Oakland Police Department for behaving like Nazi storm troopers inside his church. However, Father Neil's press conference was upstaged by the fact that earlier in the day, his brother of the cloth, Martin Luther King, had got assassinated in Memphis, Tennessee. An ugly cloud boding evil settled over the nation.

A few days prior to the assassination of Martin Luther King, Marlon Brando had flown up from Hollywood to find out for himself what the hell was going on in the Bay Area. We took him to my pad and talked and argued with him all night long, explaining to him our side of the story. We had to wade through the history of the world before everything was placed in perspective and Brando could see where the Black Panther Party was coming from. When Brando split back to Hollywood, after accompanying Bobby Seale to court next day, we felt that we had gained a sincere friend and valuable ally in the struggle.

On the third night following the raid on St. Augustine's church, members of the Oakland Police Department tried to kill me. They did kill my companion, Little Bobby Hutton, Treasurer of our party and the first Black Panther recruited by Huey Newton and Bobby Seale when they organized the party in October, 1966. They murdered Little Bobby in cold blood. I saw them shoot him, with fifty guns aimed at my head. I did get shot in the leg.

I am convinced that I was marked for death that night, and the only reason I was not killed was that there were too many beautiful black people crowded around demanding that the cops not shoot me, too many witnesses for even the brazen, contemptuous and contemptible Oakland Pigs.

A few hours later at 4 a.m. on April 7, someone somewhere in the shadowy secret world of the California Adult Authority ordered my parole revoked. While I was still in the emergency ward of Highland Hospital, three Oakland cops kept saying to me: "You're going home to San Quentin tonight!" Before the sun rose on a new day, charged with attempted murder after watching Little Bobby being murdered and almost joining him, I was shackled hand and foot and taken by Lieutenant Snellgrove and two other employees of the Department of Corrections to San Quentin.

Lieutenant Snellgrove, whom I knew very well from my stay at San Quentin and who remembered me, looked at me and said, while we rode in the back seat of the car headed for San Quentin, "Bad night, huh?" He was not being facetious—what else could he say—and neither was I. "Yeah," I said. "About the baddest yet."

Further, Affiant sayeth not.

April 19, 1968

Candidates for Public Office

ELECT WENDELL HOLMAN

REPRESENTATIVE

In this part we make a complete about-face and turn our attention to four men who have sought political power by the most traditional and accepted means: election to public office. Two of these men—Richard J. Daley and John V. Lindsay—are mayors of great cities; a third, Bobby K. Hayes, was an unsuccessful candidate for the Senate seat currently held by J. William Fulbright of Arkansas; the fourth, Senator Charles Percy of Illinois, is one of that small group of public figures who can realistically aspire to the Presidency of the United States.

In many ways the contrast between Richard Daley and John Lindsay is peculiarly revealing about the changes in American society and politics that have taken place since the end of World War II. Mayor Daley still lives in the Chicago community where he was raised. His roots are deep in what have come to be known as the ethnic populations in America—the close-knit, working-class and middle-class communities made up of the descendants of the Irish, German, Polish, Italian, and Baltic peoples who immigrated to the United States in the nineteenth century. These largely urban settlements formed the base of the great political machines that flourished in New York, Chicago, Boston, and elsewhere during the first half of the twentieth century. The network of block captains and ward heelers, supported by city jobs at the disposal of the party in power, enabled the machine bosses to deliver the vote in reliable blocs on election day. Men like Mayor Daley worked their way up in the machine, much as a corporation president in the old days might work his way up from the stock room to the board room.

What Richard Daley is to the old politics, John Lindsay is to the new. Coming from an upper-class Protestant background, Mayor Lindsay rules a city that was once controlled by Tammany Hall, the greatest of the old political machines. He has held onto his post, in the face of fierce opposition, by assembling a new alliance of voters: the black and Puerto Rican ghetto dwellers, who were largely ignored by the machine, and the politically liberal upper-middle class, which had no need of the services provided by Tammany bosses. The combination appears unnatural, bringing together as it does voters from such diverse segments of American society.

But as Robert Kennedy proved in 1968 before his death, and
as countless candidates on the liberal wing of the political
spectrum have shown since, this union of the poor, the blacks,
and the well-to-do liberal voters is a new fact of the electoral
scene.

Bobby K. Hayes of Arkansas and Charles Percy of Illinois also
provide a contrast that tells us much about America. Hayes,
a self-made millionaire, is a voice of that rural populism that
paradoxically combines a "liberal" concern for the welfare of
the poor and unpowerful with a "conservative" commitment
to religion and the old values. Men like Hayes tend to be
ignored by communications media that originate in the urban
centers of sophistication and wealth. Yet countless millions
of Americans live their lives a good deal closer to the world
of Bobby K. Hayes than to Los Angeles, Chicago, or New York.

Charles Percy is about as different from Bobby K. Hayes
as one millionaire can be from another. Growing up in a poor
urban family, Percy followed to the letter the path of the dutiful
son. Percy is the American success story in its modern,
organizational version. He rose to the presidency of a large
corporation at the extraordinary age of twenty-eight by being
the personal protégé of the old president. Suave, cultivated,
literate, Percy is the very picture of corporate success and
respectability. As a leader of the moderate wing of the
Republican Party, he speaks for the most technologically
advanced, internationalist-minded sector of the American
business world.

These four men—Daley, Lindsay, Hayes, and Percy—represent
only a handful of the political styles to be found among
candidates for public office. In this part there is no deep-South
senator, no farm-belt conservative, no big-city liberal Democrat.
Nor have I been able to include any of the countless candidates
for minor city, county, and state office whose collective effect
on American politics is so great. Despite the rapidly rising
cost of political campaigns, the electoral route is still the most
direct, and for many the most satisfying, path into public life
in America.

4. Richard Daley: An Old-Style Machine Boss

"Daley of Chicago"
by DAVID HALBERSTAM

In the political year 1968, Richard J. Daley surveyed the city of Chicago and was master of it. He exercised power as probably no man outside of Washington exercised it, and he was by most norms of the American ethic, particularly his own, a towering success. The poor of his city were afraid of him and the powerful of the nation deferred to him.

.   .   .

. . . . In a profession where municipal officials keeled over like flies after one or two terms, especially if they were effective, thrown out by angry undertaxed constituents who felt themselves overtaxed, who hated the parking and the air and their neighbors, Richard J. Daley reigned supreme, King Richard as he was called in Chicago.

Four times he was elected, the fourth by his largest majority, 74 per cent. His years of success had virtually left Chicago

without an electoral process, *that* was his achievement; in a
city where few new buildings had been started before him, the
sky was pierced again and again by new skyscrapers, each bigger and more gleaming than the last, and ever-grateful rich and
aristocratic businessmen taught from the cradle to shun the
Democratic party—that party of the machine and the Irish—
competed to enlist in Republicans for Daley, vowed to give
bigger contributions, while the most famous political scientists
of Chicago, hawks and doves, liberals and conservatives, joined
Professors for Daley. Municipal experts, technocrats with their
measuring sticks, were in general agreement that Daley was
the most successful Mayor in America—good cost accounting,
good police department, good fire department, good social-
economic programs. He was a politician with a smooth-function-
ing political machine in an age when machines were not
supposed to function. (When one reporter for a local paper
saw him at a meeting, a man who knew a machine when he
saw one, Daley would say simply, "Organization, not machine.
Get that. Organization, not machine.")

.   .   .

Richard J. Daley is the product of the politics of another
time. "I think one of the real problems he has with Negroes is
understanding that the Irish are no longer the out-ethnic group,"
one Negro says. He would be doomed in the cosmetology of
today's politics: those jowls, that heavyset look. He doesn't
look like a modern municipal leader, a cost-accounting specialist; he looks, yes, exactly like a big city boss, right out of the
smoke-filled room. "Daley will never really get a fair judging on
his abilities as a mayor because of the way he looks," an admir-
ing Chicago political scientist says. "He's much better than
people think."

When he was first elected he spoke badly—"dese" and
"dems"—but he has worked hard and now has very considerable
control over most of his political appearances; there has also
been a sharp decline in his malapropisms, though some Chicago
reporters still collect them. Two of the best are *we will reach
greater and greater platitudes of achievement,* and *they have*

*vilified me, they have crucified me, yes they have even criti-
cized me.* He is not good on the tube, but it is a mistake to
underestimate his power and charm in person. "He exudes" one
fellow Irishman says, "the confidence and power of a man who
has achieved everything he set out to do and then a little more,
but he also has the black moods of an Irishman and if you catch
him in one of those it can be pretty frightening."

He dominates Chicago and he knows it, and this adds to his
confidence. "People are always coming to me and telling me
that they're going down to see the Mayor and tell him off," one
Negro remarks, "and off they go, and of course he charms them
completely and they come back and I ask, 'Well, brother, how
did it go?' and they tell me, 'Why the Mayor's a fine man and
we *know*'—get that, we know—'he's going to do the right
thing.' " But clever, resounding speech is not his forte, and he
has learned that the less you say now, the less you have to
regret later, and indeed the problem may go away by then. He
has made a political virtue out of being inarticulate. He has
been satisfied with being Mayor, has consolidated his base
there, has never let his ambition run away with him; this is part
of the explanation for his power. He has sat there with a power
base, slowly adding to it, incorporating new men as they rose,
always looking for winners. Above all else Richard Daley loves
power and winners. An aide of John Kennedy's remembers
arriving in Chicago in 1960 for the first television debate, and
Kennedy asking again and again, "Where's Daley, where's
Daley," with no Daley to be found. "But after the debate," the
aide recalls, "the first person to break through into the studio,
with his flunkies around him like a flying wedge, was Daley.
He knew he had a winner."

He was a poor Irish boy, born in a time when the Irish felt
themselves despised in Protestant America. One reason, according to friends, that he was so close to Joseph Kennedy
was that they both shared the same boyhood scars. Daley's
father was a sheet-metal worker and an early union activist,
blacklisted at several plants. There were few avenues open to
an ambitious young Irish boy in those days and one of them was
politics; though he is widely admired by all of Chicago's business giants today for his financial acumen, it is a fact of life, of

which both are sharply aware, that he could not have made it in their world at that time.

More than most great men of power in America he is what he was. He lives in the same neighborhood where he was born, in the same house in which he has lived all his married life. He attends early Mass every day and observes the same basic tenets of the Catholic faith that he has based his life upon. His friends are the same small cluster of men, very much like himself, whom he has always known. His success has thrown him into the orbit of newer and more important men, but he has never crossed the line between association and friendship. His personal views remain rigid and he expects others to have the same; one reporter remembers a Daley son coming back from college recently with an unduly long haircut; Daley simply nodded at Matt Danaher, one of his deputies, and the boy was taken out for a trimming.

He is now the acknowledged master of the Democratic party machinery which gave him his start. The machine ethic was based upon hard work and loyalty; you worked your way up level by level. But loyalty rather than brilliance or social conscience or originality was the determining characteristic. It was and is a profession which abounded in limited men and hacks, of small men trying to throw around the power of bigger men, which often they only sniff at. Daley, apprenticing in a world of hacks, was and is no hack. He is an intelligent, strong-willed man, enormously hard-working. He set out within the party organization and mastered it, working his way up from precinct captain to committeeman to state legislator, a good one, easily distinguished from most of the men in Springfield, in his room every night studying the legislation. He was a young man who played by the rules of the game. He never frightened anyone, never looked too ambitious, accumulating political due bills all the time. He also mastered the art of finance as few active politicians in America have, eventually becoming director of revenue for Governor Adlai Stevenson.

.   .   .

Chicago is rougher than other cities. Even today its more sophisticated citizens take a quiet pleasure in talking about not only its past sins but its present vices and the current power of the crime Syndicate. The city's rough edge is often a little hard for Easterners to understand. A few years ago a Negro alderman named Ben Lewis was shot down in cold blood. A correspondent for an Eastern magazine was immediately cabled by his New York office for a piece which would include, among other things, the outraged reaction of the good people of Chicago. There was no outrage at all, he cabled back. "The feeling is that if he's an alderman, he's a crook, and if he's a crook then that's their business."

.   .   .

The Chicago machine had prospered under the New Deal, prospered to the point of venality, until it made Chicago probably the most corrupt city in the country. Everything could be bought or sold. The police force was largely concerned with street-corner traffic courts and the downtown center of the city was dying fast. So a reform movement was started behind Martin Kennelly, a clean and handsome businessman. He ran in 1951 as a reform candidate and won. The reformers were delighted; so were the Syndicate and the machine. It became easier to steal than before; underneath the surface honesty almost everything went wrong. Kennelly was totally naïve about a very tough city. To this day, a lot of Daley critics, knowing his faults and failings, think of John Lindsay and see Martin Kennelly.

The local Chicago establishment was so disturbed about the Kennelly years that an informal meeting was held to decide what to do about the Mayor. The first thing, they decided, was to destroy the myth that they themselves had created of the Good Reform Mayor. So they decided to approach a nationally known magazine writer and have him come in to expose Kennelly. Tom Stokes was selected and a leading lawyer was duly sent to visit him. Stokes proceeded to give him a lecture on why a nice businessman with high morals and fine ideals could never govern a city as tough as Chicago; he could never understand the balance between what the city required and what the politicians and crooks would permit. Chicago needed, Stokes said, a tough professional politician who understood the under-side of Chicago life and how to control it.

Enter Richard J. Daley. When he decided to run for Mayor he already wore an important political hat, clerk of Cook County, which was like being Secretary of State for the machine; it allowed him to dispense much of the machine's patronage. Before making the race he reportedly promised Colonel Arvey that he would give up the organizational job (which he didn't and it became the secret of his success). The primary was particularly bitter and it was repeatedly charged that electing Daley would be like throwing the rascals back in.

"I would not unleash the forces of evil," he countered. "It's a lie. I will follow the training my good Irish mother gave me—and Dad. If I am elected, I will embrace mercy, love, charity, and walk humbly with my God."

The machine was split (in the same ward one precinct went for Kennelly 485 to 7, while another precinct went for Daley 400 to 10). A number of reformers such as Stevenson came out for Daley, and with the help of Bill Dawson, Lord of the Negro wards, Daley won. In the general election he was opposed by Robert Merriam, an attractive Republican candidate who gave him a hard race. It was a hard fought campaign, the question being, who's going to control Chicago, State Street or the Neighborhoods (the rich or the poor)? Daley won again, de-cided to be both Mayor and organization chairman, thus to a degree breaking with Arvey. Most of his success has stemmed from that decision; it is an extraordinary achievement to hold both jobs with so little opposition for so long. . . .

.   .   .

. . . Chicago, despite all Daley's successes, is like other American cities: a place which is rotting. The pattern is not unusual—whites leaving the inner city as soon as they can afford to, jobs leaving the city too; Negroes taking over more of their old areas, Negroes bitter about their lack of jobs, their lack of power, their shabby schools, becoming more violent, their violence driving out more and more whites. The Poles and the other ethnic groups are angry and tense about the blacks *because they get all the attention,* because the country *is being run for them, all the politicians have sold out to them.* The ethnic groups hold onto their houses, bought after long and hard saving, by sheer dint of organized neighborhood feeling against the Negroes. White Congressmen from Polish neighborhoods, old-style New Deal liberals, are backtracking fast on civil rights, attacking school bussing, telling their friends, *What can I do, I try and explain, but they won't listen, they just won't listen.* The liberals are worried about the city but are moving to the suburbs faster and faster, while the traditionally liberal University of Chicago district becomes blacker and blacker. ("By the time the city is liberal enough to have a Jewish Mayor, it will have a black Mayor," one Jew says.) Those in our cities who are left to integrate with the blacks are those least prepared to understand and accept the problems of the blacks.

Perhaps 30 per cent of Chicago is black. Yet the black ghettos of Chicago are curiously powerless: they have little political bargaining power, and they have fewer jobs. A recent Urban League study on black power in Chicago showed that though Negroes composed 30 per cent of the population, they had only 2.6 per cent of policy-making positions in government and finance, and even that figure was probably optimistic.

Negro political leaders in Chicago have traditionally opted to to play the machine's game, so that blacks in general have repeatedly been sold out by their own people; their representatives are ward politicians first, and Negroes second. "They can say no to us without checking higher up," one Negro said, "but they can never say yes without checking higher up." "I sometimes wonder," one white official remarked, "why so many of the Negroes on the City Council are so docile in this day and age, and then I realize that if they weren't docile they wouldn't be there."

The black community is thus divided against itself; its representatives are largely machine politicians interested in the traditional patronage and financial benefits, sensitive about intruding or being pushy in a white man's world, down-playing civil rights—just some of the boys mimicking the style of their white colleagues. "They're not even Toms," one Negro said.

"There's no pretense at all to them. They play the game. That's what it's all about."

When on occasion a new Negro leader rises up and reflects power, Daley will try to accommodate and offer new and special privileges, with the alternative being a freeze-out. "So you have a tradition of people selling out, getting eroded. It's all too much for them," one white liberal who formerly served in the legislature said. "I know that white liberals will sit next to Negroes in the House and then the Negroes will occasionally encourage them on some liberal legislation. But when the vote comes the Negroes aren't there. So you ask them what the hell's going on, and they say, 'Look man, it's all right for you, you've got your own base, and you have something to fall back on. But this is all I've got, and if I don't do what they want, then I'm out of here.'"

All of this has probably tended to lull Daley's own view of reality. As one politician said, "The thing about him is that his machine is too successful for his own good. He allows these people so many jobs and so many positions and he thinks that he has real Negroes there and that the black community is satisfied. He doesn't realize that the community thinks that these people work for him, not for them. Then he sees the votes for him in the black wards and they're terrific votes because by the time the electoral process gets around, there's not much opposition and a lot of those people are scared to death anyway. So he decides that all this talk by civil-rights people is just that, talk."

This, of course, is true only of the South Side, which is Chicago's older, more traditional ghetto. The South Side has some organizational form, some black representation. The West Side, in contrast, is a jungle. It is the port of entry for all the young illiterate blacks coming up from the South, and it is a wild, disorganized, and pitiful section. Those Negroes who make it go on to the South Side. Those who can't remain on the West Side, hopeless, without jobs, changing homes several times a year; the business establishments on the West Side are mostly all owned by whites who live elsewhere, the landlords are largely white and absentee, even the political machinery is controlled by whites, largely by Jews who once lived there and moved away, but have kept the political control. Inside it the kids are alienated and angry, totally outside the system.

After the murder of Dr. King the West Side burned. "Now," says A. A. Rayner, an independent alderman from the South Side, "they're building it back up just the way it was before, no decisions on the part of the people who live there, just the same people from the outside making all the decisions. If they put it up the same way, then it'll surely come down the same way again."

Daley would deal with these people if they had power, but they are so hopeless they are disinterested in the electoral process, their needs too great for the ballot. For twelve years they have gotten crumbs and the Mayor has manipulated them, confident that Chicago's Negroes have nowhere else to go in a showdown. If it is a choice between siding with them and with the white ethnic neighborhoods, which would have somewhere else to go (and with whom he has a basic sympathy and identity), he will edge more toward the whites. Thus black power in Chicago has stayed so small that finally in their anger and bitterness the blacks have a power, but it is a negative one, a power to destroy.

It is really a clash of two different cultures and ethics. Daley is from and of Bridgeport, a small Irish-American community which holds steadfastly to what it was. Going through it, the small bungalows, incredibly well kept up, sparkling with paint, the Blue Star flags in the windows, one has a sense of another time and place in America. Daley has lived in the same house for more than thirty years; he goes home for lunch every day. It is a neighborhood which has produced the last three Mayors of Chicago, and it has an unusually high percentage of people with city jobs. "Just about every house on the street has someone with political connections," one critic says. It is suspicious of outsiders and new ideas; Negroes do not walk its streets at night. Nor do they buy its property.

By dint of much effort, church centered, the property is kept up and the neighborhood is maintained. Negroes are not permitted to buy. A few years ago an unduly liberal resident sold to a Negro and riots resulted, windows were smashed, and the Negro's belongings were bodily moved out and the local Democratic organization moved two whites into the house.

Daley, of course, is better than Bridgeport, but he is still a part of it, and it influences the way he looks at social problems. He is deeply religious, but his religion is pre-Ecumenical, pre-John XXIII, where there is individual sin, but little social sin. He can tolerate small and petty graft, excuse an occasional roaring drunk, a failing of business virtue, but he cannot excuse adultery, and cannot understand or tolerate a man who fathers a family and then deserts it. He seems unable to understand the forces which create these failings.

He is a product of a time when the American ethic was to succeed, and those who didn't succeed at least respected those who did. He does not like poverty programs, in part because they represent a threat to his power—federal money going directly to black neighborhoods, without his control, diluting his base and creating a new base for an organization outside his machine, *financing his opposition.* Moreover, he doesn't think these people, what one lawyer calls "the underclass," are capable of leading and governing. "In his heart of hearts," one longtime associate says, "I think he would like to grab those people by their lapels, shake them and say *Get to work.*" Two years ago a nun who was a militant civil-rights activist on the West Side went to see Daley and pleaded with him to come out there, to see the conditions, to look at the schools, to see the children.

"Look, Sister," the Mayor answered, "you and I come from the same background. We know how tough it was. But we picked ourselves up by our bootstraps."

5. John Lindsay:
A New-Style
Big-City Mayor

"Lindsay of New York"

by LARRY L. KING

Sometimes in the better regions of New York City there are spring days of such sudden sun and splendor that the austerities of winter are little more than a blur on the memory. On those days there is no sweeter garden than Central Park when viewed from the Fifth Avenue side in the East Sixties ...

There is no smog on such days, no race-baiting taxi drivers, no threats of subway strikes or unremoved garbage. Nor is there any suggestion of street muggers, rapists (four per day), murderers (two daily), narcotics addicts (perhaps 100,000), traffic nightmares, sub-par schools, or Times Square deviates. The miserable black hells of Harlem, Bedford-Stuyvesant, and Brownsville, where postmen delivering welfare checks twice monthly are escorted by armed plainclothesmen, seem worlds away. Such idyllic times and places are almost dangerous, for they disguise reality and deny the darker New York world

—sordid, bleak, restless, corrupting and corrupted—so common now to the eyes of John Vliet Lindsay.

"They say the Presidency is the world's toughest job," the Mayor of New York City said on just such a day . . . as he hurried down the City Hall steps toward yet another luncheon speech, "but the Presidency is so wonderfully insulated. In this job everyone has access to you. There's no escape." More than any other New York Mayor (including the chesty La Guardia) he has gone into the streets to seek out his constituency. In so doing he has disdained protection and exposed himself to as many dangers as the late Robert Kennedy. With the possible exception of Cleveland's Mayor Carl Stokes, a Negro, Lindsay is the only metropolitan Mayor credited with almost single-handedly cooling the black ghettos through what Bill Buckley, the conservative icon, disdains as "streetwalking."

Some critics deride John Lindsay's ghetto walks as publicity gimmicks. Old-line Harlem politicians and con men, passed over by Lindsay's person-to-person approach and thus robbed of patronage and prestige, complain that he is being manipulated by a handful of "bought-off" black militants. Lindsay admits that many whites "think of me as a nigger-lover." Criticism even comes from men of good will: Tim Cooney, a former member of the City Hall ruling class under both Lindsay and ex-Mayor Robert Wagner, credits Lindsay with excellent intentions, but calls his walks "mindless substitutes in the absence of any real intellectual approaches to problems. Neither Lindsay nor the men around him are intellectual. They are men of action unfortunately prone to ride off without considering whether they are heading in the right direction."

Lindsay himself has few illusions that his celebrated strolls will forever suffice; he has remarked that "luck and rain" may have cooled New York in a time when lesser cities have had their most violent insurrections. "It's a finger-in-the-dike operation," he says. "I hope my example inspires our city employees to more personalized public service, and I think it shows my concern and my efforts to communicate. But walking isn't everything. We do a million things you never hear about."

·   ·   ·

[On Jan. 1, 1966,] John V. Lindsay, a Republican by name if

not by nature, became the "fusion" Mayor of a city where registered Democrats outnumber Republicans 2,400,000 to 700,000. His opponents variously called him "Pretty Boy" or "Destiny's Tot" or "Mr. Clean." He was derided for referring to New York City, with its 85,000 tons of soot and other foreign matter falling from the sky each year, as "Fun City."

Today Lindsay is perhaps proudest of having restored a measure of stability to the city's shaky financial underpinnings. "When I took office the city's capital reserves were down to $53,000—that's the same as you having only fifteen cents in your bank account. We've built our reserves up to around $80 million. New York City was $500 million in the red—Mayor Wagner borrowed even for current operating expenses and we've been paying those debts off at $50 million per year. ("Hell, he even bought *pencils* on credit," Lindsay declared after his first look at the City's books).

He has gone a long way toward reorganizing the city's incredibly tangled and often self-serving bureaucracies (reducing fifty-one departments to ten), and has attracted some 500 bright young middle-management types to city government—the first mass infusion of managerial blood since Depression days. The New York City police force, largest in the world, has been increased from 27,000 to 30,000 men, and the Mayor plans to add 3,000 more within the year; despite opposition from the clannish Patrolmen's Benevolent Association, the Mayor broke up the cozy "Irish Mafia" cliques that long ruled police precinct houses. Lindsay brought forth a city income tax which was bitterly opposed in the suburbs, but which forces the suburbanite who makes his money in New York City to contribute to its upkeep.

If Lindsay has not eliminated Midtown Manhattan's traffic snarls he has—by towing away 40,000 illegally parked vehicles and hitting violators with stiff fines—at least mitigated them. Through funds supplied by corporations and foundations he has established six neighborhood "Little City Halls," operating out of storefronts and each staffed by two city employees and local volunteers.[1] His administration has enacted the

---

[1] City Council Democrats, fearful the "Little City Halls" would evolve into Lindsay campaign headquarters, thwarted the Mayor's attempts to fund them with tax money.

nation's most stringent anti-air-pollution law and has convinced Con Edison—perhaps the Interplanetary Air Pollution Champion—to switch to a fuel containing less than one per cent sulphur dioxide. By closing Central Park and six others to Sunday traffic the Mayor has restored the parks to their role of sanctuary against the rush of the city.

Critics argue that New York's new housing fails to keep pace with the city's needs. Lindsay responds that "the housing pipeline was empty when I came in" and claims that by the end of the year he will have started 25,000 new units while completing "six or seven thousand—the largest number in a decade." He boasts of building "better-quality housing than any city has in the past. We're abating taxes on the land, we're not going so heavy for high-rises. Nobody will be ashamed to live in the houses we're building. They get away from the old 'project' concept."

.   .   .

Lindsay now knows (as he once naïvely seemed not to know) that New York City's massive problems will not be met within his stewardship, and may not be wholly satisfied by Judgment Day. He has learned that individuals and special-interest groups are not above foot-dragging and demagoguery, when ambitions collide. He could not sweep out bureaucratic deadwood in his reorganization scheme because of protective Civil Service regulations, nor could he authorize his Sanitation crews to ticket illegally parked vehicles—on the grounds they make efficient street cleaning impossible—without consent of the State Assembly. He is aware that the progressive reform Mayor must do business behind the door with labor, Wall Street, black militants, minor czars of the Bronx or Brooklyn, dissident students, Washington, the Patrolmen's Benevolent Association, the proud and sensitive Liberal Party, and the reactionary shopkeepers of Queens.

Lindsay learned to accommodate those time-consuming ceremonial functions which once so nettled him. Within one spring week he received—apparently cheerfully—members of the New York Mets plugging a charity baseball game, opened a new school for the blind, gave a cocktail party for New York

Congressmen and their assistants and a formal dinner for a famous composer, greeted visitors to City Hall ranging from the senior class of New Orleans' Sacred Heart High School to the Mayor of Moscow, dined at Le Pavillon with the men who mediated the 1966 transit strike, inspected mini-cabs made in England which were said to cut down air pollution as well as occupy less space (thus drawing blasts from New York taxi drivers and Detroit's big-car manufacturers), and accepted four plaques from fraternal organizations.

Though Lindsay has called New York City "a storehouse of the nation's superlatives" and proselytes even among visiting reporters ("You should move to New York. It's where the action is. Your wife would love our theater"), there are moments when his shoulders slump. "Some people once assumed all racial prejudice to be confined to the South," he said recently, "but there are bigots in New York the same as in Alabama." A few months ago, riding in a helicopter above Manhattan after a particularly tedious day, Mayor Lindsay silently took in the smoky, jammed, and indifferent stone mass below. Then, unsmiling, he turned his thumb down, held his nose with one hand, and with the other pulled an invisible chain to flush the whole of New York City down some gigantic drain.

One afternoon this May the Mayor's helicopter came into view over the Verrazano-Narrows Bridge, one hour ahead of sundown and twenty minutes behind schedule. Men waiting on the pampered greens of a Brooklyn golf course began to straighten their ties, cock their caps, or give last-minute rubdowns to their badges. A police captain conferred with a lieutenant, who in turn spoke to a sergeant, who then rudely commanded a cop without any trappings of rank. Such strict devotion to the chain-of-command enabled a tiny segment of the NYPD to get open the right rear door of the Mayor's limousine.

John Lindsay, a long lean figure against the sun, would have made an excellent target as he ducked to avoid the chopper blades, coattail billowing in the helicopter's backwash. A group of his civilian aides huddled apart from the nervous policemen. Lindsay crossed toward the cops in long, loping strides and smiled reassuringly. He shook all available hands while Sid Davidoff crowded close to say, "We're twenty minutes late. Don't forget to stop in So-and-So's furniture store and say hello to Such-and-Such. It's cool in Brownsville the last we heard."[2]

Like most of Lindsay's community visitations, this foray into Brooklyn was unannounced. Rolling in a four-car caravan to the prosperous stretch of shops where he would march up and down, hopefully collecting Pied Piper crowds, the Mayor studied a staff memo presumably containing the last word on Bay Ridge. "This is a community of successful business-men, white-collar or professional people," a Lindsay man briefed an outlander. "Jews . . . Italians . . . Irish. Some Syrians. Buckley ran pretty well over here."

Lindsay stood at the intersection of 86th Street and 4th Avenue, hands in his pockets, his eyes flitting here and there: seeing everything, or possibly nothing. The sons and daughters of Bay Ridge stopped to ogle, though no one made any greet-ings. One was reminded of those cold, closed looks reserved for transient strangers who suddenly appear on the main streets of crossroad Southern or Southwestern towns, suspect because they wear neckties in the middle of the week. Indeed, John Lindsay's six-feet, three-inch-and-a-fraction height as he stood alone on the corner, rather aloofly ignoring his cool-eyed subjects, was a Gary Cooper scene: the new Federal Marshal, grim-jawed and still covered with trail dust, showing himself to the citizens of the erring village he has pledged to tame or sweep clean.

The Gracie Mansion cowboy rocked on the balls of his feet; with a nod of his head he motioned over two staff deputies. ("Whatcha gonna do, Marshal?" Pause. Scuffling of dust with one booted toe. "Wal, Boys, Ah believe Ah'll mosey over to the Red Dog Saloon and drink me a sasparella.") The Mayor turned to dog-trot across the street to an open-front lunch

---

[2] A reference to a crisis in the predominantly Negro Brownsville-Ocean Hill school district, prompted by the disputed firing of 19 teachers and admin-istrators by a local board against the wishes of the New York Board of Educa-tion and the teacher's union.

counter. A curious if reserved crowd collected as Lindsay—his eyes somehow sightless and his familiar face apparently unrecognized by the hefty tired-blood blonde serving him—had his sasparella in the form of an ice-cream bar.

"My, he's so *handsome*," a passing matron whispered. "May I shake his hand?" "That's what he's here for," a Lindsay aide said. Suddenly the matron was shouting that he shouldn't dare raise taxes because high taxes were breaking the good family man. "I'm having a few problems myself," Lindsay said, smiling. The woman disappeared without her handshake.

John Lindsay's elongated, slender hands moved restlessly: coat button, tie, hair. One remembered those same self-conscious gestures from John F. Kennedy's moments of public unease. The Mayor paused at the entrance to a lamp store. "How's business?" he called jovially. *"What?"* the proprietor bellowed, as if perhaps he'd been indecently propositioned. Lindsay repeated himself. "So business is business," the store-keeper said, shrugging. Lindsay shrugged back and moved on to a dress shop. A stately blonde seized the Mayor's hand, pumping it enough to raise water, and said she played tennis at the same courts the Mayor frequented. "Good," Lindsay said, "fine."

A Jewish mother straight out of Bruce Jay Friedman tugged at the Mayor's elbow: "You *eat*," she instructed, "and take care of yourself." Lindsay laughed in obvious enjoyment before turning to monitor the multiple complaints of a young, apron-wrapped butcher: excessive taxes, the crying need for Law and Order, the bullying power of labor unions. "We have certain obligations and responsibilities," Lindsay began, and along about the part where the Mayor almost had Injustice run out of town on a rail and Poverty crying for mercy the young butcher's eyes glazed over and his lip curled. Somebody on the fringe asked why all the taxes came out of white pockets only to be spent in black neighborhoods. "We have three hundred years of neglect to pay for," Lindsay said, and half the sidewalk audience was shuffling in impatience. "You should see the reception he gets in Harlem," a worried Lindsay aide whispered. "It turns him on and *he* responds." Obviously there was little to turn the Mayor on in Bay Ridge, though a few squealing teen-agers extracted autographs without complaining of taxes or garbage service.

Ten or fifteen minutes later, in Bensonhurst (an older, seedier section of Brooklyn, where elevated trains thunder and vintage trash clots the gutter), the Mayor pounced on three abandoned cardboard boxes and deposited them in a mesh-wire basket. For three blocks he walked unrecognized and once again one became aware of how truly faceless New Yorkers are to each other. Just as it seemed that New York's Mayor might stroll all the way to Canarsie unremarked, a small boy sounded the alarm. People spilled out of storefront apartments and small shops, much warmer than their Bay Ridge cousins, speaking in a profusion of tongues: Lindsay conversed easily in French with one woman, haltingly tested his less-fluent Spanish on another. He signed autographs, munched pastry, warmly greeted a Brooklyn politician, and assured a group of painted teen-age dolls that he judges The Beatles "great."

Canarsie lies at the end of the world, which places it perhaps thirty car miles from Midtown Manhattan—or approximately one billion light-years away from Truman Capote's ball or the St. Regis bar. High-rise housing projects—home for workingmen and their families—emerge from bleak flat stretches once claimed by marsh grass, sand dunes, and simple sea life. "You won't see many Negroes out here," a Lindsay assistant whispered. "These people live out here to avoid them." As the Mayor and two reporters walked at the point of a ten-man entourage they met a little girl about ten years old and a younger boy. The girl's eyes brightened in sudden recognition; Lindsay stopped and smiled. Pointing at one of the three men she shouted. *"Look!* That's Manny Perlmutter of the *New York Times."*

It was the Mayor's last laugh in Canarsie. Quite suddenly his party was encircled by loud and scruffy teen-agers. Many wore faded football jerseys, tight blue jeans or khakis, pompadoured hair, and sneers. "Hey," one youth shouted, "what's Lind-say doing *heah?* This ain't Bedford-Stuyvesant." A hard-eyed young girl in slacks and a soiled sweat shirt looked the Mayor's attendants over: "I guess all *these* boobs are his bodyguards. He may need 'em." When the Mayor met two teen-agers in front of a burger stand—one Negro and one white—he shook the black boy's hand first. "What's the matter, Rollie?" somebody taunted the white boy. "Ain't your ass black enough?"

If either Lindsay or the Negro detective trailing him by three paces heard, they gave no sign. Within fifteen minutes John Lindsay was headed to a Forest Hills synagogue where he would receive its Prophet Isaiah Award for promoting Brotherhood.

.   .   .

It is an incongruous sight to see John Lindsay (wealthy, Episcopalian, Yale: the WASP incarnate) in the pulpit of a Harlem Baptist Church. One doubts whether even the Reverend Adam Clayton Powell or Elmer Gantry could conduct such services with more vigor or dedication to the rituals of the Old Time Religion. Lindsay—who often serves various pulpits as a lay minister, and who in his youth was a choirboy—runs the holy show: he reads the Biblical text, leads hymns, prays, and preaches the sermon. He is likely to mix in a little sociological scripture, flaying bigots and poverty as well as Satan. He sways on the platform, he chants, he claps his hands; he asks rhetorical questions that the parishioners may answer with satisfying shouts of "Yes, Brother!" or "Do, Lord!" or "A-men!"

In more sedate pulpits he is another man. Recently, accepting in his home church the Bishop's Cross for Distinguished Service from the Episcopal Bishop of New York (who introduced him as "young and attractive and almost eleven feet tall"), John Lindsay was quiet, dignified, every inch the Young Statesman and the Yale Man as he talked somberly of the alienated poor and called on his fellow Episcopalians to show the way in humanitarian conduct.

One should not deduce that John Lindsay is either a bleeding heart softy or the complete choirboy: he can turn mean. To TV reporter Mort Dean, interviewing him outside a church during his 1966 campaign in a manner Lindsay found offensive, he said, "You don't know what you're talking about, you son-of-a-bitch. Don't try to interview me again." When a reporter wrote that "the White Knight was up-tight"—*i.e.*, Lindsay was tense—during a recent crisis, the Mayor bawled him out in barroom terms. Though generally cool even when heckled, Lindsay once lost his temper at a rally in Queens when baited as a "Communist" and shouted to his detractors, "You're finks. You're fairies. *Fairies!*" Once during the mayoralty campaign Lindsay, told by his brother David that he was giving unsatisfactory answers to public questions, snapped, "Only the *candidate* has the right to shout in this room. Do you want to sit in my chair, Dave? Will you take my place, Dave, and explain what *you* will substitute for the sales tax? Will you?"

John Lindsay's interest in politics began early and naturally, encouraged by a father who railed at the dinner table of the need for reformists brave enough to buck the Tammany tiger; as a small boy Lindsay visited Mayor La Guardia in his City Hall offices and gravely talked politics with him. One of his first acts as Mayor was to rescue from some City Hall dungeon an oil painting of La Guardia and one of his old desks, which he promptly installed in his own office.

After the Navy, law school, and a spell of practicing law, Lindsay was elected president of the New York Young Republicans' Club. He was active in the 1952 Eisenhower campaign and was rewarded with the job of administrative assistant to Attorney General Herbert Brownell. He came home to run for Congress in Manhattan's so-called silk-stocking district, upsetting the GOP organization and taking the 1958 general election by 7,800 votes. Two years later he won by 26,000 votes and in 1962 more than doubled that margin. In 1964 he received a staggering 71 per cent of the vote, winning by a margin of 91,000, even as Barry Goldwater, heading the GOP ticket, badly lost the district. Lindsay disavowed Goldwater as did Governor Rockefeller, Senator Javits, and then-Senator Kenneth Keating.

Lindsay loved Washington: "We had a beautiful home out in Cleveland Park and a grand family life." He was not so crazy about Congress, where, as a junior member of a liberal minority in the minority party, he was without special influence or opportunity. The House of Representatives, by virtue of the seniority system, encourages drones, party hacks, and chair-warmers. This inspires neither the activist, the bright young reformer, nor the idealist; there is a touch of all three in Lindsay.

Congressman Lindsay was suspect in the view of GOP regulars because of a liberalism that placed him on the side of the Kennedy Administration more often than not. He cast such un-Republican votes as one to repeal "right-to-work" laws and to abolish the cynical and ineffective House Un-American Activities Committees; he was among the supporters of Medicare, nuclear-test-ban treaties, federal aid to education, civil-rights bills; he became known as something of a civil-libertarian radical. Southern Democrats, in a time when a rising GOP tide threatened their conservative backwater districts, held Lindsay up as a horrible example: he opposed the oil-depletion allowance and was one of two Congressmen who voted against a ban on Communist periodicals being sold in the U.S.

.   .   .

Despite the grumbles of cab drivers, jealous fellow politicians, and suburban bigots, John V. Lindsay is generally a popular Mayor. Enthusiastic supporters once erected a billboard to Lindsay in Midtown Manhattan: "Lindsay is supercalifragilisticexpialidocious." There can be little doubt of Lindsay's dedication or sincerity: he feels real pain for the downtrodden, is often exasperated by backward-looking private citizens and politicians alike (he is embittered because neither Congress nor President Johnson, in his opinion, has been adequately impressed with the nation's three years of racial disorders and riots), and he fears that America has very few years remaining to do something about its urban blight and its neglected people. His agonizing over accepting the Senate seat was largely inspired by whether he could more effectively work for urban solutions in Washington or in City Hall.

Lindsay is obsessed with peace in Vietnam ("One of the reasons I entered politics was to work for peace. Twenty-five per cent of my graduating classes in both high school and college died in World War II") and equal opportunity. He had much to do with writing the summary of the Kerner Commission Report, ordered by President Johnson after the ghetto burnings, and is said to have authored its most famous—and most controversial—line: "Our nation is moving toward two societies, one black, one white—separate and unequal." Of this he has remarked, "Many of the nation's political leaders saw it differently. They said it was an exaggeration or that it ignored the progress in race relations of the past decade. They squirmed. They quibbled. They denied that it was so. Well, by God, it *is* so."

6. Bobby K. Hayes:
An Obscure Rural Candidate

"Bobby K. Hayes of Calico Rock, Ark.:
A 24-Hour Biography"

by PHILIP D. CARTER

He was two politicians down the hand-shaking line from
J. William Fulbright of Fayetteville: Bobby K. Hayes of Calico
Rock. It was June 1, 1968, three nights before Bobby Kennedy
was shot. He had not been at the head table at the party
dinner, but Fulbright had. He had not been asked to speak,
because Fulbright would have been embarrassed. But he was
down on the Benton County Fairground, Bentonville, Arkansas,
and he was running against Fulbright for the Senate. The senator, home from Washington in a careful gray suit, would
scarcely acknowledge he was there.

In a field of four, Fulbright was far in front, and Bobby K.—
behind Justice Jim Johnson, the George Wallace man, and
Foster Johnson, the retired encyclopedia salesman—was considered the last man in the pack. He had buttoned all three
buttons of his powder-blue jacket, a black comb peeked out

of his breast pocket, and his pants cuffs collapsed around his ankles. The senator's Philadelphia wife, Betty, was with him. Bobby K.'s Lorene, and the two kids, and Earletta, the girl who lived with them like a daughter, were far away, seeing the sights in Texas.

He lunged for people's hands, and squeezed hard, like an Indian wrestler. "How do you do," he said. "I want you to remember me: Bobby K. Hayes, candidate for the U.S. Senate." He had an Ozarks accent with odd peaks and valleys and curves. "Remember me." It was less an entreaty than a statement of fact.

"I'll get you something from the car." He excused himself and ran to the parking lot, head down and knees high, pumping his elbows. It was a 1967 Mustang Fastback, deep navy blue, with two big loudspeakers on the roof, pointed outward so the people could hear. And on the doors were words for the people to see: "Bobby K. Hayes Candidate for U.S. Senate."

His platform was mimeographed. He would bust up the big corporations and break up the plantations and redistribute the land; he would bring the boys home from Vietnam and find everyone jobs and fight for equal justice; he would stop all this foreign aid until we could build some bridges here at home, and pay at least $2.50 an hour, and provide Medicare for everyone, old and young. And he would restore prayer to public schools.

The platform had a familiar ring. It was William Jennings Bryan updated, the Populist half of Huey P. Long. He had outlasted the New Deal and the Fair Deal, the New Frontier and the Great Society, and he was still there. People said he had gotten rich.

"He's off his nut," one of the people said. Bobby K. Hayes was thirty-seven, a self-made-Ozarks-hillbilly-millionaire-with-hardwood-flooring-plants-all-over-the-map. He met payrolls and worked a few hundred hicks. "It don't make sense."

"I'm running for civil rights," he said as we stood by his car. "Fulbright never voted for a civil rights bill in his life. Fulbright is with the corporations. I'm hitting him on the issues." He doubled his fist. "He's anti-labor, and he voted against Medicare, and he's giving this money away. And there's

this Vietnam stand: you take now, he just says stop the bombing—and you see what the headlines say today, our boys are
still dying; and you can buy an M-16 rifle on the streets of
Saigon for only eighty dollars."

Five days later, Bobby Kennedy was dead, and Bobby K. was
home in Calico Rock.

Calico Rock

There were hills like worn knuckles, and mottled bluffs, a
railroad track and a bridge and the White River, rushing and
cold. There was Main Street, with its old building of sturdy
native stone, and a flooring plant where white smoke rose;
they stoked the boiler with sawdust. There were homes for
773 white people—the Indians had died off long ago, and the
town was too poor for Negroes. It was an odd corner of the
mountain South, far from the nation's heart. Bobby K. was
in his office, once a funeral parlor. He seemed both older and
younger.

Bobby K.

He waved while he talked on the phone; 2:10 p.m. Over his
inner office was a sign: "Employees Only. No loafing or visiting. Bobby K. Hayes." Under a glass counter in the outer office
were snapshots of him on a hunt, and there were antlered
heads on the wall. There were ad layouts: "Now through the
ideas of men comes the elegant new concept of Parquet Flooring by Hayes Bros." There was a notice from the federal
government: "Equal Employment Opportunity is the Law. Discrimination is Prohibited." It was a small stone building, not
unlike those in country towns like Johnson City, Texas. It
didn't look like a mortuary.

He hung up. "That's my brother, J.W. He died in an airplane
crash." He pointed at a tinted family photograph framed on
the paneled wall.

"What did you think about Bobby Kennedy?" he asked,
changing the subject. "I said don't be surprised if they kill

him. It really took the pep out of me when it happened, though. You know, my name is Bobby too. I said after Oregon, I said just wait till after Tuesday. I know. I had a close call after I got in this race. A switchblade knife."

We got into the Mustang. "I'm thirty-seven, and I'm come from nothing. I was a twenty-dollar-a-week truck driver once." We drove through Calico Rock. "Look at this. This is where to live. Have you ever been to Los Angeles? They've got every ism and chism in the world. Bobby should've been more careful.

"I lived in California for two years, in and out of there. California is worse than New York City. You go to Stockton, and you see seven hundred or eight hundred in the park— drinking, sleeping on the ground. They've got no place to go. They've give up. I had a Negro foreman on a job out there once. It was a potato-picking job. I liked him; it was picking potatoes I didn't like. That's the only job I walked off from." He was proud of it.

"I'll tell you how I got into this situation. I said, 'Mother, I've been thinking a lot. I just had to get into this.' I went down there twice to file before I did it. I went to bed at night and got up in the morning just thinking about it. I just had to do it."

On the way to see his lumberyard, we passed a car with Illinois plates going up a hill, and the other car honked. Bobby K. waved and pulled over to the shoulder, and the Illinois car drew alongside. "You're getting fat now, ain't you," Bobby K. yelled. He and the other driver bantered. "Bobby, I didn't know it was you till you passed with your name on the car." The couple in the other car used to work in Calico. They pulled away, and Bobby waved good-bye; he knew a lot of people.

"My daddy used to haul fence posts up in Missouri, haul them up to Iowa and Illinois and sell 'em to farmers. He was gone a lot." We drove into his lumberyard, down a dusty gravel road. The yard supplied his local flooring plant. "I tell you what I think. If the gap between the rich and the poor is not bridged, we'll have revolution. We've just got to."

Bobby K. showed off his flooring plant next. In one shed, he jumped in to help out, to show how it's done. He said,

"Every piece we make has our name on it." The name was "Floor-Lock Brand Calico Rock, Ark. Made in U.S.A. Hayes Bros. Flooring Company Inc." There were signs: "Danger. Do Not Watch the Arc." And there were conveyor belts and exposed gears and flying splinters and invisibly whirling saws. Some men had fingers missing. Bobby K. pointed, sighting along his finger like the barrel of a crooked gun. "There are one hundred and twenty men and women at work," he said. "That's a lot of mouths for a little guy to feed."

Home

We drove to his house; modern ranch style with carpets on carpets. "It's used," he said. "But nobody ever lived in it before we moved in. We were in it a year before we could get the final papers on it. It was part of an estate, and they had about twelve lawyers on it, just showing how smart they were."

One bedroom was barren; they had not made up their minds how to furnish in case of important guests. In the living room, there was a towel draped on Bobby K.'s reclining chair to keep it clean, and a small red rocker, child's size, sat before the picture window. Stone bluffs rose like a wall across the White. Out the back window was an old log smokehouse with a tractor and mower in the attached shed. "I bought that tractor to play with, and the new worn off it, and I didn't have time to fool with it myself."

He was restless. He took out some old family pictures, and pored over them on the couch. "That's my older brother who got killed in the plane accident, J.W.," he said. "That's my daddy and me on the running board of Daddy's first truck—a '36 Ford with a grain bed." His dad wore overalls and a black trucker's cap. "T. Hayes Gainesville, Mo," read the sign on the door of the truck.

"In '31 or '32 when he went to get that job, he had a nickel in his pocket. That was back in Prohibition, when he was doing something he ought not to have been—but he quit that job where he was making fifty dollars a week and went to driving and cutting stave bolts for fifty cents a day.

"He had been moonshining in Fort Smith, hauling and delivering it. It just shows what a man will do, but my momma, she said, 'Yessir, I'm going home,' and he quit it."

He showed pictures from army days in Germany. "I was in a motor pool there, a corporal. You know who made those pictures there? I did myself. I made them and developed them myself." Most found him staring into the camera, arms akimbo, legs parted and planted, as though against a threatened attack. "It's a hobby."

There was also his marriage license; he had married Lorene Bean in 1951 in an Assembly of God church in Harrison, Arkansas. "In Bakersville, up in Ozark County, Missouri, we lived on the same forty acres," he said. "Dad had thirty-nine, and her dad had one off of it, and that's where I got her. I was married eleven months and they drafted me. I know how to sympathize with a young man when he gets married and goes off to war."

He thought he was going to Korea, but he went to Germany instead. "We was integrated then, Negroes and whites. When it came time to ship out, they sent all the Negro boys to Korea and all the white boys to Germany, and that's when I knew that something was wrong, that somebody was *doing* it that way."

He sat on his couch and reflected. "I slept in the same room with 'em, ate together, showered together. That's when I learned to judge a man on his merits and not on the color of his skin. And that's when I learned leadership. I couldn't have run my business without it." The color TV was on in the corner, the sound was off, and the picture looked like a snowstorm. The program was about Kennedy.

He turned it off and pointed to a shortwave receiver in a corner. "Have you ever listened to one of these? I can pick up Hanoi, and I think a lot of it is true. I can pick up Johannesburg, Moscow, London, Ecuador. I listen to it a lot at night late. I don't pick up till about two o'clock at night. My mind functions better late at night, and I read a lot: trade magazines, *U.S. News, Time, Life, Post, Wall Street Journal,* the *Gazette,* the *Democrat,* the *National Review*—I try to read both sides, digest all that. I actually read about twenty hours a week; I've always been a reader and a dreamer.

Jack

Then we left the house. In the car: "You know, I've been to Susanville, California, to an auction one time, and on the way back I landed at Salt Lake. Jack Kennedy was there at the airport to dedicate a dam—you know, he pushed a button— and I took my suitcase over there where he was at, and took off my coat and put it in there. I listened at him and seen how he . . . well, he reminded me a lot of my older brother. And I said, you may not agree with him, but you have to admire him. His hair was sunburned and bushy, you could tell he'd been outside a lot. And he got right down on the ground and reached people. But I said Jack could never live his term out." He paused. "I could have had a submachine gun in my suitcase, and nobody would have known it. Three weeks later he was dead."

The People

A pickup came toward us from town and stopped, and one of the men waved and shouted as Bobby stopped: "We can't send you off nowhere there's traffic because you'll end up killing somebody. You going to be at the ball game tonight?" Bobby K. said he hoped he could; he'd played second base, but dropped games for politics.

Bobby showed off the Webb Store, Calico's new grocery. "Here's what bothers me," he said. "Can you make a tooth-paste and compete on the market? Can you make a hair spray? It would cost millions of dollars. Can you make flashlight batteries? You can't compete with these name brands." He got hot about it, then he collected himself. "But I can make oak flooring and send it anywhere in the United States," he said, and winked.

"Here's Harold. Harold, tell him about your ticker. He was a carpenter until his old ticker went bad on him. Here's a good example of why I'm for Medicare."

Harold talked about his ticker. "I draw a VA disability, which makes it all right, but a lot of guys didn't pay it in."

It was 5:20 p.m. We moved on. Bobby K.'s shirt was wide open at the neck, his tie hung halfway down his chest, and black hair poked out from under his shirt. "See her? She lost her husband. When I went up to see him in the hospital, I said, 'He'll never come home again.' "

We got back in the car and drove past the high school. "Well, look here. You've heard Mr. Fulbright talk about education, haven't you? Well, we don't have a band. And if they want to walk from one building to another, they have to walk in the rain. They built this part last year, but there's no heat or air conditioning."

We stopped at a house. "I want you to meet a woman whose husband worked for me." We stood on a bare front porch overlooking the highway. "Tell him about my stand on Medicare."

"Well, you was a lot of help for my husband." She lived on sixty dollars a month from Social Security.

"Now, this is what we've got here in America. Now, how do you expect a widow—what's your rent here?"

"Seventeen a month. I just stay weak all the time. I can't hold up." She had a wrinkled, puzzled face, and wore a dirty striped dress. "He was like myself, no education, and he couldn't get nothing but hard work, hard labor." She kept a neat yard, with a dead Chinese elm in the middle of it. She didn't know what had killed it.

We got back in the car and drove up Route Nine. He swerved, and pointed to another porch. "Now, this ole guy's got asthma. And then we give foreign aid."

We stopped at the clinic, a low modern building with several cars and pickups parked in the patient's area. A man named Herschel sat on the wall under the sycamore out front, and spat from time to time, waiting for his wife. "Tell him what happened to you, Herschel. Herschel got hold of a—what was it Herschel? About-a-hundred-thousand-volt high-power line, and it got him." Herschel showed the stigmata, red scars. "It got you, didn't it, Herschel."

"It did. They say it knocked the tacks from my boots into my feet."

Herschel had bad teeth. He told about family troubles. "My

heart's turned hard, good hard," he said. "I couldn't have took what I did. It's a fulfilling of the Bible. The last days, brother against brother."

"Tell about the hospital."

"There was a nigger preacher up there with me, holding my hand. He was good to me. He stayed right by my side. I got out. But my wife's nerves went bad. Now she comes to the doctor for her shots, comes once a week. It cost ten dollars the last time we came down here and she got aggravated and we went down to Batesville and it just cost two. She gets aggravated with these doctors."

"I just don't think a doctor has a license to steal," Bobby said, "just because he has a license. This is America."

We headed back for his office. He showed a picture of himself in Alaska with a dead caribou, and an editorial from the Pine Bluff *Commercial* that described him as a latter-day Populist in the Bryan mold. It chided him for supporting Arkansas's "monkey law" prohibiting the teaching of evolution. "They taught me evolution," he said, "but it didn't affect me because I had a good God-fearing mother who brought me up right. That was in Missouri. I believe the deterrent that keeps people from crime more than any other is the belief in a hereafter."

The editorial also warned that many Populists of the past were anti-Semitic. "One of my best friends is one of the biggest builders in this country. He is a Jew. Ask him if Bob Hayes is a Jew-hater. Paul Greenberg wrote that editorial. He is a smart young fellow in Pine Bluff; he is a Jew. I called him up and told him I didn't want my son to grow up and go on television and say he didn't believe in God like I saw one woman who was on the *Jack Paar Show* one night."

We got back in the car and drove for gas. A toothless man, small and battered, walked from the roadside to Bobby K.'s window. "Tell this man," Bobby said, "about that keg of dynamite that went off on you. Show him the hole in your head."

"I was dead for six hours," the man said. He had a large hole in his head, filled in with scar tissue, but he had a new story to tell. "A man threw me off the porch at the Bannister store."

Bobby K. changed the subject back. "Lum, tell him about that boomer that hit you between the eyes."

"I was nine days and nights coming to."

He wore a diamond ring, or good glass, his sleeves were rolled up, and oily black ringlets coiled on top of his head. One temple was bare and blighted. "See where he laid the skin off my head? He just scalped me."

"He used to be a boiler man at the mill. Now—what are you, sixty-three, sixty-four?—he works at the pool hall. Show him your money." Lum had sold out to the pool hall, but he had little to show for it. He had some deposit slips, though, and he proudly unfolded them: $100, $150. He put them back, and fastened his wallet shut with its two brass snaps.

The Speakers

We finished getting gas. "This ole world's in bad shape," Bobby K. said. We headed up Highway 5 to Mammoth, Missouri, to see the house where he was born. It was 6:45. "I don't think you have to be a college graduate to be President of the United States.

"Take Johnson. I saw him when he was Vice President make a little speech up at McCormick Place in Chicago. He was pretty arrogant that day. The photographers were taking lots of pictures, and the lights bothered him, you could tell. 'Boys, I didn't come all the way up here to take pictures,' he said. You could have heard a pin drop.

"Or you take Fulbright. The first time I saw him was at a church in Mountain Home; he made a little talk. I said to myself then, I said, 'Well, he's another human being.' The second time I saw him was at those hearings in Washington with Rusk. He looked sharp, he had on that blue shirt and that tie with doves on it. But it seemed to me his mind drifted. Maybe he just doesn't have a one-track mind; but it seems to me that if I was holding hearings I would concentrate on the hearings. I hold nothing against him personally, I think he's a handsome man. But I don't think he was the Bill Fulbright of twenty years ago.

"Look at Bobby Kennedy, the other Bobby. I believe that he

hated wealth, I believe that's what propelled him. Why should so few have the wealth and all the control? He never worked a day in his life to make a dollar. As I see it, his entire life was spent trying to help somebody, trying to redistribute the wealth in the country."

The sun was close to the cut-over hilltops, green with scrubby second growth. We drove into Norfork, Arkansas. At the gas station, there was a man in denim overalls with a truckload of cedar posts. "His pocket is his bank," Bobby said. "He carries ten thousand dollars at a time." Bobby grabbed him by the hand and they Indian-wrestled, elbow high; they sawed and puffed a little and then backed off from each other, each careful to give way. They were only fooling.

We got into the Mustang to leave, but it wouldn't start; so we pushed it around in the road and rolled it off down the hill, while the men at the station laughed. It started, and we headed back north, Bobby driving faster now because he had lost some face.

"I tell you what's bad in a capitalistic society," he said. "It's the ups and downs, the peaks and the valleys. If you're dealing with the big corporations, they can keep the valleys down as deep as they want. The deeper the valley, the more it insures they'll stay on top. If I wanted to be mean and dirty, I could break every one of the sawmills around."

It was almost dark. Bobby K. tailgated a 1959 Dodge up a winding road. "Watch this," he said, "this is something I do sometimes when I'm driving along." He picked up the microphone attached to the speakers on top, and blew into it with the volume turned so loud that it might have been the crack of a pistol. "Yes, yes, it is Hayes, Bobby K. Hayes, candidate for United States Senate, the people's choice, Bobby K. Hayes for the Senate." The Dodge swerved sharply to the shoulder, and the Mustang shot by, doing seventy along a rising curve.

.   .   .

Calico Rock

After twenty-three hours, it was time to go. We were at Bobby K.'s office. "I'm going to move out of this office for the rest of the day," Bobby said, as we left together. "It used to be funeral home, and it sounds like a morgue today. It must be the assassination."

We drove down to Main Street and parked. You could see it through his eyes.

"It was a woman who inspired me to go on my own," he said. " 'Bob, what are you doing working for your brother?' " He looked and pondered.

"I find I can kid and cut up with Jews more than with anybody else. Kid 'em about their nationality." He was silent again.

"My brother Jerry is always kidding me about having a dual personality; real mean and real good." Main Street was sunny, hot, and quiet, and there weren't many people in the stores. On the East Side there was Western Auto, Cheney's Shoe Store, Ideal Grocery, Lorene's Beauty Shop (no kin), the Home Variety Store, a Café and Pastime Pool Hall. And on the West, there was Perryman's Hardware, Matthews Insurance Agency, Rexall Drugs, Family Shoe and Ready to Wear, and the State Bank of Calico Rock. The town was pretty as a picture.

Bobby K. Hayes

The steam whistle blew at the plant; it was 12:55 p.m., Friday, June 7, 1968. Bobby K. was in the middle of Main Street, leaning against the door of a green pickup, laughing with the driver, waving as a hay truck jolted through town from across the cold White River. It was time for our last talk.

"You know, my life has more or less been thirty-seven pages. I don't know how many pages in the book. I've seen so many men my age falling to the ground beside me: friends, business associates, political idols, a brother. I don't know what it means, no one knows. I'm a very restless man. I say I'm happy, but I've always been this way.

"If I lose this fight, it won't crush me. I've had defeats. Sometimes I've asked myself, Am I running for this job, or am I running from something? I think maybe it's both ways.

"My brother would have quit. He said he was. He wanted

to fish and hunt and fly an airplane. Have you read this book *The Life Hereafter,* by Norman Vincent Peale? I think it's called that, I think he wrote it. He believes that when you die, you don't go right to heaven. Your spirit stays here on earth. Well, sometimes I get to thinking about J.W., because there's something there leading and guiding me. I think he would want me to be happy.

"Did you know this ole world is crying out for a leader? Someone who can unite the people? If there was such a man, he could get 90 percent of the votes.

"I know there is such a man, but I don't know where he's at."

Leaving

The hitchhiker was an S.A.E. from the University of Arkansas, Fayetteville. He wore a sharp blazer, and his hair was carefully cut so that it would hang just over his eyes. He smiled and nodded at the mention of Calico Rock. "I've spent summers around there," he said. "That's a bunch of red-necks, no question about it. All they do is get in fights and mess around in cars."

In the end, Bobby ran third. Fulbright won.

7. Charles Percy: A Presidential Hopeful

"The Available Mr. Percy"

by STEPHEN HESS and DAVID S. BRODER

"His life sounds like a soap opera, doesn't it?" asks Charles Percy's wife, Loraine. Actually, it has more often been compared to a Horatio Alger novel, the rags-to-riches tale of a child of the Depression working his way up to corporation president by the age of twenty-nine.

Born in Pensacola, Florida, September 27, 1919, Chuck Percy started running at age five, when he began his business career as a magazine salesman in Chicago, where the family moved while he was an infant. He promptly proved that his abilities were exceptional, winning a plaque for selling "more copies of *Country Gentleman* to city people than any other urban salesman in the United States." Within a few years he had the largest schoolboy magazine route in the city. At the time, Percy's father was doing nicely as the cashier of a small bank.

Adapted from pp. 200–242 in *The Republican Establishment* by Stephen Hess and David S. Broder. Copyright © 1967 by Stephen Hess and David S. Broder. Originally appeared in *The Atlantic Monthly* under the title "The Available Mr. Percy." By permission of Harper & Row, Publishers, Inc.

It was not until the bank failed in 1931, when Percy was twelve, that the boy's drive was also motivated by necessity.

During his high school years he held as many as four jobs simultaneously. He stoked furnaces before school, worked in the registrar's office during school, delivered newspapers after school, and on nights and weekends ushered at a neighborhood movie theater. But nothing stemmed the slide into poverty. The car was repossessed. The telephone was disconnected. Finally, Mrs. Percy sold her engagement ring.

A surprised campaign aide found out about this period when Percy was running for governor in 1964. "Why didn't you tell me you had been on relief?" he asked. "You didn't ask me," the candidate answered. "You don't go around asking members of the Chicago Club if they've been on relief," his supporter replied. "After that," writer Hal Higdon pointed out, "Percy seldom failed to mention his former welfare status."

"It was my mother's music and her religion that kept our spirits up," Percy now says. Mother's music was made on the violin. In fact, she had met her husband while on a concert tour of the South, he being from an old Southern family whose branches include a governor of the Jamestown colony and a drummer boy at Robert E. Lee's headquarters. Mrs. Percy, now in her mid-seventies, still plays in the Evanston Symphony Orchestra, and when her campaigning son toured the Illinois county fair circuit in the summer of 1963, she went along to entertain the crowds with her rendition of "Perpetual Motion."

Percy inherited little of his mother's musical ability, but her religion, Christian Science, has been a major influence in his life. Mrs. Percy organized Sunday-evening prayer sessions, had readings from the Bible and Christian Science publications at breakfast, and said grace at all meals—customs that her son continues. Like the equally religious George Romney, whose Mormon faith is as patriarchal in its orientation as Christian Science is matriarchal, Percy does not smoke or drink or swear.

Like Romney, too, Percy has a fetish about physical fitness, swimming daily if possible (he was a water polo player in college), bounding up stairs two at a time rather than taking an elevator. And like Romney, he radiates an air of purposefulness and self-satisfaction that some find a bit too much to take. The Chicago *Tribune*, only an occasional admirer, once wrote that "Mr. Percy . . . affects an elaborate piety, like a figure in stained glass."

But however it strikes outsiders, Percy draws from his religious faith a confidence and sustaining power that are almost palpable. In both the tragedies of his life—the death of his first wife and the brutal murder of his daughter Valerie—Percy has maintained a composure that has been remarked with awe by his associates.

.   .   .

If Percy needed any additional reason to cherish his religion, he could find it in the coincidence that led to his big break in the business world. The rigid formula of the Horatio Alger story requires that the hero be not only honest and hardworking, but also lucky. For Charles Percy the lucky break came when he entered the Sunday school class of Joseph McNabb, the president of a small camera company called Bell & Howell. (There is a persistent and totally erroneous story that Percy's first wife, who died in 1947, leaving three young children, was the boss's daughter.) Percy asked his religious mentor if he would give his father a daytime job so that the family could have some time together. McNabb, who liked the boy's pluck, complied. McNabb also gave the young Percy summer employment, and during one such period Percy revolutionized the customer service department by designing sixty form letters that fit nearly every situation. ("I've just taken four rolls of film and they all come out blank." "Dear Madam: Please take off the lens cap.")

.   .   .

. . . . Percy went to work full time for Bell & Howell . . . and McNabb put him in charge of defense contracts, a relatively modest activity. Within six months, however, Pearl Harbor was attacked, and Percy was soon supervising the bulk of his company's business. He was, on McNabb's recommendation, made a director before he was twenty-three—and before he left for the Navy.

.   .   .

Two years before his death in 1949, Joe McNabb informed
Percy that he was leaving a sort of "corporate will" recom-
mending that Percy succeed him as president, rather than his
son or any of the other executives. Percy delights in telling
the story of the tense days before the board of directors met
to name McNabb's successor. "I tell you," he says, "it was
Executive Suite all over again. I wasn't even a vice president
then. McNabb's lawyer and I were the only ones who knew
about the existence of the letter, and I wasn't sure whether
it had been changed since Joe had told me his plans." On the
fateful day in 1949, the letter was opened and the board of
directors, an august body of industrialists whose average age
was in the sixties, dutifully named McNabb's twenty-nine-year-
old protégé as president of Bell & Howell at an annual salary
of $40,000—plus appropriate stock options, which the young
executive declined until he could prove himself. Percy led his
company for fifteen years.

During that period sales grew from less than $5 million a
year to $160 million, company employees from fewer than
1000 to approximately 10,000, salaries from an average of $2000
to more than $7500. An employee profit-sharing plan was in-
augurated, and the company, which had been privately owned
by three families, was listed on the New York Stock Exchange.
Where Bell & Howell had been almost exclusively a quality
camera-maker, Percy diversified into business equipment, reproduction machines, automated mailing systems, and instru-
ments for the space and military programs. He pushed
expansion into foreign markets. He also, like George Romney,
went in for promotion with a flair. Living in the shadow of
Eastman Kodak—just as Romney's company was dwarfed by
the auto industry's Big Three—he tried harder.

By the mid-1950s, Charles H. Percy, having remarried (his second wife, Loraine, is a pretty Californian and fellow Christian
Scientist he met on the ski slopes at Sun Valley), having made
his company a success and himself several times a millionaire
(he estimates his personal fortune "conservatively" at $6 mil-
lion), was becoming increasingly restless and anxious to find
a new role, if not a new life, for himself. "I simply found I was

reading the political columns in the paper ahead of the business page, and I knew I was hooked," he says.

. . .

President Eisenhower, who was partial to the type, saw Percy as a comer. Right after New Year's, 1959, Percy, known to Ike as a major backer of his reciprocal-trade program and as a top fund-raiser for the Illinois Republican Party, stopped by the White House. "The nation has moved into a new period of danger, threatened by the rulers of one third of mankind, for whom the state is everything and the individual significant only as he serves the state," the thirty-nine-year-old industrialist announced to the sixty-eight-year-old President. "We need a new understanding of the problems, not only to meet a deadly menace and extend the area of freedom in the world, but also to preserve and enlarge our liberties."

The President was excited; people did not usually burst into his office and deliver a Fourth of July oration. He called his speech writers, who were then putting the finishing touches on the State of the Union message. They frantically sliced away at their lengthy draft to make room for Percy's ideas. And standing before a joint session of Congress four days later, President Eisenhower—"permit me to digress long enough to express something that is much on my mind"—announced he would appoint a Presidential Commission on National Goals.

This "goals" business was heady stuff. Having set in motion the machinery that would at last give the United States a set of "national goals," Percy now turned his attention to "party goals." Shortly after the State of the Union message, the President asked Percy to head a committee to provide the Republican Party with a "concise, understandable statement of our Party's long-range objectives in all areas of political responsibility."

The "concise, understandable statement" turned out to be a 190-page paperback, entitled *Decisions for a Better America. . . .*

It was hardly a historic document, but it was good enough to make Percy, in the eyes of Eisenhower and Nixon, the logical fellow to head the 1960 platform committee. It took some arranging, because the conservative Republican leaders of Illinois did not regard Percy as their spokesman on platform issues or anything else of consequence. But phone calls from Republican National Chairman Thruston Morton convinced them the request came from the top, so it was honored.

The platform job proved easier to get than to perform. Caught in the unexpected liberal-conservative struggle precipitated by Nixon's last-minute meeting with Nelson Rockefeller, Percy was betrayed by his political inexperience.

"He tried to do it all with charm and personality," a conservative platform committee member recalls, "and this was a situation where you had to knock some heads. When you get right down to it, Chuck was naïve."

For a full day, the revolt in the platform committee against the Nixon-Rockefeller amendments raged unchecked. Finally, Nixon arrived on the scene, and the next morning Percy quietly handed over the gavel to the committee's vice-chairman, Wisconsin's tough-as-nails congressman Melvin R. Laird, who pounded the platform through while Percy busied himself rehearsing the narration for the film that was to accompany its presentation to the convention.

One lesson Percy learned from his humiliation was that the way to have political influence was to hold public office. He explored the possibility of running for the Senate in 1962 against Dirksen, but was persuaded there was no wisdom in challenging the old master in a Republican primary. So in 1963, seventeen months ahead of the election, he announced that he would be a candidate for governor of Illinois.

.   .   .

.... The year 1964, which most Republicans would like to forget, proved especially distasteful for Charles Percy. Barry Goldwater might claim he lost with honor and Romney that he won as best he could; but Percy, as he admits, lost with little honor. "The defeat for governor," he now says, "was probably well-deserved." There were three facets to Percy's campaign that caused distress to those who saw him as a bright hope of the party.

First, he ignored the highly structured Republican county organization, relying on his own volunteer committees, and generally convincing the regular party leaders that there was no good reason for them to exert any extra effort on his behalf.

Second, Percy came across to the voters as stiff, cold, and remote . . .

Third, on substantive issues Percy managed to disturb those who had considered him a liberal without making a corresponding gain among conservatives. . . .

But what he calls "my biggest mistake" was his attitude toward Goldwater. "I was having enough trouble getting the gubernatorial nomination," he now says; "it would have been presumptuous of me to try to make a President, too." Instead, he promised to support the majority decision of the Illinois delegation, an action that, in fact, committed him to Goldwater, a candidate with whom he had little in common and one who was to prove immensely unpopular with the Illinois electorate. . . .

. . . . Badgered by both the moderates and the conservatives, Percy lost the election to Democratic Governor Otto Kerner by 179,299 votes, while President Johnson's winning margin over Goldwater was an extravagant 890,887. . . .

.   .   .

One quality of Percy's as a politician is that he is absolutely dauntless in the face of personal reversals. So, dusting himself off from the 1964 disaster, he looked around for the most productive way to employ his talents while waiting for the next electoral opportunity. He hit upon a novel plan: the New Illinois Committee. Why not try to do some of the projects— on a limited scale, of course—that he had proposed doing if elected? A sort of government-in-exile, a defeated candidate keeping campaign promises. The St. Louis *Globe-Democrat* called the idea "refreshingly new."

.   .   .

Like his decision to run for governor against Charles Carpentier in 1963, his decision to run for the Senate in 1966 was an incredibly risky one. It was the sort of choice that only foolhardy politicians or men of driving ambition make—the same sort of decision that sent John Kennedy into West Virginia in 1960 and Richard Nixon into California in 1962. What made the move so fateful for Percy was that the race would pit him against the greatest vote-getter in modern Illinois politics, Paul H. Douglas, a former University of Chicago professor whose intellectuality and independence were of immense appeal to the liberals, yet a man who had worked out an advantageous peace with the Daley machine in Cook County—the most powerful city organization left in the United States.

When the old-guard Illinois Republican leaders instantly and joyously united behind Percy, it was not hard to believe that they had discovered a painless way to be rid of this pushy newcomer. But they did not reckon with Percy's talent for adaptation.

. . .

Appearing before the Illinois Press Association on May 14, 1965, he admitted that he had been wrong to believe the real estate industry could be persuaded to adopt an effective fair-housing code, and therefore he would now support state legislation "to eliminate the evil of discrimination in housing." Later, when it was also clear that the state would not act, Percy backed a federal open-occupancy law, thus essentially taking the same position as Senator Douglas.

Douglas scored politically by describing Percy as the first public official "to raise vacillation to the level of moral principle." But he was unable to counter the major issues helping Percy in the race. Racial agitation in Chicago produced a suburban "backlash" vote that aided Percy, even though he did not court it. A sharp decline in the turnout in Negro areas plus Percy's own intensive efforts to increase his percentage there cut Douglas' margin in the central city. Downstate Republicans, worried by inflation and by the near extinction of their own party, voted the GOP ticket. Some liberals defected from Douglas because of his support of the Vietnam War. And no voter was left unaware of the difference in ages—seventy-four versus forty-seven—of Douglas and his former University of Chicago student. In all these ways, Percy's campaign was aided by circumstances that did not exist in 1964.

But the main difference between the 1964 and 1966 campaigns was Percy himself. As Howard James, the Midwestern bureau chief for the *Christian Science Monitor* wrote somewhat effusively on election night, "There is little question that Mr. Percy is a far different man from the business executive who tried and lost in 1964. Warmer, more knowledgeable, with greater feeling for the problems of the people of Illinois, white and Negro, he won because he had the people on his side."

Newspaper photographs showed Percy Indian wrestling in Franklin Park, Percy in the middle of 1200 costumed Lithuanians at a folk-song festival, Percy joining an Assyrian chain dance. Arthur Schlesinger, Jr., who flew to Chicago to try to hold the eggheads for Douglas, called Percy "the product of the black art of public relations."

Early in the 1966 campaign, John Dreiske, political editor of the Chicago *Sun-Times,* had described Percy as he was seen by Republicans across the state: "He seems so self-sufficient it is quite obvious he doesn't need you." But this picture disappeared with Valerie's murder in mid-September. There is no such thing as a self-sufficient father looking down at the battered body of his first-born. Polltakers in Illinois found little evidence of a sympathy vote. However, one had to be less than human not to feel a cold shiver and the start of tears when Percy, resuming the campaign with a bodyguard at his side, introduced his family from the back platform of a train, at his first whistle-stop, Joliet, and said, "I want you to meet my wife, Loraine, my daughters, Sharon and Val . . ."

He won by 422,302 votes—55 percent. It was an important victory because the candidate was already a national figure, because he had beaten a powerful and widely admired incumbent, because he would represent a major industrial state, because he had that elusive quality that makes reporters add the supportive clause to his name—Charles H. Percy, a potential presidential candidate.

On November 22, Percy flew to Washington for his first meeting with the capital's press corps, and the next day's headlines around the country proclaimed "A Presidential Dark Horse Talks" (Baltimore *Sun*), "Percy Disavows Presidential

Ambition, But—" (New York *Times*). It was not really what the newcomer said; rather it was the mood that the reporters brought away from the session.

Over the next months Percy complained that the newsmen had him all wrong—he was "just a fellow trying to be a good senator." Yet he lengthened his national speaking schedule, and of his first nineteen speeches away from the capital, only eight were in Illinois. Charles Nicodemus of the Chicago *Daily News's* Washington bureau interviewed one senator (described as "a veteran, widely respected political craftsman"), who was "irritated in the extreme by what he considered to be Percy's proclivity for showboating." An actor portraying Dirksen at the 1967 Gridiron Club show expressed in a song an opinion that many believe the senator secretly holds:

> Chuck Percy is only a freshman,
> As junior as junior can be.
> So why does he act like the leader?
> Oh, bring back Paul Douglas to me.

To the old hands in the Washington press corps, it was clear within weeks that Percy, ninety-ninth in Senate seniority, had his eye on something other than the slow rise to legislative leadership.

While it is conceivable for a freshman senator to seek actively the presidential nomination—Robert Taft did it in 1940—the odds against it are very long. Any calculus of the odds against Percy would have to take into account some of these assets.

Glamour and youth. At forty-eight, Percy is the youngest of the major Republican presidential prospects, and looks even younger than he is. He has a pretty wife, whose breathless voice and wide-eyed wonderment at the strange ways of politics are not unlike those of Jackie Kennedy. An effective television performer, Percy also has the Kennedy flair for providing the sort of "happening" that mass-circulation magazines dote on. When his daughter, Sharon, married John D. Rockefeller IV [in April 1967,] the guest list was a who's who of American politics and society, and the event was recorded on page after page of living color in *Life*.

Brains, Ability, and Salesmanship. The one charge that has not been made against Percy is stupidity. Nobody cracks about him, as they do about Romney, that "down deep, he's shallow," or, as they do about Ronald Reagan, that "behind that glittering facade there is—a glittering facade." His mind may be almost as facile as Nixon's, and Percy does his homework. He scurries after new ideas with the persistence of a squirrel. Between his campaigns for governor and senator, he resumed his private political science seminars, this time inviting mixed groups of academics, journalists, and politicians to meet with him for two and a half days of intensive discussion of liberalism, conservatism, urban problems, reapportionment, civil rights, and other topics, at the University of Chicago's Center for Continuing Education.

But his skill goes beyond research in the realm of ideas. As a former manufacturer of consumer goods, Percy brings to politics a healthy respect for "product development." One man who has worked closely with him for the past few years says, "Basically, he is a merchandising man. He thinks in terms of a mix of activities—research, engineering, advertising, promotion and sales." And when Percy latches on to an idea, he does not rest until it has been sold to the widest possible audience, and always with the Percy label plainly in view. Such was the case with the National Home Ownership Foundation plan, written for his campaign use by a young intellectual named John McClaughry and peddled by Percy so successfully that when it was formally introduced in April, it enjoyed the co-sponsorship of every other Republican senator and over 100 representatives.

Issues. Percy, like Nixon, is inherently a centrist; his tendency is to shun the extreme. But the homing instinct competes in him with a flair for dramatic improvisation that is also part of Percy's concept of "dynamic" leadership. In juxtaposition, the two tendencies give him a unique and probably advantageous identification in the field of 1968 presidential prospects. His eagerness for innovation in dealing with specific problems pleases progressive Republicans; his instinct for the middle of the road reassures conservatives.

Reformers

WAY

DIVORCES GROW.
CHILDREN CRY. MEN
DIE. GOD IS ANGRY.
REPENT! WOMEN, GAIN
ESTEEM! WEAR SKIRTS
7 INCHES BELOW
KNEES. I Timothy 2:8-10

America has a long and distinguished history of reformers and reform movements reaching all the way back to those stiff-necked Puritans of seventeenth-century New England who established community after community in a fruitless attempt to achieve permanent religious orthodoxy. The abolition movement, the labor movement, the prohibition movement, the women's suffrage movement, the civil rights movement, the peace movement, and now a second movement for the liberation of women—it seems sometimes that American politics is never without its marching sign carriers and leafleters.

In this part we take a look at five men and women who are carrying on today the great tradition of dissent and reform. Our first reformer is John Banzhaf III, one of a new breed of lawyers and law professors who are using law itself, the very bedrock of the Establishment, as an instrument of social transformation. There have always been gifted attorneys in America who fought for justice and the rights of minorities with the tools of the law. For a long time their principal weapon was the Constitution, and particularly the first ten amendments. Constitutional law became the vehicle for much of the reform activity in our society, and the Supreme Court emerged as a battleground of social issues.

Recently, lawyers have found that the less exalted branches of the law—contracts, torts, property law, administrative procedures—offer an even more fertile ground for reform efforts. As the administrative bureaucracy has proliferated at every level of government, lawyers have found themselves fighting for the rights of consumers, tenants, welfare clients, and civil servants. John Banzhaf, like the better-known crusader Ralph Nader, has organized law students and young lawyers into teams of investigators to search out loopholes and wrinkles in the statutes that can be used in the interests of the people.

It would be wrong to assume that all the reformers and dissenters fall on the liberal side of the spectrum. We have an equally long tradition of conservative dissent from the dominant style and direction of American society. Our second selection offers portraits of two of the best-known right-wing dissenters, the Reverend Billy Hargis and Robert Welch, founder of the

John Birch Society. The author of this twin profile is
Peter Schrag, a social commentator of a strongly liberal
persuasion who set out on a trip around the country to meet and
study a number of prominent figures of right-wing politics.
Somewhat to his surprise, he found Hargis and Welch rather
appealing people, even though he disagreed with their
opinions. Like Bobby K. Hayes in the last part, Hargis and Welch
typify a style of political thought and action that is wide-spread
and deeply rooted in American society, even though it gets
relatively little sympathetic attention from the major
newspapers, magazines, and television networks. Reverend
Hargis, in particular, voices the fears and hopes of many
Americans for whom fundamentalist Christianity is still the
dominant philosophical influence in their lives.

The remaining pair of selections might as appropriately be
put in the part devoted to revolutionaries, for the Women's
Liberation Movement is potentially the most revolutionary force
for social change yet to appear. I have classified Connie Dvorkin
and Alice de Rivera as reformers simply on the grounds that
they do not call for the use of violent or illegal methods. I am
aware, however, that this is very shaky justification for
classifying them with Billy Hargis, Robert Welch, and
John Banzhaf rather than with Ted Gold, Eldridge Cleaver,
and the Berrigan brothers.

The personal testimony of Connie Dvorkin and Alice de Rivera
is significant in a number of ways. They are the youngest
persons to appear in this volume—Frank Madison was their age
when he served as a Senate page (see Part 4), but his
experiences date from the 1950s. One of the most striking
features of the recent American political scene has been the
appearance of younger and younger participants. First college
students in large numbers entered the political arena; now
high-school teen-agers are writing underground newspapers,
attacking restrictive school practices, and rejecting society's
patterns of work, study, and sex.

Equally important is the fact that these two students begin
with their own personal experiences. In this way they resemble
Eldridge Cleaver rather than John Banzhaf. The Women's
Liberation Movement has from its start insisted on its roots

in the felt emotions and daily frustrations of its followers. Any
theoretical framework must come afterward and be built
on the foundation of those experiences. History suggests that
this is the way all genuine social movements begin, and as
Alice de Rivera and Connie Dvorkin grow older, we can be
certain that we shall be hearing a great deal more from them
and their sisters in the movement.

8. John Banzhaf III:
A Lawyer-Reformer

"The Law Professor Behind Ash, Soup, Pump and Crash"

by JOSEPH A. PAGE

The career of John Banzhaf III demonstrates the diversity of what some see as a crusade and others as simply an exciting new branch of the legal profession. Banzhaf, a 29-year-old champion of consumer causes, is on the one hand a baiter of powerful corporations and bureaucrats, and, on the other, a specialist in something that has already earned a respectable title—"public interest law." He crusades under two different hats, as an associate professor at George Washington University's National Law Center in Washington and as executive director of ASH, Action on Smoking and Health, an organization that he created in 1968 as "the legal arm of the anti-smoking community." This fall, he will again dispatch groups of his students, dubbed "Banzhaf's Bandits" by the press, on various missions in the nation's capital. Inevitably, he is compared with Ralph Nader, inspirational leader of "Nader's Raiders."

In some respects, he seems to be consciously adopting an approach that is at least 90 degrees from Nader's. While the latter is known for what one of his Raiders has termed "an endless capacity for indignation," Banzhaf admits that he does not get himself terribly worked up over his causes. Nader projects an aura of self-effacement and humility, but Banzhaf does quite the opposite. Nader is extremely difficult to contact, while Banzhaf still keeps his listing in the phone directory. The two men, both bachelors, have completely different life styles. Nader, who may be the first secular monk, is now diverting a substantial portion of his earnings to subsidize his own public-interest legal research group. Banzhaf believes in the good life. He drives a car, dates, takes vacations and would like to have the time to indulge in more creature comforts. He also feels very strongly that public-interest advocates need not be underpaid. Including his pay as a law professor and an $18,000-a-year salary from ASH, his earnings now approximate $35,000 annually.

Banzhaf and Nader have met but are not in close contact or coordination. They have already taken somewhat opposing sides on one issue, smoking on airlines. Nader petitioned the Federal Aviation Administration to ban smoking altogether for reasons of safety. Banzhaf and his students filed a petition stressing the rights of the nonsmoker and arguing for segregated smoking compartments. The F.A.A. denied Nader's petition and is considering a ruling favorable to Banzhaf's position. Meanwhile, Nader is appealing to the courts.

Banzhaf works out of a pair of tiny offices at the law school. ASH, which gets funds from health groups as well as doctors and other individuals, pays for his two secretaries, who help administer the antismoking legal action campaign. One wall of the narrow cul-de-sac corridor which leads to his base of operations is virtually papered with his press clippings. "Proof of his oversized ego," critics charge. "Just something to arouse student interest," he explains.

A casual dresser, he looks younger than many of his students; but for the receding and thinning of his closely cropped brown hair and his recently expanded girth, he would easily pass for a college undergraduate. His carefully modulated voice, however, exudes a self-assurance belying the cherubic expression that occasionally brightens his smooth-skinned face-in-the-crowd features. It is a self-assurance appropriate to a man who, while still in law school, convinced the Government that copyright laws should cover computer programs; who at the age of 27 filed a complaint with the Federal Communication Commission which eventually forced TV stations to provide an estimated $75-million worth of annual free time for antismoking commercials; and who today is becoming known as one of the most resourceful and controversial of the new public interest, or *pro bono publico,* advocates.

His motto is, "Sue the bastards." As he explains it, "You can often get best results by suing the hell out of people, using all the legal pressure points you can find. And if you're going to spend the rest of your life suing, you might as well sue the *bastards.*"

Students have the opportunity to put this philosophy to work in Banzhaf's fall semester course in unfair trade practices. He encourages members of the class to identify some specific unfair practice and to try to do away with it by filing their own complaints with the courts and administrative agencies. The students form groups, to which they give inventive acronyms as names, and plunge into battle.

The group that attracted the most attention last year was SOUP (Students Opposed to Unfair Practices), which attempted to get the Federal Trade Commission to take action against Campbell Soup Company television ads that, SOUP charged, used marbles at the bottom of bowls to make soups appear to hold more solids than they actually contained. The F.T.C. wanted to issue a cease-and-desist consent order and leave it at that. SOUP argued that the commission should make Campbell run advertising to counter the effects of the deception.

The commission ruled 3 to 2 against SOUP, rejecting the students' bid to participate as consumers in the proceedings against Campbell, and issued a final cease-and-desist consent order. However, the majority opinion admitted that the F.T.C. did have the power to issue the type of order SOUP sought. The students view this language as a victory. Moreover, they have just filed a petition for review with the U.S. Court of Appeals, asking for the right to intervene.

.   .   .

The law school scene in which Banzhaf now operates differs considerably from the ambience in which he began his legal education. Columbia Law School in the early nineteen-sixties was a pillar of the legal education establishment. The professors on the whole could fit Ralph Nader's description of their Harvard Law counterparts, who he said employed "professorial arrogance as a pedagogical tool." The predominant mood of much of the student body was, "Let's all go down to Wall Street and make a buck."

Banzhaf was not about to let this atmosphere intimidate him. A graduate of M.I.T. with a degree in engineering, he entered the law school in September, 1962, and soon won a reputation as one who would not hesitate to speak his mind in class. By the end of the first year his colleagues were making book on how many oral contributions he would make during each class hour.

His first-year grades were high enough to qualify him for membership on the Columbia Law Review. Top-flight legal journals tend to breed pomposity, and the straight-laced, tradition-oriented Columbia Law Review was no exception. Thus its editors were dismayed to discover that they had a maverick on their hands.

Banzhaf's first project for the Review took advantage of his engineering background and involved research into whether computer programs could be copyrighted. A standard approach would have required first an examination of the copyright laws and the legal decisions interpreting them, and then the development of finely reasoned recommendations on how the question should be resolved. Banzhaf went one step further. Since no one had ever tried to copyright a computer program, he decided to make the attempt himself. To his surprise he succeeded, and on May 8, 1964, the news, garnished by his photo, made The New York Times.

This was John Banzhaf's first legal action project and his first savor of publicity. He enjoyed both immensely. Student writings in the Columbia Law Review are published anonymously, however, and so his name did not appear on the note which he subsequently authored. A footnote did refer to the first successful copyrighting of a computer program, but did not disclose that this was a direct result of the preparation of the note; nor did it mention the name of the person who had obtained the copyright.

The Review's tradition of student anonymity did not sit well with Banzhaf, who approached several technical journals in the data-processing field, one of which wanted to reprint the note with his name on it. The board of editors of the Review, claiming that they had a copyright on everything printed in that journal, refused to grant permission for republication on those terms. They were thoroughly chagrined when their contentious colleague pointed out to them that they had been putting their copyright notice on the wrong page of the Review, and hence none of the articles were legally protected. He then thumbed his nose at the board, rewrote the substance of his note in language comprehensible to a nonlegal audience and had it published under his name in the other journal.

This was not the only occasion that Banzhaf piqued his fellow editors. In his senior year he decided to write an article applying a mathematical analysis to weighted voting as a means of reapportionment. He offered to submit it to the Review, but the notion of publishing a full-length article written and signed by a mere student was unheard of and contrary to all rules and regulations. Undaunted, Banzhaf sent his manuscript to the Rutgers Law Review, which did not hesitate to print it. The Columbia editors fussed and fumed and even talked about expelling him from their ranks. As a parting shot, he wrote a tongue-in-cheek letter on abortion to Playboy, and signed it as a former editor of the Columbia Law Review.

In June, 1965, John Banzhaf received his law degree *magna cum laude.* The presence of a metal plate in his arm, souvenir of a fall from a bicycle when he was 15, kept him out of the draft. After passing the New York and District of Columbia bar exams, he did a research project on reapportionment for the National Municipal League and then went to work for a year as a law clerk for Judge Spottswood W. Robinson III of the United States District Court for the District of Columbia (now on the United States Court of Appeals for D.C.).

During his summer vacations while at law school Banzhaf had worked on the social staff of a cruise ship, and after an arduous year with the hard-working Judge Robinson he went off on a series of short cruises to the Caribbean. Between sailings he stayed at home in the Bronx with his parents, where, while watching football games on television on Thanksgiving in 1966, it dawned upon him that the cigarette commercials which were constantly popping into view might be considered "controversial" in legal terms.

The significance of this moment of inspiration stems from the so-called "fairness doctrine," under which the Federal Communications Commission required radio and TV stations to present fair and adequate treatment of both sides of controversial public issues being aired. "Why not apply the doctrine to cigarette commercials?" he asked himself, and a week later, before leaving on another cruise, he wrote a letter to C.B.S. requesting that the network provide equal time for antismoking commercials. Upon his return home in late December, he fired off a second letter to C.B.S. and on Jan. 5, 1967, in the purser's office of the Swedish-American Line's M.S. Kungsholm, he typed up a formal complaint which he mailed to the F.C.C. On the next day he set sail on a 92-day cruise of the South Seas.

This was the first antismoking effort for John Banzhaf, himself a nonsmoker. "I felt reasonably strong about the problem of smoking and about the misuse of the airwaves," he now reminisces. "And I decided that here was something that I as an individual could do." After returning home from his cruise, he went to work for a New York City patent law firm. Two weeks later, to his astonishment, the F.C.C. upheld his complaint.

Subsequent accounts of Banzhaf's crusade have stressed its David vs. Goliath angle. This may be a bit misleading. At the time he filed his complaint, there were important elements within the F.C.C. who were favorably disposed toward the arguments he was making. The growing concern over smoking as a cancer risk strengthened the hand of members who disapproved of the habit and the commercials.

This does not, of course, diminish his contribution. As one of his friends in the public interest law movement has observed, "John had the ability to see certain forces moving in certain directions and to seize an idea whose time had come. This is a creative talent—no doubt about it." Another *pro bono* specialist has put it more colorfully: "The F.C.C. had within it an ovum, and Banzhaf supplied the sperm."

.   .   .

Law students and young lawyers have been for some time expressing their distaste for the profession's traditional preoccupation with representing powerful, vested interests, and with what one of their number has termed "the degeneration of the large law firms into servicing affiliates of big corporations." They are repulsed by travesties such as a recent American Bar Association committee report which opposed allowing consumers to bring class-action suits against defrauding corporations and was signed by nine lawyers whose clients include large companies and trade associations.

Until recently, *pro bono* practitioners confined themselves to the representation of individual indigent clients in criminal and civil cases and to the test-case approach of organizations such as the American Civil Liberties Union and the National Association for the Advancement of Colored People. The new breed of public interest lawyers provides legal services to a variety of citizen's groups which have just begun to demand access to the legal system and vindication of their legal rights. They are trying to give the same quality of representation that business interests customarily receive to consumer organizations, conservationists, poor people and minority entrepreneurs.

At its most imaginative, the practice of public-interest law often intervenes in proceedings which have never before been recognized as adversary, and helps create new constituencies among people who stand to benefit from campaigns for legal reform—for example, the consumers of a certain product. The public-interest advocate, in Ralph Nader's words, "seeks distributive justice for the greatest number of people, practices before all branches of government and other large institutions [such as corporations and labor unions], responds to his own conscience and dedication to professional goals, and remains undeterred and undetoured by parochial client interest or control."

Public-interest lawyers in Washington are experimenting with a wide range of organizational structures. Among these are: Berlin, Roisman & Kessler, a firm which handles *pro bono* matters exclusively and hopes to find enough paying clients to survive; Asher & Schneiderman, a firm 75 per cent of whose work is in the public-interest field; the *pro bono* division of the large Washington law firm, Arnold & Porter; Benny L. Kass, a lawyer-lobbyist who works on consumer problems for non-profit groups and individuals; the Citizens Communications Center, a small, foundation-financed office which specializes in representing citizens' groups before the Federal Communications Commission; the Urban Law Institute, an affiliate of George Washington University which provides representation for Washington community groups; and the Washington Research Project, which focuses primarily on civil-rights issues.

One of the more interesting experiments is the Stern Community Law Firm, a foundation-backed group which is challenging the legal profession's own prohibition against soliciting business. (Director Monroe Freedman, who claims the ban is unconstitutional because it prevents public-interest lawyers from telling people about their rights, plans to advertise for clients.) Another is the Center for Law and Social Policy, a foundation-funded organization which trains students from universities such as Yale during part of their law school careers and recently helped win a court order requiring the Department of Transportation to reopen an investigation into certain G.M. pickup trucks. (Along with *pro bono* counsel from Arnold & Porter, the center's lawyers argued that the department's engineers had found the truck wheels tend to develop cracks and collapse without warning.)

Ultimately, Banzhaf hopes that public funds will be forthcoming for a kind of organization of ombudsmen.

"What I would like to do," he muses, "is to continue with an organization having a principal legal focus, and go into areas where I can find a confluence of important problems and a point of legal leverage. The idea is to accomplish a large result with a relatively small input.

"It would be great to establish the proposition that there can and should be organizations whose purpose is to take legal or law-related measures to benefit some aspect of the public interest, and that they should be supported at least in part by the public, either directly through contributions or by grants from other organizations. This would also provide lawyers with an institutional framework within which they can work professionally on a full-time basis to advance what they see as the public interest. The success of such a venture would demonstrate that lawyers and law students can initiate legal action which can have an important catalytic effect on society. The result would be a revolution within the system to avoid a revolution outside the system. Of course, I may be just a perpetual optimist, but I think all this can be done."

.   .   .

Though a legal activist, Banzhaf is by no stretch of the imagination a radical. He firmly favors working through established channels: "I believe there's a great deal that can be done through the system by prodding it and operating on the periphery. I recognize many things that can't be achieved through legal action. You can't sue to stop the Vietnam war or get student power. But I stay within the system because that's where I have my expertise."

.   .   .

Nader has termed Banzhaf "one of the most imaginative legal start-up advocates in the country. He provokes his students into creative application of old bottles with new wines." Commissioner Mary Gardiner Jones of the F.T.C. has said that "he has a philosophy of how a citizen fits into the government and is doing concrete, positive things to make the government respond. We surely need this kind of effort."

There are those, on the other hand, who accuse Banzhaf of being abrasive, egotistical, immature, opportunistic and politically inept. His fondness for publicity has alienated some of his students. ("Talking to him about this problem is like throwing water at a wall," one of them complained.) It is no secret at the law school that he is in tenure trouble. A not insubstantial number of his colleagues take an exceedingly dim view of him and his manner of operation. He is one of two members of the faculty under 30 and is not given to treating his elders with deference. "A saint he is not," was the succinct appraisal of one professor who is favorably disposed toward him. The faculty will decide this fall whether to grant him tenure. He could lose, and would have to leave.

To a certain degree these problems derive from the fact that John Banzhaf has always been a loner, a fierce individualist who does not much care how people react to him. This quality has motivated and sustained him throughout his career. It may also compromise his effectiveness.

The survival of ASH, as well as that of all the public interest groups, depends in large part upon publicity. Private contributors and foundations are much more likely to support an operation which has enjoyed widely heralded successes. John Banzhaf has never taken a backward step in the competition for public attention. His critics contend that he overdoes it. For example, law students in a group called GASP (Greater Washington Alliance to Stop Pollution), which took legal action against the overemission of exhaust from D.C. buses and which had no connection with the Bandits, were very upset by what they saw as his attempts to take credit for their successes.

Still, it is not true, as some have charged, that he is motivated solely by a desire to see his name in print. On the evening after a minor police riot on the George Washington campus during a demonstration to protest the verdict in the "Chicago 7" trial, he went to the lockup and quietly bailed out several law students who had been arrested. And when the university hospital refused to admit a 105-pound law student who had been gratuitously clubbed by police, he brought the boy back to the hospital and invited officials to explain into his tape-recorder exactly why they would not treat the injured student. They quickly changed their minds.

Public-interest advocacy can be a tricky business. At times it requires aggressive persistence, a quality John Banzhaf has displayed in abundance. At other times, political acumen is indispensable. In this latter respect, his shortcomings may run deeper than an apparent talent for rubbing people the wrong way.

Pro bono advocates are reluctant to criticize others doing similar work for fear of harming the movement. Yet some have privately admitted misgivings about Banzhaf's tactics, which have been termed unwise and even childish. Testifying at a Bureau of Motor Carrier Safety hearing in July (dressed in what appeared to be a tennis outfit), Banzhaf warned that unless smoking were banned on interstate buses the passengers might resort to self-help. To illustrate what they might do, he pulled a cylindrical tube which he said was a smoke bomb out of his pocket and challenged Isaac D. Benkin, the bureau's counsel, to give him a legal reason why he should not explode it on the spot. His argument was that if smokers had a right to pollute a bus, he could discharge smoke in the hearing room. Benkin, visibly alarmed, threatened to report him to the bar association—whereupon Banzhaf disclosed that the "bomb" was a harmless flare.

At the conclusion of his recent testimony in favor of a broad consumer class-action bill before a Senate committee, exuberance lapsed into indiscretion when Banzhaf boasted: "Give us these kinds of tools, give me 500 law students in the District of Columbia, and I would turn the F.T.C. and the Justice Department and the major advertisers upside down and shake them." Industry lobbyists opposing the bill are delighted to have such hyperbole on the record, and are expected to make good use of it in their efforts to help pass the Nixon Administration's watered-down class-action bill.

There are skeptics who consider the public-interest law movement a fad and view Banzhaf as a shooting star who will soon fade from sight. They dismiss the students as dilettantes who are having a thoroughly enjoyable time in the pursuit of trivial causes. But the commitment of so many young people—with talent and training and experience—suggests that the movement is here to stay. The fact that it has been able to accommodate a quintessential individualist like Banzhaf testifies to its vitality.

9. Billy Hargis and Robert Welch:
Right-Wing Reformers

"America's Other Radicals"
by PETER SCHRAG

"It is Communist. It is a Communist revolution. The people who are burning down the campuses, they're not right-wingers, they're not Birchers, they're not Ku Kluxers, they're not conservatives. They are Communists. . . . You better wake up, brothers. The Communists feel they've got the college-age youth in their pocket. Now they're concentrating on the high schools. . . . They may feel that this is the time to go for broke. And what are you going to do about it? Are you going to keep doing nothing?"

It was getting hot. Two hundred people in the Church of Christ in Angus, Nebraska. Old farmers in their rimless glasses, clerks from the hardware and the feed-and-seed, young couples with babies, Birchers from Northern Kansas passing around petitions against trade with the Russians. Hot. The church wasn't meant for this. Last Sunday they'd had thirty-four for the worship service, but on this Tuesday night some of them had driven 100 miles to hear this man, Billy James Hargis, of Tulsa, Oklahoma, deliver The Message and collect the contributions. *Anyone who doesn't have an envelope—the ushers have more.* The Christian Crusade: For Christ—Against Communism. There's a blank check inside. Fill in the name of your bank and the amount.

Hargis takes off his jacket and wipes his brow. The wavy hair is still in place but the blue shirt is getting damp. It is hard work, especially for a man of 260 pounds who is trying to lose weight and found it impossible that day to fit his belly into a restaurant booth. A few years before, he traveled in a $50,000 air-conditioned Greyhound bus that had been fitted with sleeping accommodations, an office, recording equipment, and other facilities. But the bus has been given up because, Hargis said, there had been an accident—fumes had backed into the ventilation system—and he no longer felt it was safe. So now he travels by chartered plane and car, and the road is harder. Two hours per evening in one-night stands, exhorting, collecting, preaching. Last night in Norton, Kansas; tomorrow in Scotia, Nebraska; Thursday in North Platte; Friday in Miller, then back to Tulsa for the Conference of Orthodox (Fundamentalist) Ministers. Two hundred appearances a year: churches, auditoriums, meeting halls. Two thousand in Indianapolis. Three thousand at the annual Christian Crusade dinner at Knott's Berry Farm in Orange County, California. Five weekly radio broadcasts on 115 stations; a weekly newspaper; a summer conference center in Colorado called The Summit which "trains Teen Agers and College Youth in Christian, Anti-Communist Leadership"; books, pamphlets, records, bumper stickers, and, beginning this fall, American Christian College in Tulsa, of which he will be president. Privately he is diffident, almost touching, about his country background in Texarkana and his lack of formal education. "I'm going to be president of that college," he says. "Now can you imagine anything more ridiculous than that?" But publicly he is in charge; he understands about the Communists and the liberals and the demons outside. In Angus or Lima or Shreveport, and maybe even in the Baptist Temple in Indianapolis, Hargis *knows.*

The right hand waves the glasses, and sometimes the left holds a newspaper or a pamphlet with the story of new atrocities. Devils dance, old ones resurrected, new ones conjured up from the headlines: the liberal ministers and the National Council of Churches, Martin Luther King and the Black Panthers, sex and pornography and dirty movies and sensitivity training, the Eastern press and the college radicals, the Ford Foundation and the Council on Foreign Relations, J. William Fulbright and Richard Nixon and sometimes even Agnew.

"The National Council of Churches can't back our men in Vietnam, but I see that they can take holy tithe money and support those draft dodgers in Canada. We could win this war in a month if we supported an all-out solution. We shouldn't let 'em lose; we should let 'em win. That's the American tradition and the only American tradition."

"Amen."

.   .   .

I spent all that day with Hargis, sitting in his motel room in Grand Island, and, after his speech, late into the night, driving across the dark, flat Nebraska countryside, consuming steaks at roadside restaurants, talking about America and the churches and the people who come to listen, trying to decide how much of this man was hustle, how much conviction, and trying to separate the general madness of the country from what could be called serious politics. . . .

.   .   .

As we drive north from Angus, up Route 14, then west on Interstate 80, he fiddles with the radio, trying to get the returns of the Alabama primary between Wallace and Brewer, saying, almost offhand, "Now that Wallace, he's a real Populist," then talking about Bryan and Lester Maddox, and of how Maddox went on television when his son was arrested for holding up a filling station, not to disown him but to declare his father's love; then talking again about Wallace, and how he brought Wallace to his national Christian Crusade convention a year ago because Wallace was a drawing card and would help fill the hall; and about General Edwin "Pro Blue" Walker who had used Birch literature to indoctrine his troops in Europe, and who, after his retirement, spent time on the circuit with Hargis. Walker had been a poor platform performer, sometimes incoherent, and Hargis always took the collection before Walker spoke. "Walker is a good man," Hargis said in explanation, "but he never understood the way the country treated him." He stopped for a moment—he didn't like running people down—and then he returned to his favorite topic, the liberal churches, how they had been losing members, and spoke of the huge congregations of the fundamentalist churches in the large cities, Detroit, Indianapolis, Kansas City, Los Angeles, churches "where they have ten thousand in Sunday school," and then about his own career as a preacher in Arkansas and Oklahoma, of how he had grown up "in an awkward age" after the great evangelists had retired, and of an old evangelical preacher named A. B. McReynolds who had helped and encouraged him: "He turned my life around. He gave me a book, *The Road Ahead* by John T. Flynn, and it explained how even then the churches were going liberal, how they were going from the salvation gospel to the social gospel. It explained all my frustrations to me. In the churches *I* knew it was all Bible, but in the ministerial schools you'd hear all the other. Mac explained it to me; little by little he fed me this material. One day he said, 'God is going to raise up some young minister who's going to keep the church's feet to the fire, who's going to start a great movement,' and I asked, 'Could I be that young man?' and he said, 'What do you think I've been doing all this for?' . . . Brother Mac was a real renegade, he's part of my anti-Establishment life. He took orders from nobody but God."

It was hard not to like him. "I'm an evangelist at heart," he had said earlier that day. "I always talk on the Bible." *The Bible is inspired. I'd be a wildcat if I didn't believe in hell. I'd live it up if I didn't have to confront an angry God at judgment.* But in his public appearances the Bible always seemed to lead to other things, to Martin Luther King, "who didn't believe in the Virgin Birth, who said the Virgin Birth was a white man's trick to exploit the ignorant Negro," to *Playboy* and Hugh Hefner ("If Satan gives a medal, Hugh will get it"), to sex and pornography, to *Midnight Cowboy,* "with homosexuality and three acts of intercourse on the screen" (it occurred to me, as he mentioned that in Angus, that I never counted them), to a school in Chicago "where six- and seven-year-old kids are modeling sex organs *right in class,*" to Abbie Hoffman and Jerry Rubin and William Kunstler, "the Communist-front lawyer," to the war and the liberal press, and, then, inevitably, to the pitch, to the collection, to the table of records and books: a transcription of a Black Panther meeting—"filthy, dirty, vulgar"—in two versions, bowdlerized and unabridged, a booklet entitled *The Black Panthers Are Not Black—They are Red* and another *Those Red Bears in Their Clergy Collars,* an exposé of the Ford Foundation (it bankrolls the Left), taped sermons by Dr. William Ward Ayer, $5 each, Christian sex-education records, one for boys, one for girls (in Angus he had run out of the boys' record), American flag lapel pins, copies of *The Christian Crusade Weekly,* and a biography of Hargis himself. *The ushers will move among you. Can you give even a dollar a month to save your country? I want you to give your time, your money, your prayers to help get the message out. If I fail to touch your pocketbook I've failed completely.*

He had been crusading for twenty-four years. He started preaching in little churches when he was sixteen, began his first radio broadcast a few years later, and now conducted an annual business of some $3 million employing 104 people, most of it, he said, supported with small contributions and subscriptions. "Whoever thinks we're in this for the money is just kidding himself. There's no money in being a right-winger." Each night he takes the checks, the one-dollar bills, and the ten-dollar bills and stuffs them in his attaché case: $600 in Norton, $400 in Angus, $2,000 in Indianapolis. A few years ago, the Internal Revenue Service revoked the Crusade's income-tax exemption—the work, he said, of J. William Fulbright and Lyndon Johnson—but he has taken the matter to court and hopes to have it restored. He speaks as if the Republicans will be more understanding. Christian Crusade is not a political organization but a religious and educational movement; it supported no one for President. (It is impossible, I remember Welch saying, for any truly anti-Communist organization to get a tax exemption.) "I've gotten some support from Walter Knott [the California entrepreneur who turned a roadside fruit stand into a huge business] and a few others, but only a little. Money's always been hard. I have to work for every dollar." As we ride through the Nebraska dark he wonders out loud if he should work harder with organizations of businessmen, corporation officers, luncheon groups, but somehow he knows that most of them live in another world, and that even he doesn't quite understand it. He speaks about the Crusade's investments, land in Texas and Oklahoma, a hotel in Tulsa ("I prayed and prayed to find out what the Lord wanted me to do about that hotel; we bought it for the college as endowment"), but he seemed more to be playing at it than doing it. Obviously he lived well; he occupied a $44,000 "parsonage" that the Christian Crusade had bought for him, he rode in cars that the organization provided, he owned a little farm in Missouri, and several times a year he and his wife led "tours" overseas—to Rhodesia, to the Oberammergau Passion Play, to Israel ("the most anti-Communist country in the world"). And yet, it still wasn't his world or his time. When I asked him why he hadn't served in World War II (he turned eighteen in 1943) he explained that he was then already a minister, that he automatically received a clerical exemption, and that only men with college degrees could become chaplains, but he seemed to know that the explanation wasn't impressive, and he obviously didn't like the subject. (Since then he has received a bachelor's degree from the Burton College and Seminary in Manitou Springs, Colorado, and a couple of honorary doctor of laws degrees, one of them from Bob Jones University, the other from Belin Memorial University in Chillicothe, Missouri. Belin's founder, Dr. Clyde Belin, has since served a year in prison for mail fraud.)

Three ninety-five Concord Avenue in Belmont, Massachusetts, the home office of the John Birch Society, looks like the central headquarters of a suburban school board: tile floors, cinderblock walls, fluorescent lights. The American flag hangs over the front door twenty-four hours a day; it is illuminated at night, which, I assumed—given the place—was proper flag etiquette. There are a few flag decals on the cars in the parking lot—

Chevys, Buicks, an Imperial—and one sign that says, "I'm a Secret Member of the John Birch Society." Next door, the employees of the Belmont Post Office make certain that the spill-over of Birch cars doesn't come to rest in the socialist parking spaces of the government. Just inside at number 395 is an American Opinion Bookstore, one of the 350 or so that distribute the literature of the Society and its affiliate, Robert Welch, Inc.—some five million pieces a year—and beyond that there are the offices, billing machines, duplicators, and mailing rooms of the Society itself. During the day I saw no end of wall maps with pins marking the location of the bookstores and the 4,000 JBS chapters (Southern California was clogged, ditto for the northern suburbs of Chicago, Dallas-Fort Worth, Houston, Northern New Jersey, and Long Island) and a scattering of pictures of John Birch heroes and authors, many of them the waxy paintings resembling holy cards that *American Opinion* magazine uses on its covers: Eddie Rickenbacker, the film writer Jack Moffitt, who testified against the Hollywood Ten in McCarthy days, General Patton, General MacArthur, Taylor Caldwell, Professor E. Merrill Root (author of *Collectivism on the Campus* and *Brainwashing in the High Schools*), J. Edgar Hoover, Greek Premier Papadopoulos, and George S. Schuyler, once a writer for Mencken's *American Mercury* and now for Birch journals. Schuyler is—how would he like to be described? —a colored man.

It all looked normal—the plain cinderblock walls, the desks, the editors, the managers, the bookkeepers and secretaries (very few single women), the crowded halls and offices, which had already forced expansion into other buildings. A few bulldog types, second-string football tackles twenty years later, some YMCA faces, and more Southerners than you'd expect in a Boston suburb, all straight, typing, answering telephones, dictating, doing what most people do in offices. You had to keep trying to square the words with the faces and the behavior; after a few hours even the language seemed quite ordinary and proper. Hermetic reality.

It should be noted and remembered [Welch wrote in the May *Bulletin*] that, even in 1917, both Lenin and Trotsky were nothing more than agents, employed and supported by the top Conspirators above them. And that neither of them could even have got to Russia in that year, or have had any chance to leading and sustaining the Bolshevik Revolution, but for the huge sums of money turned over to them, and the vast influence exerted on their behalf by far more powerful Conspirators in England, Germany, other countries, and especially in the United States. The fact that these countries were at war with each other had no bearing on the community of interests among the top....

After 1917, however, two very important factors gradually changed the nature of the Conspiratorial advance. One was the establishment (in 1922) of a physical base and headquarters for the Communist arm of the Conspiracy, in the form of the Union of Soviet Socialist Republics....The second was simply the evil genius and ruthless ambition of Stalin, which contributed so mightily to this physical progress....

Communism is never anything but a drive for power or position or glory or wealth on the part of the *Insiders* at the top, or of those climbing to the top. These *Insiders* impose the components of Communist tyranny on a people and on the world, subtly, skillfully, deceptively, and with patient gradualism....This is why nothing else that you do to oppose collectivism or immorality or revolutionary vandalism really matters, unless you expose the Conspiratorial drive behind them.

From Robert Welch all things flow. It is his organization, his employees, his work, his words. Then an executive of the Welch Candy Company, Welch launched JBS in 1958 at that now-famous two-day meeting in Indianapolis, where he spoke to some of his corporate friends for endless hours, telling them of the menace, and asking for their help. (The speech, which was to become the *Blue Book of the John Birch Society*, did not mention *Insiders* or the higher Conspiracy, or his allegation, spelled out in his book *The Politician*, that Dwight Eisenhower was a Communist agent.) Of all the Radical Right organizations, JBS became the only one that succeeded in building a broad base of membership, and in getting that membership to work faithfully on the projects Welch outlines in his *Bulletin* each month: circulating petitions against trade and aid with the Communists (more than 1,500,000 signatures to date), writing letters to politicians and newspapers, persuading merchants to carry California grapes (Cesar Chavez is a Red agent) and not to stock Polish hams, demanding an end to sex education and pornography, recruiting new members, supporting local police, and harassing the Supreme Court. (The Welch magazine *Review of the News* has been calling for the impeachment of Justice Douglas, but JBS has not elevated that cause into a project for members because Burger and Blackmun aren't much better.)

The organization that Welch created consists of two separate entities, JBS itself, and an affiliated publishing arm, Robert Welch, Inc., which includes *Review of the News, American Opinion,* and a book-publishing house, Western Islands. Together they employ more than two hundred people and operate on a budget of nearly $5 million a year. ("We spend whatever we can raise," Welch said.) The field work of the Society is managed by 74 paid "coordinators" and "major coordinators" who direct the activities of chapter leaders and members (ten to twenty people in each chapter), recruit new volunteers, run monthly "study clubs," advise the front groups, MOTOREDE, SYLP, TRAIN (To Restore American Independence Now), and TACT (Truth About Civil Turmoil), and try to keep the bookstores staffed with chapter volunteers. And yet it is still Welch, now seventy, who sets the policy, writes the *Bulletin*—15,000 words a month, in longhand—hires the staff, and selects the members of the National Council, a group of businessmen, doctors, and lawyers who advise him and help give the organization a look of corporate respectability. In Belmont, he is always *Mr. Welch,* and if anyone believes that his vision of the Conspiracy is wild, he doesn't say it very loud. "Mr. Welch," someone explained, "is a driven man."

The tone, inevitably, is considered, with a kind of anal reasonableness that seems stranger on paper than in the environs of a chapter meeting or the offices in Belmont. You learn all sorts of things: that it was no coincidence that Earth Day, April 22, was also the one hundredth anniversary of Lenin's birth; that the Chinese satellite was not Chinese but Russian; that the "incredible distributive drug network" sponsored by the Communists is delivering drugs produced in China; that "the international financiers" sponsored anti-Semitic attacks on themselves to preclude serious scholarship on their machinations; that youth revolt in this country is sponsored by the

Communists, but that student demonstrations in Prague and Belgrade are locally sponsored phonies designed to throw us off the track; that most young radicals were, at one time, on the payroll of the Office of Economic Opportunity, or workers in OEO-supported programs; that the Soviet Union never took its missiles out of Cuba, and that "they've paraded them through the streets of Havana" to maintain pressure on the United States and thereby justify the ever-increasing scope of government in this country; that international disarmament is a fraud which would really involve the transfer of weapons from national (*i.e.* American) control to the control of a world government.

Words. From *American Opinion* (which has more editorial latitude than the *Bulletin* and does not necessarily reflect the Birch line):

> When they come to get your gun, are you going to let them have it?...One of the good things about Marlboro country and such, where men are men and pack something besides Marlboros to prove it, is that everybody is more polite....
>
> In December, Berkeley radicals actually held ceremonial burial services for Christmas trees. It is interesting to recall that one of the first moves after the Communists' November Revolution in Russia was the banning of Christmas trees....
>
> When disciples of the Marquis de Sade demonstrate against the atomic bomb they are just insanely jealous.

Inevitably—and beneath most of it—there is the vision of a smaller, simpler world, of less government, of a lost innocence, and—at the same time—of a nation so powerful that only treason and conspiracy could have created its contemporary problems. (It is not suggested that the military is also part of government, and hence should be reduced. It is assumed that if the generals were allowed to win—in Vietnam or wherever —the armed forces would atrophy of their own volition.) "What about the FBI?" I asked Scott Stanley, Jr., the editor of *American Opinion.* "The potential danger is there," he said. "Suppose Hoover were replaced by a man of the Left, by someone like Nick Katzenbach [Attorney General under Johnson]. It's scary." And yet, there is also the sense—certainly on their part, and perhaps on mine—that the world's version of chaos has moved closer to theirs. "The young people," Stanley said, "are conditioned to be anti-Establishment. They're concerned about oppression of the individual. They feel lost in their environment without a feeling that they can control it. We agree on the problem—the growth of bigness, the destruction of individuals. They don't see how a rational man can turn to government." The whole object of the revolution in the streets, he explained, is the extension of collectivism and repression. The revolution is being manipulated to justify a repressive Congressional reaction—an expansion of the power of the state and the *Insiders,* the Conspiracy "which we call for convenience the International Communist Movement."

The literature flows and the speakers mount their platforms; retired colonels and little priests in white socks, ex-Green Berets and crewmen from the *Pueblo:* brainwashing, drugs, "Our Families—Under Attack," "The John Birch Society—The Myth and the Reality," "The Glorification of M. L. King—a Victory for World Communism," "Communist Target—Youth: Cannon Fodder for Revolution," "The American Military: Target of a Smear." One week's schedule: Bellaire, Texas; Marion, Michigan; Moline, Illinois; Petoskey, Mich; Kalkaska, Mich.; Tulsa; Elkhart, Indiana; Schenectady; Holland, Mich.; Tyler, Texas; South Bend, Ind.; Rockville, Minnesota; Plattsburg, New York; Sturgis, Mich.; Columbus, Ohio; Minneapolis; Syracuse, N.Y.; Battle Creek, Mich.; Cleveland; North Branch, Minn.; Buffalo, N.Y.; Hastings, Mich.; American Legion halls, school auditoriums, hotels, community centers, the Knights of Columbus, the Grange hall, the "Memorial Opera House."

In the basement recreation room of a development house on Staten Island, the most conservative borough of New York City, the monthly meeting of a local chapter. We sit around a large table covered with white cloth. Eleven people. All but one of the five women sit around one corner; the men sit opposite. We stand to say the Pledge of Allegiance, then a moment of silent prayer. The leader is a lady in her thirties (Italian Catholic, bleached hair, well-preserved; most of the others are

older, but they are all first generation out of the city: Little
Italy, Chelsea, Yorkville Irish or German). We do the *Bulletin.*
Like school. *Explication du texte* and projects. Things to do this
month. Write letters to the Senate Foreign Relations Committee opposing adoption of the Genocide Treaty. Side reference to
the Supreme Court: "Democracy is the worst of all government," says the leader with a little difficulty, echoing Welch's
First Principle. ("This is a Republic; Keep it That Way.") Petitions against trade and aid are collected: twenty-seven sheets
with seventeen names each. Mr. Welch says he has something
big planned when they get two million. . . . We recently recruited some students. One of them said the Radical Left didn't
offer him anything so he joined the John Birch Society. There'll
be some people with petitions going to the hard-hat parade; the
construction workers—their hearts are in the right place—but
they don't understand either. Not Peace with Honor; Victory.
And the way to win, says Mr. Welch, is to stop supporting the
Communists. Stop trade. Did you know that Nixon has just
taken 1,300 items off the strategic materials list, so now they
can be sold to the Russians?

.   .   .

Welch's own claims for the society are modest; he suggests
that it was the Society's work that made the Ford Motor Company reluctant to build an automobile plant in the Soviet Union,
that its attacks on Earl Warren and the Supreme Court helped
drive Fortas off the bench and produced a more general suspicion of the Court, and that its campaign to Support Your Local
Police has alerted people to the attacks on local law-enforce-
ment agencies. The Panthers and the SDS were gullible tools, he
explained. What they were doing was to create, on behalf of
the *Insiders,* a public demand for "more stringent laws against
freedom of speech and for suppression by the federal government of freedom of assembly," and the way to stop that was
to "take the handcuffs off the police and put them on the
criminals."

It was all part of the same plot, going back to 1776 and a
crowd of Conspirators called the *"Illuminati"* and their hand-
picked successors. For some time we spoke about the *Insiders,*

about Colonel House and Christian Herter, who, he said, were planning World War II at the time of Versailles, about the central bankers, and of how the income tax, the Federal Reserve System, and the foundations were planned together. The *Insiders* were hard to fight because "they've had all the experience" but it was not clear from the conversation whether the members of the Conspiracy in the United States were working for the Communists or vice versa. Perhaps it didn't matter. What was clear was that it was hard for *us* to use *them*—that *they* inevitably succeeded in manipulating us because they were so adept at the use of human psychology. (Marx, Lenin, and Trotsky, I was told again, were just agents.) It was all in the book, in the pamphlet, documented in the latest issue of the *Bulletin. Go do your homework.*

. . .

I kept trying to define Radical Right; it was easy a decade ago, but that map no longer served. Too much had happened, too much has come unstuck; it had now become fashionable to confuse error with treason, ignorance with racism, and revolutionary rhetoric with Conspiracy. "Democracy," says a character in John LeCarré's novel *A Small Town in Germany,* "was only possible under a class system. . . . It was an indulgence granted by the privileged. We haven't time for it anymore: a flash of light between feudalism and automation, and now it's gone. What's left? The voters are cut off from parliament, parliament is cut off from the government, and the government is cut off from everyone. Government by silence, that's the slogan. Government by alienation. . . ." As I left Welch's office, loaded with literature, I asked him who the real *Insiders* were in America. "I wish I knew," he replied. "I wish I knew."

10. Connie Dvorkin and Alice de Rivera: Women's Liberation in High School

"The Suburban Scene"

by CONNIE DVORKIN

I was born March 4, 1955, in Doctor's Hospital in New York City. All my life I have lived in an unincorporated area of the town of Greenburgh, though my mailing address is Scarsdale and the school district is Edgemont, Greenburgh Union Free District No. 6. I am in the eighth grade and have been a pacifist and a vegetarian since October 1968. I live in a Republican stronghold and the conservatism that usually goes along with that is very evident here. My prison's name is Edgemont Junior-Senior High School, grades 7-12, with approximately 850 inmates. I am the so-called secretary of Edgemont Students for Action to which all the activist radicals and more radical liberals more or less belong.

I think I first heard of the Women's Liberation Movement on WBAI (Radio Free New York), most likely on "Radio Unnameable." Like Eldridge Cleaver in *Soul On Ice,* I never realized how oppressed I was until someone brought it into the open. I wrote a letter asking for some literature on the Women's Liberation Movement that I could read. It was for a Social Studies report that never materialized. But that is irrelevant like school is. The important thing is that I read the stuff and immediately agreed with everything. Ironically the very night I was reading it I was babysitting and watching TV. The show, "I Love Lucy," was an episode where the two women were to be equal to the men for one night—no courtesies "due to a woman," no shit like that for *one* night, eating out at a restaurant—and they couldn't do it. They *had* to depend on their husbands. They couldn't face life out in front, they had to hide behind their husbands' names and souls. The kids I was sitting for laughed their asses off, and I realized that I would have, too, five months earlier.

Now, with awakened eyes, I could see all the brainwashing of my sisters that goes on at school. It starts almost the instant they are born, by their mothers, and by fathers encouraging the boys to take an interest in cars, baseball, etc., and discouraging girls. A girl I know who was always a "tomboy," now, in the compulsory intramural volley ball we have with the boys, always seems to hang back and doesn't seem as "boyish" as she always is. I feel particularly sorry for the snobs or society "chicks" of my grade. Everybody knows the type. They will probably never hear the gospel and if they do would never accept it. I once thought it was "fun" to wear miniskirts (I had a really good figure then, but no longer worry about that shit) and look good for boys and men generally. I rationalized. "Why not? It's fun and they like it." I read all the literature on women's liberation and still wore skirts. But then I heard about the momentous decision by the judge who said that principals could no longer tell girls what to wear, and I went up to my principal; he said he couldn't stop me, but he thought slacks "were in bad taste." Anyway, since that, I've worn dresses or skirts about five times—one time it was to the Passover Seder. Since I began wearing pants I have discovered two things: 1) I feel more equal with boys, and 2) I no longer have to worry as to how my legs are placed and all that bullshit as I had to when I wore skirts. I no longer feel myself fighting other girls for the attention of boys, and am generally much more at ease with the world.

In seventh and eighth grade you have the trimester along with the regular report card. The trimester consists of three subjects—Music, Art, and Home Ec "for girls" and Shop "for boys." I began thinking about a groovy idea—taking Shop instead of Home Ec. So I talked it over with my mother (whom I consider far more liberal than my father) who sent a note off to the junior high girls' guidance counselor. She said I couldn't, but she didn't really tell me why. Then my mother sent a letter off to my principal, repeating that I wished to take Shop and could he please voice his opinion on that. Three weeks later his reply came back. I thought this was a deliberate delay tactic on his part. He is a very clever conservative always having this fantasy that he's on the students' side, which of course is bullshit. Anyway, in his letter he cited several reasons why I couldn't take Shop: 1) it was traditional that a girl took Home Ec, 2) there wouldn't be enough room in Shop for one more pupil, 3) the teacher in Shop would be overworked. He knew that we would go over him to the school supervisor, Dr. Larson, so he sent Larson a copy of his letter. I obtained an appointment with Dr. Larson five days before Home Ec was supposed to start. I explained to him my reasons why I didn't want to take Home Ec. I said I thought that the school system is the mold for people in this society and that in giving a course in Home Ec just for girls and Shop just for boys they were trying to mold girls into being "homemakers" and boys into what molds people thought define "masculinity." I was very impressed by the interview because Dr. Larson, outside of one understanding teacher, was the only school official who took me seriously and listened to me while discussing school affairs. Well, Dr. Larson passed on the request to the district superintendent, Dr. Russo. Larson sent me Xerox copies of the letter to Russo and Russo's letter to an official up at Albany, so I could trust him. Word was passed along to me that nobody in Albany wanted to touch the issue, and they finally sent down an edict that I could do what I wanted to.

While this was going on Home Ec and Shop had already started and I was given a Study Hall during the period that

Home Ec/Shop was in. I requested this since I am a pacifist and do not believe in confrontation politics. I wasn't trigger-happy for a confrontation like many SDSers are. (I don't mean to offend any SDS people reading this. Some of my best friends are in SDS.)

The first day I started Shop I was very apprehensive about how the boys were going to react to me being in the class. I have two very good friends in that class (including Dr. Larson's son Mark), and they congratulated me on my success. One of the boys is very condescending toward me, always speaking in the patronizing, gentle voice that really makes me angry. "Connie, let me help you," they say. "Well! I just want to tell you—fuck you, damn it, and go home and stop farting out all that chickenshit, man, just quit it!" I say furiously, but silently. But Shop is fun if the "teacher" isn't paying attention because you can goof all you want to. One thing I realized when I walked into the room the first day was that I could *never* cut, because my absence would be too noticeable.

The whole scene at a suburban school I realize is different than a city school in many ways, of which the maybe most important is that Edgemont is very isolated from other schools and the things you hear about other schools are from either the *New York Times* (who believes them?) and the lower-county paper, the *Reporter Dispatch,* based in White Plains (truthfully called the Distorter Repatch). And you can guess from their nickname what they print. The whole middle-class values, including the meek, passive, "feminine" girl and the strong, overpowering, "masculine" boy are very evident here as in any suburb but especially here since Westchester is such a wealthy suburb-county. The whole bit with the school dances where the boys ask the girls helps brainwash girls and boys into thinking that girls' places in the social caste of a social life and school and elsewhere are lower than boys. As a girl, I often find myself tongue-tied when trying to argue points with older boys, but can talk with boys my age successfully.

I am sure some people when reading this will say, "But surely there's a contradiction in Connie being a pacifist and trying to break down the old definition of femity as passivity!" I became a pacifist simply because I do not believe that wars solve anything but only create new ones such as new hates, refugees, etc. That is also why I think that Joan Baez is correct in saying all the New Left has is anger and that anger doesn't solve anything just as war doesn't. (I assume I am misquoting her out of context and putting things in her mouth that she never said.) My belief as a vegetarian has grown out of my belief as a pacifist and a lover of life.

"On De-Segregating Stuyvesant High"

by ALICE DE RIVERA

Before I went to John Jay High School I hadn't realized how bad the conditions were for students. One of the things that changed my outlook was being involved with the hostilities of the New York City teacher strikes in the fall of 1968. Students were trying to open the school and the teachers were preventing them. I was disillusioned by the low-quality, high-pay teaching we received afterwards, and soon became involved with expressing my discontent.

It was then I found that students had no rights. We had no freedom of the press: many controversial articles were removed from the newspapers by the teacher-editors. We were not allowed to distribute leaflets or newspapers inside our school building, so that press communication was taken away from us. We also had no freedom of speech. Many teachers would put us down in class for our political ideas and then would not let us answer their charges. If we tried to talk with other students during a free period about political issues, we were told to stop. The school was a prison—we were required by state law to be there, but when we were there we had no rights. We had to carry ID cards and passes. We could be suspended; we were considered guilty before proven innocent.

It was this treatment which made me as a student want to change the schools. When I talked to students from other public high schools in the city, I found they had been oppressed within the schools in much the same way.

I have been writing about the student's plight in general because it was my first encounter with oppression. It is such a familiar experience to me now, that I think I can try to define it. Oppression, to me, is when people are not allowed to be themselves. I encountered this condition a second time when I realized *women's* plight in the high schools. And for the second time I tried to help change the schools so that I and other girls would not be hurt.

The first time it really occurred to me that I was oppressed as a woman was when I began to think of what I was going to be when I was older. I realized I had no real plans for the future—college, maybe, and after that was a dark space in my mind. In talking and listening to other girls, I found that they had either the same blank spot in their minds or were planning on marriage. If not that, they figured on taking a job of some sort *until* they got married.

The boys that I knew all had at least some slight idea in their minds of what career or job they were preparing for. Some prepared for careers in science and math by going to a specialized school. Others prepared for their later jobs as mechanics, electricians, and other tradesmen in vocational schools. Some just did their thing in a regular, zoned high school. It seemed to me that I should fill the blank spot in my mind as the boys were able to do, and I decided to study science (biology, in particular) much more intensively. It was then that I encountered one of the many blocks which stand in the woman student's way: discrimination against women in the specialized science and math high schools in the city.

Many years before women in New York State had won their right to vote (1917), a school was established for those high-school students who wish to specialize in science and math. Naturally it was not co-ed, for women were not regarded legally or psychologically as people. This school, Stuyvesant High School, was erected in 1903. In 1956, thirty-nine years after New York women earned the right to vote, the school was renovated; yet no provision was made for girls to enter.

There are only two other high schools in New York which specialize in science and math: Brooklyn Technical, a school geared towards engineering, and Bronx High School of Science. Brooklyn Tech moved from the warehouse, where its male-only classes were started, into a modern building in 1933. It was renovated in 1960, yet still no provision was made for girls.

This left only Bronx Science. Bronx High School of Science is

the only school where girls can study science and math intensively—it is co-ed. It became so in 1946, the year it moved into
a new building. However, although it admits girls, it still dis-
criminates against them; it admits only one girl to every two
boys.

Out of these three schools I could try out for only one. This
one, Bronx Science, is one and one-half hours travel time from
my home. It presents very stiff competition because of the
discriminatory policy which allows only a certain number of
girls to enter, and also because all the girls who would other-
wise be trying out for Stuyvesant or Brooklyn Tech have Bronx
Science as their only alternative. I became disgusted with this,
not only for my sake, but for all the girls who hadn't become
scientists or engineers because they were a little less than
brilliant or had been put down by nobody having challenged
those little blank spots in their minds. After talking about it
with my parents and friends, I decided to open up Stuyvesant
and challenge the Board of Education's traditional policy.

I took my idea to Ramona Ripston, co-director of the National
Emergency Civil Liberties Committee, and she accepted it
warmly. Pretty soon I became involved in trying to get an application for the entrance exam to Stuyvesant filled out and sent.
It was turned down and we—NECLC, my parents, and I—went
to court against the principal of Stuyvesant and the Board of Ed.

The day on which we went to court was the day before the
entrance exam was scheduled to be given. The Board of Ed
granted me the privilege of taking the test for Bronx Science
(which is the same as the one given for Stuyvesant), and the
judge recognized that the results of this test would be used in
another court hearing to resolve whether or not I would be
admitted. Five days after the other students had received their
results, we found out that I had passed for entrance into both
Stuyvesant and Bronx Science.

We went to court again a couple of months later, in April.
Our judge, Jawn A. Sandafer, seemed receptive to our case, but
he reserved his decision. Later we were told that he wished an
open hearing for May 13. This was a great break for us because
if what the judge needed was public support, we had many
important people who were willing to argue in my favor. How-

ever, on April 30 the New York City Board of Education voted to admit me to Stuyvesant High School in the Fall. The superintendent had wanted to continue the court fight.

This seemed a victory to us at first, but in actuality it would have been better if we could have continued the case and received a court order. We hoped to establish that public funds could not be used to support institutions of learning which discriminate against women. Such a ruling would have been the key to opening up the other sexually segregated high schools in New York City.

There are a great many battles yet to be fought. Aside from being discouraged to study for a career, women are discouraged from preparing for jobs involving anything *but* secretarial work, beauty care, nursing, cooking, and the fashion industry. During my fight over Stuyvesant, I investigated the whole high-school scene, and found that out of the twenty-seven vocational high schools in the city, only *seven* are co-ed. The boys' vocational schools teach trades in electronics, plumbing, carpentry, foods, printing (another example of Board of Ed traditional policy— there is hardly any work for a hand-typesetter today), etc. The girls are taught to be beauticians, secretaries, or health aides. This means that if a girl is seeking entrance to a vocational school, she is pressured to feel that certain jobs are masculine and others feminine. She is forced to conform to the Board of Education's image of her sex. At the seven co-ed vocational schools, boys can learn clerical work, food preparation, and beauty care along with the girls. But the courses that would normally be found in a boys' school are not open to girls. There are only two schools where a girl can prepare for a "masculine" job. Charles Evans Hughes High School in Manhattan is co-ed for teaching technical electronics. Newtown High School offers an academic pre-engineering course of study for boys and girls. However, this school is zoned for the Borough of Queens only.

In conclusion, there are three types of schools, twenty-nine in number, that the Board of Ed has copped out on. These schools are composed of the specialized science and math school Brooklyn Tech, twenty vocational schools which teach students their trade according to what sex they are, and the eight traditionally non-co-ed academic schools.

These eight academic schools are zoned schools which admit only boys or only girls. The argument against these schools is that "separate but equal" is not equal (as established with regard to race in the Brown Decision). The psychological result of the school which is segregated by sex—only because of tradition—is to impress upon girls that they are only "flighty females" who would bother the boys' study habits (as a consequence of girls not being interested in anything but the male sex). This insinuates immaturity on the part of girls—and certainly produces it in both sexes. A boy who has never worked with a girl in the classroom is bound to think of her as his intellectual inferior, and will not treat her as if she had any capacity for understanding things other than child care and homemaking. Both sexes learn to deal with each other as non-people. It really messes up the growth of a person's mind.

Out of the sixty-two high schools in New York City, twenty-nine are now sexually segregated. I believe that it is up to the girls to put pressure on the Board of Education to change this situation. I myself cannot live with oppression.

All girls have been brought up by this society never being able to be themselves—the school system has reinforced this. My desire at this time is to change the educational situation to benefit *all* the students. But I'm afraid changes *could* be made that benefited male students, leaving the status of females pretty much as it is. Female students share the general oppressive conditions forced upon everyone by the System's schools, plus a special psychological discrimination shown to women by the schools, the teachers, *and* their fellow students. So, since I don't want *my* issues to get swallowed up in the supposed "larger" issues, I'm going to make women's liberation the center of my fight.

Figures of the Establishment

Some years ago, the term "Establishment" was coined to describe the interlocking group of politicians, diplomats, prelates, educators, financiers, and intellectuals who dominated the political and cultural life of England. Very quickly, the term was taken over by American social critics, who condemned what they believed to be a similar ruling elite in American life. Whatever the appropriateness of the term "Establishment" to the much more diverse American scene, there does seem to be some truth to the notion that certain men and women are, by birth, education, and corporate or professional affiliation, "established" as influential figures in our life and politics.

The first two men in this part make an odd contrast Roger Baldwin has the sort of family background that is perfectly suited for an Establishment type: old New England Protestant aristocracy, the right schools, the right friends. Yet his life has been an unremitting protest against injustice, discrimination, and political repression. Dean Rusk comes from humble Southern origins, and yet he rose to the presidency of a great foundation and the Secretaryship of State. Baldwin, who founded the American Civil Liberties Union half a century ago, stands in a long line of aristocratic WASPs (White Anglo-Saxon Protestants) who have acted as voices of the public conscience. Freed by their family background from the need to succeed in the world of business and the professions, these tribunes of American society have frequently devoted themselves to the most unpopular causes. Secretary Rusk's career illustrates a different feature of the American Establishment, namely the interrelationships among the military, diplomatic, philanthropic, and educational directorates. Rusk began as a career military officer, moved into the Department of State, left to take over leadership of one of the largest foundations in the world, returned to head the Department of State, and has now "retired" to a prestigious professorship at the state university of his native Georgia. The only thing missing to make the picture complete is a stint as senior partner of an elite Washington or Wall Street law firm.

I depart from the format of this book in the second pair of selections in order to achieve a unique perspective on the most established enclave of American politics, the U.S. Senate. The first selection is the famous chapter from William S. White's book on the Senate in which he coined the phrase "inner club" to describe the exclusive circle of powerful senators who dominate the upper house of Congress. The old saying has it that to get an English lawn, you plant some grass seed and roll it for six hundred years. Similarly, it might be said that the best way into the Senate inner club is to get elected and just sit for two decades. Those of you who seek a short road to power and position in American politics had best look elsewhere than the Senate!

One point that White makes especially deserves to be underscored, for it is a clue to the power and influence of men and women in many institutions, not merely in the Senate. White points out that the senators who devote themselves entirely to the Senate, without treating it as a stepping-stone to higher office or as a public forum, are more likely to enter the influential inner club. Thus John Kennedy and Richard Nixon were not members of the inner club during their time in the Senate. In every institution real power tends to collect in the hands of those whose time, energy, and loyalty are totally at the service of the institution itself. Paradoxically, therefore, those who most want to use the institution as an instrument of some further purpose are least likely to be able to, whereas those in a position to do so will rarely if ever wish to. This same truth explains why the most influential members of a university community are rarely those well-known professors who use the university as a launching platform for public careers.

The concluding selection is a series of extracts from the delightful diary of Frank Madison, a former Senate page. It offers us a sprightly, irreverent view of imposing Senate figures through the eyes of a young man with more than a normal dose of adolescent cynicism. By a happy accident, a significant Senate decision concerning congressional control of the CIA is described by both William S. White and Frank Madison.

11. Roger Baldwin:
Spokesman for the Public Conscience

"The Roger Baldwin Story: A Prejudiced Account"

by ROGER BALDWIN

1971

This is the kind of a view of myself that writers of obituary notices favor, and since they will be written in the not-distant future (I am now 87), I will anticipate them. I do so because I have been asked for biographical notes quite often as I get along toward the end, and I have nothing to offer but the one-page summaries of my career that the American Civil Liberties Union office sends out—hardly more than what *Who's Who* got from me.

I call myself a political reformer, and it is about as near as I can come to describing the unclassified occupation that marks my whole public life. I have been at various times a social worker, teacher, executive, and organizer, but the field was always political—the relationship of people to government. That might make me a political scientist, but I can't claim it as a teacher and anyway I don't believe in science in politics. However, the American Political Science Association has been my trade union for many years, just as previously the National Conference on Social Welfare was in my early social work and reformist years. I never did quite accept the pretensions of most social work to doing people good. I never have had them, I hope. I have tried to base reforms, from personal cases to the destiny of mankind, on what I thought people really wanted, not what I wanted for them. That got me into a lot of confusion because so many people have conflicting wants. But I have stuck pretty close to the underdog and his wants on the principle that he should be given his chance.

I guess I was conditioned that way ever since I was a kid. I was born into a time, place, and family where concern with social problems was inescapable. My parents were liberal Unitarians, and I a natural product of a suburban Boston community where Unitarians were among the best people, or we thought so. My paternal grandfather was a sort of lay preacher, president of the Boston Young Men's Christian Union and friend of nonconformist Brahmins, and he must have influenced me more than I knew. I caught the spirit of public service from Unitarian "lend-a-hand" concerns and the good people I looked up to. I started my infantile social work at about ten, went to church with unquestioning belief in man, if not God, and read history outside of school with a reformer's eye, always on the side of the underdogs and rebels. Not that I did not like our society. I did. I liked it so much that I was certain democracy would perfect it and that good people like us would prevail. Was I not the picture of the liberal of my time, with Negroes at our dinner table, my Uncle William a trustee of Tuskegee Institute and sponsor of Booker Washington, my father a business associate and friend of Jews, my mother an agnostic and something of a feminist?

Harvard, the inescapable, after my Wellesley High School days, changed nothing of my direction. Social work with adult education and help to the Boston settlements were my outside activities. I had no advanced ideas but I enjoyed being helpful. Perhaps that's what has always influenced me in my social relations, because I enjoy people of all sorts, curious about their problems, happy to share whatever I can. I never worked much at ideas and theories, and what I got came from my sympathies. I guess that explains why, after a year of pure fun and adventure with my family in Europe, I accepted the offer that came to me to go into social work and teaching. I had consulted my father's lawyer, Louis Brandeis, who urged me to accept as against a business offer from my father's partners. He saw that I was already committed and that St. Louis, where he began his career, would fit me better than Boston, where I had too many ties.

It was a good choice. To prepare I took a Harvard summer course in sociology, which I was to teach at Washington University (1906 to 1910). For the job at a neighborhood slum settlement, I went to New York, where my Aunt Ruth Baldwin, widow of my Uncle Will, introduced me to all the uplifters. I never have regretted St. Louis or the jobs with the Ethical Society and the university. Both have been my havens for over half a century on my numerous St. Louis visits. Washington University gave me an LL.D after sixty years, and the Ethical Society heard my final "sermon" (I hope) when I was 85. My friends in St. Louis are the sons and daughters of my contemporaries (now almost all gone), who treat me like one of themselves, with canoe trips on my old rivers and some new ones, camping out, and indulging my lifelong adventures in natural history—birds, trees, plants, whatever moves and grows outdoors.

In recent years I have added to nature study a worried concern with conservation of the whole natural habitat. That interest was embedded years ago in my boyhood association with Bradford Torrey, the naturalist author I read weekly in the *Boston Transcript,* editor of Thoreau's journals, and my neighbor. Birds became a major concern, and all my life I've been attracted to feathers and organizations of naturalists— the Nuttall Club in Cambridge, the American Ornithologists Union, and much later the National Audubon Society, in which I served as a director and vice-president. But those Missouri rivers! I spent my happiest days in a canoe, there and elsewhere, alone or with a companion, in a spiritual unity with the universe. Floating in silence in the wilderness I became just a point in time and space, part of the whole and the whole a part of me.

St. Louis lasted eleven years, from 1906 to 1917, when the war uprooted me. I had been tempted to leave before by New York job offers—one, rather ironically as it turned out, was the job that Harry Hopkins later had: director of the Association for Improving the Condition of the Poor. Lush as it was in salary and prestige, I could not bring my democratic soul around to such a mission. I had been a social worker, a university teacher, chief probation officer of the Juvenile Court for three years, and secretary of the Civic League, the vigorous good-government organization of the reformers and the elite.

I had strayed from these conventional ties, not in occupation but association. I had developed a curiosity about challenges to the social system in which I worked. I sought answers to poverty, injustice, and inequality, and I was exploring ideas and movements, any road to salvation. I fraternized with the socialists and found them too doctrinaire, too German, too old. I worked with the labor leaders and found them to arrogant, too defensive and scornful of intellectuals and reformers. But I found Emma Goldman and anarchism, a philosophy of freedom and individualism with revolutionary overtones that I could accept in principle, even if I never joined anything more than a subscription to Emma's paper, *Mother Earth*. She had the influence on me of opening vistas I had hardly glimpsed. I studied the literature of protest, the utopias, the kind of nonconformist authors not taught at Harvard, particularly the Russian Peter Kropotkin, to whom I was most drawn and some of whose works I later edited. Emma remained from St. Louis days to her death one of my dear friends.

The IWW men came to St. Louis and claimed my attention by their demonstrations for unemployment aid. I found them kin, men with vision and courage and a simple working-class resistance to "capitalism." It was years later, in 1920, that I joined the IWW for a brief period when I needed a card to experiment with manual labor for a few months. It was the only radical organization I ever joined, but despite so brief a membership I kept my friendships with many of the members I knew in civil liberties cases, especially with the sensitive poet who edited the IWW paper. I loved both him and his family until their deaths years later.

I left St. Louis for Washington and New York in 1917, when I was thirty-three, to serve as a volunteer director of the American Union against Militarism, of which I had been the St. Louis representative. I knew at once when World War I broke that I could have no part in it; it was against both my then-radical ideas and my later pacifism. I sensed my unity with the British C.O.s as I read the accounts about them featured in the press. Right then I became aware I was a complete pacifist, unwilling to take part in organized violence for any purpose, however good, and I have never faltered since. But the war issues that faced us at once in 1917 were civil liberties—freedom of speech, press, and assembly by critics and opponents of the war, and of conscience by youths refusing military service. And they were immediate. The Union became so involved that a bureau was formed under my direction to handle the flood of cases. It quickly became independent under a strong committee of tough-minded pacifists in New York, led by a Quaker lawyer, Hollingsworth Wood, with board members Norman Thomas, my life-long comrade in everything that mattered to me; Max Eastman, a charming, challenging Red; Dr. John Haynes Holmes, as near my minister as I ever had; Dr. John Lovejoy Elliott, my old Ethical Society mentor; Oswald Garrison Villard, of the *Nation*; and like-minded colleagues.

We did our wartime duty without fear and with some successes until toward the end of 1918, when the bureau was raided as suspect of encouraging the very conscientious objection we were defending. I quit at the time because I was about to be drafted and to resist. The bureau was later cleared of such suspicion, and I went to prison on a plea of guilty for the maximum term then, a year, with no loss of rights. I started serving my sentence on Armistice Day, going to the city jail in Newark, N.J., through the confetti-filled streets of New York. I spent six months in the Newark jail under an Irish warden who'd have none of "England's war," and four months in the County Penitentiary at Caldwell, to which I was moved as a troublemaker—I had organized the prisoners to help one another.

I enjoyed the whole experience, both as adventure and as a sort of testimonial to what I believed. I liked many of the prisoners, no better and no worse than those outside, with a few exceptions; they were just those who got caught. One of my great friendships grew out of prison, with Mrs. Caroline Bayard Colgate, a New Jersey woman who was active in helping prisoners. She developed quite a coterie of my young friends in jail she wanted to and did help. She wrote up the experience in her only book, *Off the Straight and Narrow.* Our contacts lasted beyond prison, and my friendship with her lasted until her death many years later.

When I left prison in 1918, I had one novel purpose, to spend a few months as a manual worker in basic industries, dependent entirely on my earnings, to get the experience of working-class life first-hand in a turbulent period. It lasted four months, enough to learn even more than I expected. I worked all over the Middle West in mill, mine, smelter, and railroad yards, and I wound up in Pittsburgh during the great steel strike as a spy for the union at the request of the head of the union. It was a good adventure I would not repeat, and I survived on my own earnings. I had vaguely thought of a job with a union, but my colleagues insisted on my getting back into civil liberties, then in as critical a state as during the war. I was willing if nobody objected to a jail-bird. None did. So the American Civil Liberties Union was formed in January 1920, with me as director.

In 1970 the ACLU was fifty years old and I have been with it all this time, not with intention but because I never seemed able to quit for more than brief leaves of absence. Always there was some new challenge, some new task to intrigue me, for it is an endless but always hopeful struggle that has to be won over and over. So I have kept at its manifold tasks, as executive director from 1920 to 1950, when at the age of 65 I retired of my own choice to serve as an adviser to the ACLU on international affairs. I was for some years, not by my choice, the nominal chairman of the ACLU National Advisory

Committee, and have always been a member of it, a tie to my colleagues as well as to the staff. I have never departed from the line taken by the Union; it is mine, with the inevitable exceptions. But I have approved of almost every action. We had our internal splits over communist influences, which were healed by excluding them in a long and sometimes turbulent controversy over the method. Since then, in 1940, no political intrusion has troubled the Union. It is as vigorous as when it started, but it has grown and changed in structure, doubtless for the better, from a tight New York directorate to a diffused national network of affiliates.

But the Union has not claimed all of me. My reformer's drive has led me into many other movements, all related in my mind, if not in the minds of my critics. For twenty years I headed a small agency in New York of nonpartisan liberals to help free political prisoners in foreign lands. We protested, pulled diplomatic wires, visited European prisons, and helped free some prisoners. For twenty-five years I was a board member of the National Urban League. Issues of academic freedom enlisted me as a member of the Harvard Overseers' Committee on the Economics Department for almost twenty years of interesting if somewhat futile effort. During this time I was invited to give the 1934 Godkin lectures on industrial conflict under the New Deal. For almost as many years I was a board member of the National Audubon Society.

These were all very reputable connections. Less so, but still acceptable because Christian, was the Fellowship for Reconciliation, uncompromisingly pacifist and anticapitalist, on whose board I long served despite my objections to sectarianism. But I left behind any claim to the acceptable in hailing the Russian Revolution, critical as I quickly became over its police state, publishing in 1924 *Letters from Russian Prisons,* a collection of letters written by leftist opponents of the Bolsheviks. In 1927 I spent three months in Russia, where I inquired into liberty and repression, later publishing a book titled *Liberty under the Soviets,* which was much too hopeful, as I soon found out, of the forces of education and "proletarian freedom" to modify a tight party dictatorship. I just did not understand, as Emma Goldman and others did, the nature of a dictatorship that "coordinated" everybody as did the communists and fascists. I was later ambivalent about Russia and its dictatorship. When fascism and Nazism threatened to triumph in 1934, I was disturbed enough to write some pro-Soviet and procommunist sentiments that really represented no retreat from my commitment to freedom but appeared to do so, and they have provided embarrassing quotes for my opponents ever since.

The Nazi-Soviet Pact of 1939, a traumatic shock to me, ended any ambivalence I had about the Soviet Union and all co-operation with communists in united fronts. I know that peace and world order require the divided world to find a common base, but unlike many pacifist colleagues I am not trying to anticipate it. I was confirmed in my rejection when I returned to Moscow in 1967 after forty years and found even more evident that beehive quality of life that spells total con-formity to the state's dictates. I was appalled, not frightened as Mrs. Roosevelt wrote she was.

With communists at home I had many contacts, ending in 1939, in defense of their rights and in united fronts for good causes. I was in most of them, but the three I really worked at were peace and democracy, anti-imperialism, the Loyalist cause in the Spanish Civil War. They were my major concerns and losing causes at the time, all of them. In none did the communists control except negatively: if they had quit the front would have collapsed, and in each of the three cases it did. I do not regret my participation but it earned me quite unfairly a procommunist reputation in circles not entirely con-fined to the right wing. Neither my later public identification with anticommunist agencies nor my efforts against com-munist infiltration in other agencies seemed to counteract their fixed impressions and repudiated quotes.

The greatest single change in my public life came in 1947 at the age of 63, when I was quite unexpectedly invited by the War Department to go to Japan and Korea to assist in developing civil rights agencies. It was an amazing offer, but as I was to find out, the military occupation was using every resource it could find to democratize those peoples, American style. Of course I accepted, and the Union gave me a leave of absence with its blessing as its agent. Objecting to a role as a government representative, I arranged to go as a private citizen dealing with Japanese private citizens. I was a little fearful that among generals my pacifism and radical record would create difficulties; they must have known my record, but nobody in Japan and Korea ever mentioned it or treated me other than as a VIP.

The three months in Japan and Korea, where General MacArthur and General Hodge opened every door for me, were the most exciting I ever spent, keeping me keyed to the top of my abilities. Every minute I was occupied with interviews, inquiries, conferences on every aspect of occupation policy and Japanese practice on civil rights. I had to learn a lot fast. I was invited to meet the Emperor, and found him a friendly and understanding simple man. Twelve years later his chief chamberlain invited me again to the palace in the Emperor's absence in the country, and he, with other old friends of 1947, gave me a banquet. I had established a Japanese Civil Liberties Union and stimulated both the occupation and Japanese government to protect civil rights, and they seemed to see in me a genuine friend. A few years later the Japanese government awarded me the Order of the Rising Sun at the embassy in Washington, with jewels and ribbons to match.

Following the Japanese experience in 1947, which had drawn me into a new world of activity, I was invited next year to Germany by General Lucius Clay to do the same service of waking up the Germans to protect their own rights. The invitation was for the Civil Liberties Union's delegation, so I was accompanied by Arthur Hays and Norman Cousins. General Clay was as cordial and helpful as General MacArthur, but I did not find in him or any other general General MacArthur's philosophic outlook on the problems and prospects of mankind. Vain, the critics said, but I found him free from pride or self-importance. General Clay was the executive who got things done. He laid the way for me to return to Germany, as I did three times in the following years to help the new German organization, which was, however, far less effective than in Japan because of the division of Germany and the traditional dependence on government and authority.

These experiences under American occupation strengthened my international interest, already expressed in the human rights ambitions of the new United Nations. I had worked in Geneva with the now-defunct League of Nations in its mandate and minorities commissions, but they were useless; no government would heed them. But the United Nations held better prospects, and the work was in New York, where we already had functioning under French refugees an International League for the Rights of Man. So when I retired from the Union in 1950 I was quite prepared for the international field. I became the League chairman and held the post for fifteen years, devoting my major time to its work at the United Nations. It has taken me far afield too, in one trip around the world in 1959 under UN auspices to examine the activities of nongovernmental organizations; trips to the Middle East on the Arab-Israeli refugees; trips to Cuba, Venezuela, Costa Rica, and Peru in behalf of Latin American democracy; many trips to European conferences; one to Africa to celebrate Nigerian independence under my old friend Dr. Zik (Azikiwe); and in 1967 after a UN conference in Warsaw, a return after forty years to Moscow.

Ever since 1954 when the issue of Puerto Rican self-government came before the UN, I have visited that island regularly as the guest of my old friend Governor Luis Muñoz Marin. First I helped him set up a study of civil rights and liberties, then a commission to protect them. To that was added an appointment at the University of Puerto Rico Law School to help handle a constitutional rights seminar, so that I've been going to Puerto Rico, happily in the winters, for the last ten years. I've taken on the Virgin Islands, too, where I have helped with getting more home rule.

It seems to me amazing that the late years of my life should be the most exciting and varied, if not the most productive. But they have coincided with my involvement in the first attempt in history for universal human rights. They have brought me new friends all over the world, fresh knowledge and interests in the search for freedom, peace, and world order. They have brought me, too, my first specific occupational title, that of professor, reinforced by doctor of laws degrees from Yale, Brandeis, and Washington Universities. So far, health and energy have held up. No ills, no pills. Plenty to do; never retired nor tired. Failures and disappointments there are, of course, but extroverts recover fast!

It's been a good kind of life in a crazy, confused era. Despite the dominance of armed power, I am sure the forces of law and freedom are growing, and I am grateful for the chances I have had to play a part in the struggle. I keep intact my faith in mankind's progress toward an ordered world of peace, law, and freedom. It will be that or nothing.

Good show; I'm glad I came!

12. Dean Rusk:
Executive Appointee

"Incidentally, Who *IS* Dean Rusk?"

by MILTON VIORST

To hear Dean Rusk explain it, we'd be in the same fix in Vietnam today no matter who was Secretary of State—or, for that matter, who was President. Foreign policy, he argues, comes out of the "big enduring things" about the country and doesn't respond to the whimsy of one individual or another, even if he happens to be nominally in charge.

Rusk says that sure, he reexamines foreign policy all the time. "But the people who preceded me were not fools," he declares, so foreign policy hasn't changed much since Dean Acheson decided to "contain" the Communists some twenty years ago. Just about the only difference between Secretaries of State in all these years, Rusk says, is that John Foster Dulles had a particular addiction to summoning God to make his case.

Not only does Rusk insist that personality has little to do with foreign policy, he also maintains that it shouldn't. One of his major objectives, he says, is to "depersonalize" his office. He speaks with a hint of condescension of Acheson's flamboyance. His own aim is to keep himself off the front page, he says, and to turn foreign policy into a humdrum routine. He's pleased that journalists, despairing of understanding him, refer constantly to him as "inscrutable" and "Sphinx-like." Rusk won't quite concede that the logical conclusion of his conception is the conduct of foreign policy by computer. But he does say that the kind of man he is has virtually no relation to the way the United States runs its affairs in Vietnam or any other part of the world.

.   .   .   .

Dean Rusk was born in 1909 in Cherokee County, Georgia, on a remnant of the land that stories say his great-grandfather had taken from the Indians in the time of Andrew Jackson. He was the third and youngest son among five children. His brother Roger, just three years older, remembers how backward Cherokee County was when the Rusks were children. "When I went to Williamsburg many years later," Roger reminisced, "I saw the culture of the eighteenth century. I was amazed to see that it was identical with the culture of my grandfather in the beginning of the twentieth century." Only indirectly, however, did this rural culture make an impact on Dean. In the Summer of 1912, heavy floods made it impossible for the Rusks to get out the crop. "The land didn't want us," said Roger. In 1913 the family picked up and moved to Atlanta, some thirty miles away. It was in Atlanta that Dean Rusk was raised.

Though the Rusks were poor, it is not true that they were "poor whites," in the sense that the term (sometimes rendered as "white trash") is classically used in the South. Robert Rusk, Dean's father, had somehow managed to put himself through Davidson, a small Presbyterian college but one of the South's best, before going on to the Louisville Seminary to become an ordained Presbyterian minister. Dean's mother had attended normal school and did some teaching before she married. In the Rusk household, there was, in contrast to the "poor white" attitude generally, a considerable respect for learning, if not for erudition. Parks, Dean's oldest brother, was too busy in the cotton fields throughout most of his boyhood to get much schooling, yet he went on to a respectable career in journalism. The two younger brothers both had the importance of education drilled into them, and Dean determined early to follow his father to Davidson. Robert Rusk, because he lost his voice, was unable to pursue his career in the ministry and spent much of the rest of his life as a mailman, but neither he nor his wife was persuaded by poverty to abandon the ambitions they had for their sons.

Dean Rusk readily acknowledges the influence that his father's Protestant religion had on him. He has said that when he was young, most of his home life was built around the church. He was faithful in his attendance at Sunday school and midweek prayer meetings. After church on Sunday, the funnies forbidden, he and his family spent the day reading the Bible and memorizing the psalms and the catechisms. Throughout his school years, he was active in the Christian Endeavor, an organization of young people devoted to encouraging Protestant spirituality. Rusk says that, as a matter of fact, until his second or third year in high school, he planned to make a career in the Presbyterian ministry.

Roger Rusk, now a physics professor at the University of Tennessee, maintains that it is impossible to understand his brother without grasping the meaning of Southern Protestantism—a set of tenets which all the best authorities agree is fundamental to the culture of the South. Basic to it is a rigid Calvinism, with the commitment to Original Sin and the essential evil of most men, with the obverse that the Saved will eschew frivolity and lead lives of abnegation and sacrifice. Southern Protestant Christianity was hewn among the rigors of the frontier, where there was little place for subtlety, intellectuality or dissent. Closely bound up with danger, it exalted force, tolerated violence and generated the deep feelings which have evolved from sectionalism into patriotism. Inevitably, Southern Protestantism was identified with the white race, the Scotch-Irish in particular. This is the doctrine, says Roger Rusk, on which Dean was raised and which built civilization on this continent.

"Love of God, love of country," Roger said, "they were exactly the same and they were as natural to us as living and breathing. Even though it's stylish now to downgrade the W.A.S.P.'s, this belief was common to all the families who got here first. Part of the teaching of our homes and of our church was complete devotion to the country.

"We were also taught a sense of service, to be self-effacing. We were taught to abandon personal ambition for the sake of others. I myself have sacrificed my life to the service of the people I've loved here. [He nonetheless drives a new car, owns a handsome home, dresses in elegant tweeds.] Dean has made his sacrifices to humanity. I teach science out of Christian motivation; Dean strives for world peace.

"What people also don't understand about Dean is how deep are his military inclinations. It's part of our Anglo-Saxon heritage. The South always had a military disposition. It's part of our stock.

"During World War I, Dean and I cut out pictures of soldiers from the newspapers and pasted them on cardboard. We had thousands. We dug trenches twenty- and thirty-feet long across our backyard and built fortifications. We followed all the battle plans. There wasn't a rich kid in town who had as many soldiers as we did. [Roger also says that when they were children, he and Dean used to test which one could outstare the other. That's the origin, he says, of the Secretary's famous expression after the Cuban missile crisis: 'We were eyeball to eyeball and the other fellow blinked.']

"I have no apology for saying it, but we never considered war immoral. War is one of the consequences of sin. As long as men are sinful, we'll have war. War is an error to be endured."

. . .

Having learned to read from Roger at home, Dean Rusk skipped right into the second grade when he enrolled at the local grammar school. By chance, it was an experimental school, to which the city had assigned its best teachers in an effort to upgrade its programs. Later, Dean went to Boys High, where he received a solid grounding in the "classical" subjects, including Latin and even Greek. His Greek professor remembers him as one of a handful of students, over a long career, who "seemed to be born mature." Old friends say Dean was a neat, well-scrubbed lad, playful enough but, in school, already something of a drudge. They agree, however, that he was by far the smartest kid in the class. It was in high school that Dean Rusk got the notion from a Presbyterian missionary, a former Oxonian himself, to aspire to a Rhodes scholarship. Though he had the benefit of what was probably the finest public education available in the South, it was young Rusk's own industry and intelligence that laid the scholastic foundation for his luminous future.

After taking two years off to earn some money for college by working in a law office, Dean Rusk went on to Davidson as he had planned. He settled down to a full program of studies, found a part-time job in a bank and was elected president of the freshman class. He joined a fraternity, played varsity tennis and center on the basketball team, and acquired a steady girl friend. He attended chapel daily, undertook missionary work for the Y.M.C.A., passed his two compulsory years of Bible and never missed church on Sunday. Having already lost most of his hair, he was given by his friends the nickname "Old Folks," which also reflected his solemn countenance and serious view of life. Nonetheless, he was popular and, according to the best recollection, a thoroughly good fellow. In his senior year, he and some chums took a trip to New York for a lark, the first time he had left the South. In 1931, he was graduated from Davidson, with a Phi Beta Kappa key and a Rhodes scholarship.

When he applied for the Rhodes scholarship, the examining board asked Rusk, in view of his proclaimed interest in world peace, to explain his obvious predilection for military values. He had taken four years of R.O.T.C. at Boys High and had risen to the command of all the R.O.T.C. units in Atlanta. At Davidson, he took four more years of R.O.T.C., attained the student rank of colonel and graduated with a reserve commission. Later Rusk explained: "Well, of course, in the South most of us as we were growing up just took it for granted that if there was to be trouble, if the nation was at war, that we would be in it. I had eight years of R.O.T.C., both in high school and college. The tradition of the Civil War was still with us very strongly. Both my grandfathers had been in it. We assumed that there was a military duty to perform if one is required on the part of all citizens, so we took that for granted as a perfectly natural part of being an American." Rusk said he handled what the board of examiners considered the paradox in this way: "I did at that time point out that the American eagle on the great seal has the arrows in one claw and the olive branch in the other and the two have to go together." Thus Dean Rusk has, from that day to this, looked upon armed force and world peace as simply two sides of the same coin.

The times were grim when Rusk sailed for England, but at Oxford, where he read politics and philosophy, he was insulated from the Depression's miseries. In his second year abroad, Rusk went to a German university for a semester, just as Hitler's regime was beginning to flower. Clearly, his experiences in these years did not fire Rusk with any reformer's zeal. By the time he returned to America in 1934, Southern contemporaries like Lyndon Johnson and Abe Fortas had already staked out careers in the New Deal, while diplomatic contemporaries like Charles E. Bohlen and O. Edmund Clubb were questioning American policy toward Russia and China. Rusk, however, was content to go off to Mills College in California, where he taught political science, married Virginia Foisie, one of the students, and rose to the rank of dean of the faculty. In six years as an academic, he wrote nothing of record and acquired no reputation as a scholar. He did, however, attend law classes at the University of California and he faithfully acquitted his obligations as an officer in the Army Reserve. In 1940, a full year before Pearl Harbor, Dean Rusk was called into the military service.

Assigned to Army headquarters in Washington, Rusk, as a former Rhodes scholar, was given responsibilities in British Empire affairs. But after the United States entered the war, he was sent to the China-Burma-India theater, where he helped plan operations on the staff of General Stilwell. Though he was stationed chiefly in New Delhi, he had an opportunity to travel rather widely throughout Asia. It was Rusk's first exposure to the Orient and it was an intensive one. He spent three years in the C.B.I. and rose to the rank of colonel. Near the end of the war, General George C. Marshall, the Chief of Staff, asked that a group of outstanding young officers be brought back to the United States to do postwar planning. Thus, shortly before V-E Day, Rusk returned to Washington, to work in the heady atmosphere generated by the furious preparations being made for peace. He was in a group headed by Colonel C. H. Bonesteel III (now a general and Commander of the U.S. Army in Korea), who had been Rusk's best friend when they were both Rhodes scholars a decade earlier.

Over the course of the next few years, Rusk crossed back and forth between the Pentagon and the State Department in various staff capacities. He went first to State after his discharge in February, 1946, then back to the Pentagon a few months later as special assistant to the Secretary of War. It was at this point that he was offered a regular commission in the Army and, as he said, "had more or less agreed to take it," when Marshall was appointed Secretary of State. Anxious to have men around him familiar with his military ways, Marshall invited Rusk back to State and he accepted. Specializing in United Nations affairs, he gradually worked his way up the ladder until he became an Assistant Secretary. Since the United Nations, at least in those days, was thought of largely in terms of the peace-keeping forces envisaged in its charter, Dean Rusk had no trouble dedicating his energies to it. He could conceive of it much as the American eagle, with an olive branch in one claw and arrows in the other.

The bright young men who worked around Rusk in those days, almost all of whom have gone on to considerable achievement elsewhere, remember him as exceptionally competent and dedicated, modest and affable, serious but not grim. Almost unanimously, they describe him as fresh, intellectually flexible, rich in ideas, and without arrogance.

His great strength, they agree, was in lucid articulation of a problem, in which, as one put it, "he knew the value of a fact." Even those who object to his current conduct of the

State Department—and that applies to almost every one of them—concede that they saw in him none of the smugness and dogmatism of which he is now accused. At least one of his former colleagues dissents, however, insisting that Rusk's open-mindedness reflected not wisdom but uncertainty and that Rusk was an intellectual second-rater. Another former colleague said that, in retrospect, he recognizes that Rusk was unduly submissive to authority, unwilling to fight for any idea to which his superiors did not immediately subscribe. A third argues that this submissiveness was in reality an intense loyalty to his superiors, "the military side of Dean Rusk," a staff officer's acceptance of the responsibility of his chief for the final decisions. However interpreted, this last quality, combined with his genuine talents, singled out Rusk among his peers and made him a functionary prized at the highest level of the government. One former diplomat remembers a party back in the late Forties in which a group of colleagues toasted Dean Rusk as "a future Secretary of State of the United States."

Rusk began to come into his own in January, 1949, when Dean Acheson became Secretary of State. Obviously, he concurred with Acheson's new "get-tough" policy toward the Communists and the elevation of the Cold War to the first rank of diplomatic priority. On March 12, Rusk announced the United States was abandoning its frigid attitude toward Nationalist Spain, on the grounds that an anti-Franco policy was no longer "realistic." A week later, he joined in the advocacy of the North Atlantic Pact. "We haven't been able," he explained, "to get through the worldwide security system that we hoped to work out through the United Nations." Shortly afterward, Rusk was promoted to Deputy Under Secretary, the third ranking post in the Department, with general administrative and policy responsibilities. It was clear that Acheson had the highest regard for him.

But Rusk remained in his new job only a few months. By the end of 1949, the Communists had taken over the Chinese Mainland and Dean Acheson, who earlier had ordered an end to American support of Chiang Kai-shek, became the target of a high-powered anti-Red crusade. In the beginning of 1950, the post of Assistant Secretary for the Far East became vacant. As Acheson tells the story, Rusk "came to me and said, 'I am applying for demotion. I'd like to go back to being Assistant Secretary, and I'd like to take over this job.' And I said, 'You get the Congressional Medal of Honor and the Purple Heart all at once for this. Do you really want to do it?' And he said, 'I fit it.'" Exactly why Rusk felt he "fit it" is not clear. He points out now that he had taught a little Far Eastern history at Mills and, of course, had spent the war on China's periphery. But even he cannot say with certainty why he volunteered for what was known to be the hottest job in the Department. What is clear is that he felt very deeply about the "loss" of China. George Kennan has said that Rusk was one of the members of the Department who experienced genuine "moral indignation" over Mao's conquest. Rusk has himself said privately it was unfortunate that the United States demobilized too quickly after World War II to have an army ready for deployment in China. From Acheson's point of view, Rusk was an ideal lightning rod "and so we of course kissed him on both cheeks and gave him the job." From Rusk's, it was apparently an opportunity to make personally sure that the United States would stop Communist China dead in its tracks.

.   .   .

. . . Rusk's career, despite the sensitive post he held, moved along flawlessly. Rusk proved invulnerable to McCarthy's rampage. Bohlen had stumbled because he had gone to Yalta with Roosevelt, Clubb because he had found faults in Chiang Kai-shek, but Rusk stayed clean. "He was insulated from the McCarthy trouble," said one old colleague. "He had come in from the Pentagon, which meant he had a safe beginning. He retained a close association with the Defense Department. He was on the right side in Korea. He never pushed any audacious proposals or offended anyone. Rusk was always very secure." Despite McCarthy's siege of the Department, Rusk continued to find favor with people in high places.

One of the friends Rusk made was John Foster Dulles, who happened at the time to be Chairman of the Board of the

Rockefeller Foundation. A prominent Wall Street lawyer, expert in foreign affairs and a Republican, Dulles had been confident in 1948 of becoming Thomas E. Dewey's Secretary of State. After Dewey's defeat Truman appointed Dulles an adviser to the State Department to impart a quality of bipartisanship to his foreign policy. When Dulles, in 1951, was given responsibility for negotiating the Japanese Peace Treaty, he had among his advisers Dean Rusk and John D. Rockefeller III who had known each other at the Pentagon at the end of the war. The three men got along famously. Some months later the presidency of the Rockefeller Foundation became vacant, and Dulles and Rockefeller agreed that their friend Rusk with his combined academic and diplomatic credentials would be ideal for the job. For his part, Rusk had three growing children and he felt that to bring them up he needed more money than he earned at State. When the Rockefeller job, with its substantial salary (around $50,000 a year) and prestige, was offered to him in 1952, Rusk resigned from the State Department to take it.

Dean Rusk, it should be noted, distinguished himself at Rockefeller by reorienting the foundation and its funds, previously dedicated to domestic concerns almost alone, to the needs of the underdeveloped countries. "We should be fully aware of the historical significance of what is happening in those areas which lie outside the English-speaking democracies, Western Europe, and the Iron Curtain," he wrote in A Memorandum to the Trustees in 1955. "Ideas and aspirations which were generated in the course of democratic, national and economic revolutions in the West are now producing explosive demands for far-reaching changes in other parts of the world. . . . The underdeveloped countries of today are borrowing ideas and aspirations and have examples of more 'advanced' countries before their eyes; but they lack capital, trained leadership, an educated people, political stability, and an understanding of how change is to be digested and used by their own cultures." Under Rusk's leadership, the Rockefeller Foundation undertook remarkable experimental projects in education, resource development, population control and leadership training in many of the backward regions. Rusk's work endowed him with the reputation of someone who appreciates the problems of those countries that threaten one day, by poverty and people, to swallow up their rich industrial neighbors.

Throughout his eight years at the Rockefeller Foundation, Rusk continued to endear himself to the powerful members of the business and financial community in New York. His leadership was considered innovative and efficient. He found time to lecture occasionally on international affairs and serve in the Council on Foreign Relations, an esteemed body of rich, public-spirited citizens. He also was in constant touch with Dulles, now Eisenhower's Secretary of State, advising him of this policy and that. Meanwhile, he lived quietly with his family in Scarsdale, the *right* upper-class suburb, where he dabbled in community affairs and local Democratic politics. Though he was always the first to insist that he was, deep down, still just a simple Southern boy, Rusk acquired a veneer of Eastern sophistication from his New York life. If not a member of the "Establishment" family, he certainly became a first cousin. Highly respected and financially secure, Rusk undoubtedly wanted nothing more than to spend the rest of his days at Rockefeller, but the position he had attained, by chance, gave him just the right qualifications for the dazzling new career that awaited him in Washington.

Well-prepared as he was for the office, John F. Kennedy was elected President in 1960 without knowing whom he wanted as Secretary of State. He had a list of candidates, to which Dean Acheson had added the name of Dean Rusk, but it seemed to stand near the bottom. One by one, however, those who stood higher on the list were eliminated for various reasons. Adlai Stevenson's own personal following was too strong; Chester Bowles was too identified with the liberal left; Senator J. William Fulbright had voted against civil rights; Douglas Dillon was a Republican; David Bruce and Averell Harriman were too old; McGeorge Bundy was too young; Robert Lovett was in poor health. Before long Dean Rusk alone—the first choice only of Acheson—was left on the list.

Kennedy did not even know Rusk, but he was attracted by

his credentials. There was no disputing that the man was well-informed, efficient and familiar with the workings of the State Department. All reports agree that he was self-effacing, not likely to challenge Kennedy's primacy in the making of policy. Most important of all, he had the recommendation of men whose support Kennedy now solicited. As President-elect by the narrowest of margins, Kennedy felt himself in an unstable position. He wanted to change old Eisenhower policies, but he could not risk being branded as brash, to say nothing of radical. He needed the "Establishment" behind him and to win them over he wanted the Republican Dillon for Secretary of the Treasury. He had offered a choice of cabinet posts to Robert Lovett, former Under Secretary of State and Secretary of Defense, New York investment banker and board member of countless corporations and foundations, including Rockefeller. When Lovett said he was too ill to take any post, Kennedy asked him for his recommendation for Secretary of State. Lovett proposed, among a group of five, the name of Dean Rusk, who had served him in various subordinate capacities since the war. Kennedy was impressed by the endorsement of Lovett, since it meant that Rusk had the approval of precisely the powers he was anxious to reassure.

.   .   .

From the beginning, . . . it is clear that Kennedy was dissatisfied with Rusk. The new Secretary brought neither administrative efficiency nor intellectual rejuvenation to the State Department. He was notably deficient in providing Kennedy with fresh ideas. Perhaps most disappointing of all, he was painfully reticent in foreign-policy discussion, so that Kennedy felt that the State Department was without an advocate. To be sure, Rusk was excellent at laying out all the facets of the problem, no matter how complex, and Kennedy was grateful for his faithfulness, as well as his pleasant disposition. But he was scarcely satisfied with Rusk's irresolution and he often said that in State, he was pressing up against a "bowl of jelly." Rusk has been credited with having had the wisdom to see the weakness of the Bay of Pigs operation, only he failed to convey his reservations to Kennedy while there was still time to stop it. Throughout the three years of his term, Kennedy was not so much angry at Rusk as frustrated at his passivity.

.   .   .

After he became Secretary of State, Rusk seemed to lose interest in anything but standing firm against the Communists. He showed indifference to the administration of the Department, though he was once known as a fine administrator. He gave little attention to long-term policy planning, though under Marshall he was instrumental in setting up the Department's current planning machinery. Perhaps most disappointing, Rusk paid small heed to the problems of the underdeveloped world, for which he had shown so much understanding at the Rockefeller Foundation. Here was Rusk's opportunity to make history, to redirect the energies of the United States and, perhaps, the entire Western world to the threat of overpopulation and engulfing poverty. Yet, according to a member of Kennedy's original task force on foreign aid, Rusk was so preoccupied with other matters that he seemed bored by the issue. Kennedy, of course, established the Alliance for Progress, but Rusk's contribution to it was inconsequential. Though there is no suggestion that Rusk was remiss in his duties as Secretary of State, it is clear that in his preoccupation with communism he had a single-minded view of his responsibilities.

What is not true is that Rusk was out of tune with Kennedy's liberalism in domestic matters. Though not intimately concerned with them, Rusk was certainly sympathetic to Kennedy's objectives at home, including civil rights. On racial matters, Rusk's upbringing had been conventionally Southern. As one of his classmates at Davidson put it: "It never occurred to us in those days to question our society's treatment of Negroes, neither Dean nor any of the rest of us." But something happened to Dean Rusk when he went out into the world, and if any Southerner ever tried hard to overcome racial biases, it was he. Ralph Bunche remembers that it was Rusk who insisted successfully on the integration of recreational facilities when they were both young officers in Washington in the early days of the war. It was this liberal attitude to which Roger Rusk referred when he noted sadly that "Dean, more than I, has sought to transcend Southern values." If it is evidence of his achievement, his eldest son, David, works for the Urban League, while his daughter, Peggy, recently married a Negro. Rusk explains his liberal outlook as the product of Southern Populism, modified by three years in the C.B.I., "where I was surrounded by a sea of Indian and Burmese faces." Few of Kennedy's people, whatever their criticism of Rusk as Secretary, challenged the sincerity of his liberal convictions.

.   .   .

Kennedy's death, of course, changed everything, including the course of American foreign policy. . . .

.   .   .

"Lyndon Johnson," said a friend of the President, "showed a great deal of respect for Rusk's judgment from the very beginning. Being from the South was, of course, a natural recommendation, but Lyndon Johnson was impressed further by Rusk's achievements—Phi Beta Kappa, Rhodes scholarship, Rockefeller Foundation and all the rest. Johnson's got no respect for what he calls a 'stay-home boy' who never leaves the South, but for a Southern boy to go where Rusk went, is, to him, really something.

"Besides, the President saw Rusk as the outcast of the Kennedy Cabinet. He knew a kindred spirit when he saw one. Both had been kicked around by the Arthur Schlesingers and the Dick Goodwins of the world. The President saw Rusk as wounded and he came to his support. Rusk never forgot that. Rusk immediately acquired a feeling of belonging he never had with Kennedy."

.   .   .

Still profoundly a Southern Calvinist, Rusk is instinctively convinced of the ubiquitousness of sin and of his own duty to extirpate. His view of mankind is not complicated: there are good guys and bad guys and he's for the good ones. In a television interview on the nature of his office, Rusk once said, "One of the consequences of the fact that the world is round is that at any given moment, two-thirds of the world is awake and *up to something.*" An unreconstructed Calvinist would think of mankind in such mischievous terms, suspicious and on guard, conscious of his own role in the process of salvation. Like his brother Roger, Rusk sincerely sees his work in terms of self-sacrifice. "I never wanted to be Secretary of State," he said in the same interview, "up until the moment that I *had to* be and then I *had to* do my duty. . . ."

.   .   .

A close associate once asked Dean Rusk whether it had ever occurred to him that he might be making a mistake in Vietnam. "Well, if I am," he snapped back, "it's a beaut." But apparently, it had never really occurred to him. For Dean Rusk doesn't stay up nights worrying if he's made a mistake. As sure as there's a God in Heaven, he knows he has not.

13. The Senate Inner Club: The Congressional Establishment

"The Senate and the Club"

by WILLIAM S. WHITE

When one unexpectedly needs a room in a good, and crowded, hotel in New York like the Pierre, which is not so very long on tradition, his best course is to approach the clerk in masterful determination, allowing no other assumption at all than that he will be accommodated. When such a need rises in a traditional hotel abroad, say Brown's in London, the wiser attitude is precisely the reverse. There it is better to approach the subject wearily and a bit hopelessly and to say to the clerk, of course I know it is hardly possible that you could find a place for me.

When one enters the House of Representatives, or becomes an official in the Executive Department, the sound attitude is not simply to put the best foot forward, but to stamp it for emphasis—in front of the photographers if any are present, and if official superiors are not. But when one enters the

Senate he comes into a different place altogether. The long custom of the place impels him, if he is at all wise, to walk with a soft foot and to speak with a soft voice, and infrequently. Men who have reached national fame in less than two years in powerful non-Senatorial office—Saltonstall as Governor of Massachusetts, Duff as Governor of Pennsylvania for recent examples—have found four years and more not to be long enough to feel free to speak up loudly in the Institution. All the newcomer needs, if he is able and strong, is the passage of time—but this he needs indispensably, save in those rare cases where the authentic geniuses among Senate types are involved.

The old definition of the Senate as "the most exclusive club in the world" is no longer altogether applicable, as perhaps it never was. It *is*, however, both a club and a club within a club. By the newly arrived and by some of the others the privileges are only carefully and sparingly used. To the senior members—and sometimes they are senior only in terms of power and high acceptability—privilege is inexhaustible and can be pressed to almost any limit. I have seen one member, say a Lehman of New York, confined by niggling and almost brutal Senate action to the most literal inhibitions of the least important of all the rules. And again I have seen a vital Senate roll call held off by all sorts of openly dawdling time-killing for hours, in spite of the fact that supposedly it is not possible to interrupt a roll call once it is in motion, for the simple purpose of seeing that a delayed aircraft has opportunity to land at Washington Airport so that a motorcycle escort can bring, say a Humphrey of Minnesota in to be recorded.

Lehman was, of course, a member of the Outer Club, which is composed of all the Senate. But Humphrey is, in part by the mysterious operation of acceptability-by-association, in or very close to the Inner Club. The inequality indicated here has nothing to do with political belief or activity; both Lehman and Humphrey are liberal Democrats and both have records of distinction. Humphrey simply got along better.

The inner life of the Senate—and the vast importance to it of its internal affairs may be seen in the fact that it has on occasion taken longer to decide upon the proper salaries for a handful of Senate employees than to provide billions of dollars for the defense of the United States—is controlled by the Inner Club. This is an organism without name or charter, without officers, without a list of membership, without a wholly conscious being at all.

There is no list of qualifications for membership, either posted or orally mentioned. At the core of the Inner Club stand the Southerners, who with rare exceptions automatically assume membership almost with the taking of the oath of office. They get in, so to speak, by inheritance, but at their elbows within the core are others, Easterners, Midwesterners, Westerners, Republicans or Democrats.

The outer life of the Senate, in which all the members are theoretically more or less equal at the time of decision that comes when a roll-call vote is added up, is defined by its measurable actions on bills and on public policies. But this outer life, even in its most objective aspects, is not free of the subtle influence of the inner life of the Institution.

The inner life is in the command of a distinct minority within this place of the minority. This minority-within-a-minority is the Inner Club. This Inner Club, though in spirit largely dominated by the Southerners, is by no means geographic.

Those who belong to it express, consciously or unconsciously, the deepest instincts and prejudices of "the Senate type." The Senate type is, speaking broadly, a man for whom the Institution is a career in itself, a life in itself and an end in itself. This Senate type is not always free of Presidential ambition, a striking case in point having been the late Senator Taft. But the important fact is that when the Senate type thinks of the Presidency he thinks of it as only *another* and not as really a *higher* ambition, as did Taft and as did Senator Russell of Georgia when, in 1952, he sought the Democratic Presidential nomination.

The Senate type makes the Institution his home in an almost literal sense, and certainly in a deeply emotional sense. His head swims with its history, its lore and the accounts of past personnel and deeds and purposes. To him, precedent has an almost mystical meaning and where the common run of members will reflect twice at least before creating a precedent, the Senate type will reflect so long and so often that nine times out of ten he will have nothing to do with such a project at all.

His concern for the preservation of Senate tradition is so great that he distrusts anything out of the ordinary, however small, as for example a night session. Not necessarily an abstemious man (and sometimes a fairly bibulous one as a convivial character *within* the Institution) he will complain that such sessions, especially along toward the closing days of Congress, will be unduly tiring on the elders of the body. Often he really means here that prolonged meetings, tending as they do to send the most decorous of men out to the lounges for a nip, may wind up with one or more distinguished members taking aboard what never in the world would be called a few too many.

This Senate type knows, with the surest touch in the world, precisely how to treat his colleagues, Outer Club as well as Inner Club. He is nearly always a truly compassionate man, very slow to condemn his brothers. And not even the imminent approach of a great war can disturb him more than the approach of what he may regard as adequate evidence that the Senate may in one crisis or another be losing not the affection of the country (for which he has no great care) but the *respect* of the country.

He measures the degree of respect being shown by the country at any given time not wholly by what he reads and hears through the mass media, and not at all by the indicated attitude of any President, but by what is borne in upon his consciousness by his contact with what he considers to be the more *suitable* conveyors of *proper* public thought. He, the true Senate type, has this partiality toward the few as distinguished from the many all through his career even though he will hide it skillfully in his recurring tests at home when, up for re-election, he *must* depend upon the mass.

As the Southern members of the Inner Club make the ultimate decisions as to what is proper in point of manner—these decisions then infallibly pervading the Outer Club—so the whole generality of the Inner Club makes the decisions as to what *in general* is proper in the Institution and what *in general* its conclusions should be on high issues. These decisions are in no way overtly or formally reached; it is simply that one day the perceptive onlooker will discover a kind of aura from the Inner Club that informs him of what the Senate is later going to do about such and such.

For an illustration of the point, there was this small but significant incident in 1956: Some of the junior members had set out to put some Congressional check on the Central Intelligence Agency by creating an overseeing Joint Congressional Committee. A majority of the whole body became formally committed to the bill, and all seemed clear ahead. Suddenly, however, some of the patriarchs—among them the venerable Alben Barkley of Kentucky, who was soon to die in his seventy-ninth year while smiting the Republicans from a speaking platform at Washington and Lee University—found themselves disenchanted. They decided, for no very perceptible reason except that they felt they had been inadequately consulted, that a joint committee would not do at all. Under their bleak and languid frowns the whole project simply died; a wind had blown upon it from the Inner Club and its erstwhile sponsors simply left it.

The Senate type therefore—and his distillate as found in the Inner Club—is in many senses more an institutional man than a public man in the ordinary definition of such a personage. Some of the Senate's most powerful public men have not been truly Senate types. The late Senator Arthur Vandenberg of Michigan, for all his influence upon foreign relations after he had abandoned isolationism for internationalism, was never in his career a true Senate type, no matter how formidable he was as a public man. Incomparably the truest current Senate type, and incomparably the most influential man on the inner life of the Senate, Senator Russell of Georgia, has never had one-tenth Vandenberg's impact upon public and press in objective, or out-Senate, affairs.

Russell's less palpable and less measurable influence, however, was infinitely greater in the *Senate,* on all matters involving its inner being, than was Vandenberg's, as indeed was Taft's. For Russell could actually command the votes of others upon many matters, even some entirely objective matters. Vandenberg spoke to the country and occasionally to the world. Russell (and the other Senate types as well) speaks primarily to the Senate. Going back a good deal farther, Huey Long of Louisiana spoke also beyond the Senate, specifically to the discontented and the dispossessed outside, while one of his greatest critics of the time, Carter Glass of Virginia, spoke to the Senate, as Byrd of Virginia does to this day.

The non-Senate types, it thus may be seen, are in the end influential only to the degree that they may so instruct or so inflame a part of the public sufficiently large to insist upon this or that course of political conduct. The Senate type in the last analysis has the better of it. For not only does his forum generally resist change and all public pressure save the massive and enduring; it also will tend quickly to adopt *his* proposals unless they are quite clearly untenable.

The Senate Democratic leader in the Eighty-fourth Congress, Lyndon Johnson of Texas, once was able to pass more than a hundred bills, not all of them lacking in controversy, in a matter of a little more than an hour. There were a variety of reasons for this wholly untypical burst of speed in a body devoted to the leisurely approach. But the most important of these reasons was simply "Lyndon wants it." It is hardly necessary to add that "Lyndon" is pre-eminently a Senate type, so much so that, highly realistic politician though he is, he is quite unable to believe that the public is not in utter fascination of the parliamentary procedures of his Institution.

Again the Republican Senate leader, Knowland of California (and like Johnson he is senior only in terms of place and power and not in years) is a curious example of the power of the Senate type. Knowland, who inherited the leadership in a personal laying on of hands from the dying Senator Taft, was in both the Eighty-third and Eighty-fourth Congresses in what one might have thought to be a position scarcely likely to win him great popularity in his party or in the Senate.

A young Republican of the old school, he was faithful in his fashion to the newly arrived Republican in the White House, General Eisenhower, but he persisted, it will be recalled, in rebellious notions about Asian policy and about dealing with the world Communists. There were many times when, in the Senate and before the world, he was clearly contradicting an almost ecstatically popular Republican Président of the United States and all the powerful forces in that President's train.

Outsiders could not quite see how Knowland could in these circumstances remain the President's party spokesman in the Senate. The Senate types, for their part, simply could not grasp what the outsiders were talking about. To the Inner Club it was sheer nonsense to talk of Knowland as the *President's* leader; plainly he was the *Senate's* leader, on one side of the aisle.

There arose some talk among the "Eisenhower Republicans" of trying to displace Knowland as leader. It died, embarrassedly, in the throats of its utterers before the stern reproof of the Senate type—in both parties, if it comes to that.

A man, therefore, may be a Senate type in good standing in the Inner Club if he is wholly out of step on fateful matters with his own Administration (as with Knowland on Asia in regard to Eisenhower). He may be the same if he is wholly out of step with his own party, as for illustration Byrd in regard to the regular Democrats who control the party nationally. He may be the same if, like McClellan of Arkansas he comes fortuitously and reluctantly to national attention only because he becomes involved in something widely televised, like the Army-McCarthy hearings.

Equally a man may be a powerful Senate type with never a great legislative triumph to his credit, by a mysterious chemical process that seems to be transforming now so relative a newcomer as Payne of Maine. Why such progress for Payne? It is a little awkward to explain; perhaps the explanation is that Payne, who was a rather hard-handed politician as Governor of Maine, simply generates a warmth about him because he so wholeheartedly performs, without fuss or trouble, such Senate chores as are handed over to him.

The converse is similarly so. William Fulbright of Arkansas, a Rhodes Scholar, an ex-university president, a young and literate man with many useful years ahead of him, was credited as a member of the House with promoting this country's turn to internationalism before the Second World War. He has been credited since in the Senate with many achievements, not the least of which is the cumulative achievement of an experience and a seniority that are very likely one day to make him chairman of the Foreign Relations Committee.

He is not, for all of this, quite a Senate type. Nor, for another example, is Paul Douglas of Illinois, with his academic background, his ability in the field of economics, and his not inconsiderable feat in winning re-election in 1954 over assistance given to his opponent by President Eisenhower. Is scholastic achievement or "intellectualism" then—considering the cases of Fulbright and of Douglas—some bar to the Inner Club? Not at all. For, standing well inside the doors of the Inner Club, at least, is Humphrey of Minnesota, who used to teach political science. And at the very heart of the Inner Club in the Eighty-fourth Congress sat the man with what many would consider the most truly intellectual character in the Senate, Eugene Millikin of Colorado.

Does being liberal put a barrier on the way to the Inner Club? No, for few in the Institution can be more liberal than the old indestructible, Senator Theodore Green of Rhode Island, a member of the very hierarchy of the Club.

Does being "unpopular" and remote keep out a man? No. The ordinary conversation of Carl Hayden of Arizona, whose manners are as leathery as his face, consists largely of sour grunts. And Hayden could very nearly be the president of the Club, if only it had officers.

Does wealth or social status count? Not really. One of those men in the Senate who are wholly without commercial instinct and must get along strictly on their salaries is Mike Mansfield of Montana. He spent his young years in the mines of Butte; he largely educated himself—and he, like Humphrey, is well across the threshold of the Inner Club. And, unlike Humphrey, Mansfield has no gift at all for gregariousness; at Senatorial parties one sees him standing aloof, his eyes and voice quiet, smoking his pipe and leaving as soon as departure is at all possible. Knowland, too, is less than a relaxed social being. Earnest, conscientious and loyal though he is, he is almost without a sense of humor—but not without a sense of tolerance.

Indeed, it may be that this is one of the keys to the qualities of the Senate type—tolerance toward his fellows, intolerance toward any who would in any real way change the Senate, its customs or its way of life. And, right or wrong, it is the moral force of these men that gives to them an ascendancy in the Institution which they never assert and which most of them do nothing consciously to promote.

It is, then, against all this background of the human facts in the case that answer must be made to the question whether and how the Senate is "the most exclusive club in the world" and whether, indeed, it is exclusive in the ordinary understanding at all.

Certainly there is in the common definition nothing exclusive in a place in which a Taft, with his almost religious feeling about party orthodoxy, for years sat so amicably and by choice beside an Aiken of Vermont, whose Republicanism had, by Taft's standards, some sadly thin spots in its fabric. Where the son of an Alabama sharecropper, Sparkman of Alabama, has shared so many projects in social legislation with the rich, aloof Murray of Montana. Where the son of Huey Long, Senator Russell Long of Louisiana, so atypically carries on the dynasty by habitual quietude and responsibility in the seat that his father made so clangorous and so irresponsible. Where a Prescott Bush of Connecticut, late of St. George's School, Newport, R.I., and still later of Brown Brothers Harriman & Co. of Wall Street, has shared a forum with a Pastore of Rhode Island, late of the public schools of the city of Providence and of Northeastern University.

There *is,* however, for all of this, a quality of exclusiveness, too. Though some arrive more or less by accident in the Senate, most have worked a passage that has required more than luck, than money, than family or political position. In a sense at first there is the exclusiveness of success and then, as test succeeds test, the exclusiveness of both success and understanding. All these may be, and are, attained without reaching the final quality of exclusiveness that is involved in acceptance in the Inner Club.

To be in the Inner Club a man must be many things—some important and some mere accidents of life—but the greatest of these things is to have the character that will pass the severest scrutiny (if carried out blandly and seemingly casually) of which nearly five score highly understanding and humanly perceptive men are capable.

It is not character in the sense intended in the forms prepared by personnel offices. It has not got much to do with questions like "Does applicant drink?" or "Does he pay his bills?" It is character in the sense that only the true traditionalists will understand.

It is character in the sense that the special integrity of the person must be in harmony with, and not lesser in its way than, the special integrity of the Institution—the integrity of its oneness.

14. A Senate Page:
A View of the Inner Club from the Bottom Up

from *A View from the Floor: The Journal of a United States Senate Page Boy*

by FRANK MADISON

January 3, 1956

My living accommodations are ideal. I live overlooking Admiral Farragut, who supposedly said, "Damn the torpedoes! Full speed ahead," or something equally discourteous. It is very difficult to find a statue of anybody in Washington but generals and the like. The Admiral's cannons are very handy for nesting birds. The place is infested with pigeons and squirrels as fat as capitalists.

On my first day I walked all over town finding out where everything is and looking at the exteriors of things. The Washington Monument is rather disappointing, much smaller than it seems on postcards. The memorials to Lincoln and Jefferson, on the other hand, suffer from the postcard treatment. Jefferson's view of the Potomac is magnificent. The most beautiful building externally houses the Federal Reserve; it has much better grounds than the White House, for instance. There is an interesting international Christmas display back of the White House, highlighted by the official tree, from South Dakota, reaching from here to there and with Christmas balls a foot in diameter. As sideshows there are a crèche with live donkeys and all of Santa's reindeer looking the worse for their one-night stand. Dasher, Vixen and Cupid had passed out and were asleep on the hay.

I showed up on schedule at the office of Bobby Baker, Secretary for the Majority, an important position for a man of twenty-seven. On his secretary's desk was a sign that read, "You don't have to be crazy to work here, but it helps." She pressed the green button on her telephone and picked up the receiver. She said, after a minute or so, "Yes, Senator," and then pushed the yellow button and said, "Bill, Senator R. wants a case of White Rock in his office immediately. Oh, and by the way, stop by and pick up some documents while you're at it." Having been sworn in (I am to uphold the Constitution) and being now worth $4,000 in the event of my death (a worthy investment, as Washington drivers drive on the assumption that when the light turns the pedestrian will leap wildly toward the sidewalk), I proceeded to the Democratic cloakroom, where Democratic telephones were being answered by young Democrats. It was 12:02, two minutes after the gavel had first struck, and the sound of 96 senators chortling and backslapping simultaneously was creating quite a racket in the next room. I met the Head Page (wearing a brown suit rather than the customary blue), who said I was the person they had been expecting who didn't fit in anywhere. That was as far as I got the first day, as he said there wasn't much use in my trying to learn anything that day and I should return the next day.

I was sitting in the outer office of the Sergeant at Arms shortly after the breakup of some of the longer New Year's Eve parties waiting for some papers. The secretaries were waiting for one of the six phones to ring while idly sniping at one another. Then a senator burst into the room. I did not know him yet, but he had those unmistakable characteristics, large grin and potbelly. The secretaries instantly girded themselves for joviality. "Say," said one, in her best jolly-good-fellow tone, "that was a wonderful box of candy you sent us up at the office. And do you know who is eating it all up? The chief! Every day he comes in and says, 'Where's that brown box of candy?'— that's yours, Senator." She slapped her thigh in amusement. The Senator slapped his thigh in amusement. Then he burst into the office of the chief, without knocking.

.   .   .

January 20, 1956

The senators from the gas-producing states, Monroney of Oklahoma, Fulbright of Arkansas and Daniel of Texas, to name a few, all presented excellent arguments in favor of the natural-gas bill. Their argument is that all Gaul is divided into three parts, the producer, the pipeline, and the city distributor. Senators Pastore and Douglas contend that all Gaul is divided into four parts, the fourth being the consumer. Lyndon Johnson, in an eloquent speech, his first open advocacy of any measure in this session, said it was a question of whether or not we trust the capitalistic system. On all sides it has been a magnificent debate with all the Senate's really fine men making their first debating appearances of the session. Senator Pastore is a strange man with black hair and a moustache. He has a sickly grin; he bares his teeth and utters something resembling a death rattle. He can be very vehement. It is almost comical to see Pastore and Douglas, leaders of the opposition to the gas bill, together. Pastore, small and dark, is about half the size of the majestic, white-haired Douglas. The debate has been a great strain on Douglas, who has shown magnificent poise courtesy and restraint.

I can now boast of having seen Congressman Tumulty of New Jersey, who weighs more than 350 pounds and whose stomach arrives approximately two feet before he enters the room officially. If Douglas and Pastore form a strange contrast, that formed by "Tummy" and Senator Clifford Case is even more pronounced. The Congressman appeared a couple of feet wider beside the gaunt Senator Case.

It is an excellent custom to have freshmen senators do most of the presiding over the Senate. It familiarizes them with Senate procedures and with their fellow senators and does not cut out a senior senator from his debating on the floor. The presiding officers usually have very little idea of what is going on and merely repeat the offical words whispered to them by the Parliamentarian.

The big event of January 19 was a two-hour smear of Dulles by Republican Jenner of Indiana. He said that the Secretary was well-known for deceit and that his recent bellicose attitude is merely a front to hide a weak-kneed retreat before the Communists. He decried attempts to bathe the heathen when the heathen will not fall in with our military ambitions and do not live up to our time-honored principles.

Senator Humphrey showed today (January 20) that he still has plenty of spleen to vent. Two other speeches were also made on the "Case of the Blundering Secretary." Neely of West Virginia delivered an unashamed smear. Mike Mansfield of Montana gave a sober analysis, saying that the Democratic policies adopted by the Eisenhower administration were applicable until world conditions changed. At one point in his speech, he said, "I believe Mr. Dulles is an honorable man." I expected him to say, "So are they all—all honorable men." Humphrey showed himself on the side of ire by praising Neely, while questioning Mansfield.

I learned the other day how it was possible for Wayne Morse to break the filibuster record a year or two ago with a speech of almost 23 hours. He whiled away the hours by discussing how he courted his wife and how his ten-year-old daughter was doing in school and by reading letters from constituents. He would say, "Now here is an example of just what we've been discussing in regard to this bill." Then he would read an article from *Reader's Digest* about the hazards of being a milkman or "How I Became a Forger."

.   .   .

April 12, 1956

Senator Jenner is a reactionary, but he is an absorbing reactionary. He gave a thrilling speech on why we should junk the farm program and particularly all contacts with foreign countries. "Our Government is like Penelope of Greek legend. Penelope knit by day and unraveled by night. That is what our Government is doing with the farm program. What little is knit by our agricultural officials is quickly unraveled in the stealth of the night through the State Department." An example of this foreign foolishness is sending United States technical assistants abroad to raise productivity of famished nations because this competes with artifically stimulated United States prices. Jenner always goes around with his head thrust forward in a gesture of intensity, pursing his lips in a grimace of fierce determination.

It is impossible to convey how droll Senator Dirksen sounds when delivering a speech in his precise oratorical style and in the most devastatingly beautiful voice imaginable. It rolls like the ocean; it undulates with the pathos of humanity. His big soulful eyes have all the heartrending quality of those of a discontented cow.

Nine-year-old Lucy Johnson, daughter of the Majority Leader, was cavorting around in the Democratic cloakroom on the evening of the vote to approve the conference report on the farm bill, which restored the rigid 90 percent of parity. There was some talk about Mother Ladybird's attempts to keep candy out of her daughter, and various political remarks also slipped out. On the possibility of Kefauver getting the nomination: "Not if my father has anything to say about it." On the possibility of Johnson himself getting the nomination: "We love our daddy. We don't want him to be President and have another heart attack." Lyndon came into the cloakroom and found Lucy in the phone booth. She was talking to some chum. He dragged her out, saying: "I want you to meet a very important person who came in here just to meet you. This is the Vice-President, Alben Barkley." Cordialities were exchanged. Afterwards, Lucy said, "Aw shucks, and I was right in the middle of a nice conversation, too."

The only significant piece of legislation discussed during the past week was a proposal by Senator Mansfield of Montana to set up a supervisory joint committee of Congress, modeled after the Joint Committee on Atomic Energy, to supervise the activities of the Central Intelligence Agency. Senator Mansfield based his pleas on the fact that the President and the White House pretorian guard have during the past twenty years been arrogating congressional prerogatives, while the Congress has stepped limply aside. He feels that the Central Intelligence Agency is a prime example of this trend.

All the operations of the CIA, down to the salaries paid its officials, are cloaked in ominous and, for all we know, guilty silence. Senator McCarthy has one hundred pages of conclusive evidence of staggering graft, inefficiency and Communist infiltration that have completely incapacitated the agency, in his view. No one seemed dreadfully impressed with that, but McCarthy was hard to refute because no one really knew what the situation was. Through either congressional ineptness or executive adroitness officials of the CIA have appeared before the Armed Services Committee on only two occasions during the past year and before the Appropriations Committee only once, when they came to ask the benighted senators for a lump sum.

Senator Saltonstall was the administration spokesman and argued that after all ignorance has its blissful points, that there are certain things that it is not wise for him, as a senator, to know. This got Wayne Morse all riled up, if indeed anything in particular is necessary to bring him to a boil. He said that he had gotten sick and tired, as a member of the Armed Services Committee, of having army officers come before the Committee and, raising an Olympian eyebrow and glancing meaningfully at a shoulder covered with brass, state mystically that their achievements are beyond comprehension, more particularly the comprehension of the Senate. Morse conceded that it might be better for him not to know certain things, but he was damned if he was going to let someone else decide what he should and should not know, especially some brass-plated knucklehead.

Well, more powerful if not necessarily wiser heads prevailed, and Senators Russell and Hayden, Chairmen of Armed Services and Appropriations, had their way; the proposal was defeated. Russell said it was one of the disillusioning things about the Senate that it only took a couple of days for something reported in a closed session to get into the papers. It could be said, however, that Senator Mansfield accomplished his purpose of focusing attention on the lack of supervision of the CIA, and the Armed Services Committee will probably pay a little more attention to it in the future.

.   .   .

May 17, 1956

.   .   .

Votes in the Senate are always rigged and often farcical. There are two examples from this week. First, the presiding officer said, "All in favor say 'aye' "; silence; "All opposed, 'no' "; silence; "The 'ayes' have it."

Then the most uproarious one happened Wednesday night at 7:00 p.m., just as the Senate was preparing to adjourn. Johnson asked for speedy passage of a routine money bill. At the time, following the main vote of the evening, there were only twenty Republicans and ten Democrats left on the floor. Democrat Humphrey was presiding. When the "ayes" were called for, the ten Democrats made a respectable noise. When the "nos" were requested, the twenty Republicans obviously made more noise. But, as Humphrey knew that the bill was scheduled to pass, he said, "The 'ayes' have it." The Republicans requested a division, in which all senators stand to be counted on a vote. Now as everyone realizes it is rather a touchy matter to say that ten Democrats outnumber twenty Republicans, Johnson went to work fast. And, while the Parliamentarian spent thirty seconds counting each senator, as instructed, Johnson had a little word with Senator Knowland, Minority Leader. He told him that he knew perfectly well that the Democrats could pass this bill if they got all their senators there, but it was simply being ornery to force all of them to come back for a vote. Knowland had no real desire to be unpleasant and unreasonable, so the request for division was withdrawn, and again they had a voice vote. Again the "nos" completely drowned out the "ayes." "The 'ayes' have it," said Senator Humphrey.

. . .

June 20, 1956

This is a typical example of my exhausting work schedule: On Wednesday, I came to work at 11:00 a.m. Between 12:00 and 2:00 we passed a new accounting procedure for the Federal government that is supposed to save $5 billion by eliminating unexpended balances. At 2:00 Senator Clements called me to the office to "gladhand" the four top 4-Hers from Kentucky. The Senator was busy and could not get off to show them around Washington, so he detailed me to the task. We climbed into our chauffeured black Cadillac for a three-hour jaunt around town. Senator Clements does not have a car in Washington, and so when he needs one he borrows one of the two Cadillacs of the Sergeant-at-Arms or one of the two of the Secretary of the Senate. Beside these, Cadillacs are provided for the Financial Clerk, the Attending Physician, the Secretary for the Majority, and the Majority and Minority Leaders. Well, we toured in great splendor from the Russian Embassy to Arlington Cemetery, from the National Gallery of Art to the Pentagon. I dropped off my friends on the other side of town and rode back to the Capitol in solitary splendor in the back of my black Caddy. I arrived a few minutes after the Senate had adjourned for the day, and I had the ego-stimulating thrill of arriving in style just as one of my various bosses was flagging down a cab. Come to think of it, he's practically the only boss I have who doesn't have a furnished Cadillac of his own.

. . .

June 26, 1956

. . .

By far the most memorable speech was that of Senator George, Chairman of the Foreign Relations Committee. It was the most moving experience I have ever had in the Senate. I actually find it very difficult to say anything appreciative about anything after having heard months of nauseating and meaningless eulogies and praise. After hearing people refer to Herman Welker as the "great and distinguished Senator from Idaho," those adjectives are very difficult for me to use; yet, truthfully, I thought George's speech was moving and eloquent. He spoke with more force than he is physically capable of. His voice cracked and broke with emotion. While I ridiculed McCarthy for not being able to hold onto his speech and letting it fall all around him, the same thing added poignancy to Senator George's speech. As he pounded on his desk, books and papers mounted around his feet; he was oblivious of them. With deep reverence Senator Mansfield moved quietly into the seat beside him to make sure that nothing more would fall on the Senator. Quite often he lost his train of thought in the middle of a sentence. He spoke in broken phrases and often referred to "these things" when he couldn't place the right word. All of this, while calling for derision in another, added great force to the impassioned plea of Senator George. I think that after his speech other senators felt as I did: that superlatives and compliments have become so commonplace that they are trite and fulsome. Not a soul said a word in commendation of the speech. They all gathered round and silently shook his hand.

The Men and Women in the Ranks

Thus far we have concentrated our attention on the stars of the political firmament—the personalities, the names in the headlines, the famous few behind whom the troops rally. In this concluding part we shall look at, and listen to, some of the unfamous men and women whose activities support the careers of the notables and give American politics much of its flavor.

The first selection is a remarkable and rather unsettling portrait of some of the female aides who have dedicated their lives to serving a senator or governor or president. These are the able, self-effacing assistants who are on call, day and night, seven days a week, to retype a speech, hunt down a fact in the library, brew coffee, fend off unwanted callers, make travel arrangements, and attend to all the wants of men considered too important to bother with such matters themselves. Working side by side with the aides are speech writers, advance men, public relations experts—a crowd of people distinguished both by their technical skill at the daily business of politics and by their readiness to submerge themselves totally in the careers of their bosses. In an important sense they are voluntary slaves, for as Sara Davidson's portrayal shows, the female assistants to powerful Washington figures are willing to sacrifice home, marriage, career, money, free time—all for the chance to be next to power and success.

The second selection portrays a group of young political activists as different as one could imagine from the political aides described by Sara Davidson: the McCarthy kids who trooped to New Hampshire and California during the presidential primaries of 1968 to support the antiwar candidacy of Eugene McCarthy. The female aides are what we have been calling political professionals. They love the political life itself, and when their man dies or is voted out of office, they are likely to seek out another notable and join his entourage. The McCarthy kids were political amateurs. A few have remained in elective politics on a regular basis, and many have gone on to fight for other causes, but most of them retired from the political arena after the debacle of the 1968 Democratic Convention in Chicago.

The outpouring of student energy and commitment that Senator McCarthy himself called a "second children's crusade" can teach us a great deal about the power and the limits of reform movements in American politics. On the one hand, the students and other McCarthy supporters had an impact on presidential politics all out of proportion to their numbers. This is, after all, a nation of more than two hundred million men and women, and the antiwar campaigners numbered only in the thousands. Nevertheless, their efforts are widely credited with having influenced Lyndon Johnson to step down from the presidency without seeking a traditional second term. On the other hand, the Democratic nominee who took President Johnson's place on the ballot, Hubert Humphrey, defended a position on the Vietnam war that was no more than marginally different from the President's. When push came to shove in the nominating convention, there simply was not enough support for the antiwar position. The election of Richard Nixon confirmed this indication that the McCarthy movement had failed to win a majority of the American voters.

One of the frustrating facts of democratic politics is that when all the money has been spent, all the doorbells rung, all the books written and positions argued, it is still necessary to win a majority of the votes. To a dedicated political activist who believes that he knows what is best for his country, it is terribly disheartening to fight the good fight and still be rejected by the voters. Needless to say, the majority is not always right. Indeed, history suggests that wisdom more often lies with the few than with the many.

Not all the disappointment and frustration lies on the left of the political spectrum, as our portrait of Billy Hargis and Robert Welch in Part 3 showed. In this concluding selection, we listen to an angry voice from that silent majority of middle Americans to whom President Nixon has directed his appeal. Robert S. Moga is everything that Ted Gold despised, just as Ted Gold is everything that Robert S. Moga despises. Both are the descendants of immigrants who came to the United States in search of a better life, and both are American through and through. Yet each of them, given the chance, would read the other out of American society. It would be comforting to end this book with the confident assertion that America is big enough for both the Ted Golds and the Bobby Mogas, as well as the Eldridge Cleavers, the Richard Daleys, and the John Lindsays. But this is not an easy time for optimists, and I do not think we can take it for granted that American society will hold together over the coming years.

In my opening remarks, I called attention to the kaleidoscopic variety of styles of action which occupy the political arena in our society. It remains to be seen whether Americans can share that arena, if not in peace or harmony, then at least without open warfare.

15. Female Assistants:
The Faceless Workers Behind the Great Men

"The Girls on the Bandwagon"
by SARA DAVIDSON

Susan, a slim girl with a red pageboy and a perfect summer tan, crouches on the hot asphalt in front of the Biltmore Hotel. Behind her, an impatient crowd is waiting for the motorcade that will bear John F. Kennedy to the Democratic National Convention. It is Los Angeles, July, 1960. Susan, just graduated from Palisades High School, has never heard of Kennedy.

A brass band blares "High Hopes." Motorcycles roar through the emptied street, and an open car with Kennedy in back stops in front of Susan. The crowd surges forward, pinning Susan against the car. She reaches out her bare, freckled arm; Kennedy grasps it, smiles at her, and she loses her balance. She squirms back through the crowd and makes her way to the Kennedy headquarters, where she takes ten campaign buttons and signs up as a volunteer. All through that summer, Susan worked for Kennedy, twelve hours a day, often seven days a week. As she addressed envelopes, she imagined Kennedy visiting the headquarters, seeing her, and whispering to one of his aides to have her come to his room late at night. That fall she went to college and studied American history. The next three summers she worked around Washington. She found that the intoxicating sex-power attraction was not unique to Kennedy, but applied to almost every political figure, even those who, by objective criteria, would not be judged to have great physical appeal. "When I saw Lyndon Johnson on television, I thought he was totally unattractive. Then I saw him about a foot away at a reception, and he had an aura of power so thick you could feel it. I suddenly thought, What a handsome man! I have this theory that successful men in public life have an inherent sexual pull. Even someone like Arthur Goldberg, who is not that good-looking, has this quality about him that is physically moving."

Susan is 27 now and still in Washington, working as a legislative aide to a Senator. She does not think of herself as a career girl: "I'm waiting to get married." She looks at the women in their fifties who have been on Capitol Hill all their lives and thinks, It won't happen to me. Yet she works eleven hours a day, always Saturdays, sometimes Sundays, has lunch at her desk, takes only one week's vacation a year. "It gets down to commitment. It's a thrill to be right in the center, working with people who make the country move." The words used by friends to describe Susan—bright, capable, attractive, unmarried—apply to a great many women in Washington who are known variously as political spinsters, boiler-room girls, pol molls, or, recently, political groupies. The term groupies is inaccurate in its literal sense; in the rock world, where it originated, it implies open and total sexuality. The rock groupie, a hedonist, with a strong streak of masochism, sleeps her way to status by pursuing musicians and gains her identity by sexual submission.

Political girls are vastly different: they are serious, idealistic, work-oriented, and devoted to one politician or political philosophy. Their submission is emotional, more than sexual. They gain their identity by affiliation with a powerful man, to whom they devote all their energy and time. Peggy Harlow, who was brought up in a political family and works for Vice-President Spiro Agnew, says, "Women here give everything to the men they're working for. They get so totally involved in the man, his ideals, and his career that they often have nothing left over for themselves. Some women never realize this until they wake up at fifty and panic, 'What am I going to do when I leave this job?' I used to be that way—living my work. I did *not know* what to do with myself when I had even one day off from my job."

The career of a political girl in Washington seems to progress in three stages. When she is young—in her twenties up to her early thirties—she is not committed to a career, but thinks of her job as stimulating, glamorous work to bide her until she gets married. She moves frequently, living with other girls in apartments or houses in Georgetown, avoiding buying furniture and acquiring trappings of permanence. Claudia Bourne, twenty-seven, a puckish blond with wide blue eyes who is a press aide to Senator Charles Percy of Illinois, says, "I don't think I've ever thought of a career for myself. This is something I do because I enjoy it." Kathie St. John, who holds the frenetic job of executive secretary to Mayor John Lindsay, in New York, believes a career girl has to be "cut-throat and tough. I'm not that at all. I'm waiting to get married."

In Washington, though, a girl's chances of meeting eligible men are probably worse than in other cities of similar size, not only because there are many more single women than men in the capital, but because the girls work so many hours that they have little time for outside socializing.

.   .   .

Peggy Harlow and three girl friends organized a Monday Club shortly after President Nixon was inaugurated, for young people in the lower echelons of government to get to know one another. They would meet each Monday at a different restaurant, buy their own drinks and dinner, and talk, invariably, about their jobs. The club fell apart rapidly, Peggy says, "because people started getting too busy."

By their mid-thirties, the girls begin to say, "It's unlikely I'll get married," and throw themselves even more into their work. They set up permanent homes, and their personal life becomes wholly enmeshed with that of their boss. Pat Donovan, secretary to Senator George McGovern of South Dakota, last year bought and furnished a summer house for herself at Rehoboth Beach, Delaware. "My life revolves around the job," she says. "I couldn't give it the time and energy I do if I had a lot of other responsibilities." Pat makes more than $15,000 a year, has traveled around the world with the Senator on a Food-for-Peace trip, and is close to the McGovern family. They take her out to dinner with them, to the theater, and to their home for weekends. "I'm totally dedicated to the Senator," Pat says, "and I thoroughly love this work."

Past the forties, the women are set in their roles and could not imagine another way of life. They have met and worked with a chain of influential people, can reminisce through conventions and Congresses, and have had books dictated and dedicated to them. They have been to state dinners at the White House, met ambassadors and astronauts, and learned the capital from the inside out. Some, like Rose Mary Woods, secretary to President Nixon, have made a lifetime commitment to one man, in or out of power. Others follow the election tides: when one man leaves office, they find a newcomer to serve.

There have been a few cases where politicians have married staff members. Senator Russell Long of Louisiana married his secretary, and Senator George Aiken of Vermont married his administrative assistant. But politicians, unlike rock stars, must be circumspect to the point of paranoia about their romantic lives. In New York, women still hiss and turn their backs on Governor Nelson Rockefeller because he left his wife of thirty-two years to marry Happy Murphy. That Rockefeller risked his career for love, and that Mrs. Murphy was willing to sign away custody of her four children to gain her freedom to marry the governor, only made the crime more heinous to people who demand Victorian behavior of their officials. In Massachusetts, where financial scandal and internecine treachery enhance a politician's image, the one sin that will finish him off with the public is womanizing.

Political figures have to endure fishbowl marriages and must maintain the illusion of a happiness family even if they have grown apart from their wives. They are the subject of rumors so elaborate and persistent that the rumors become accepted as facts. One New England figure was widely believed to have been cited in a paternity suit, which never existed. A rumor that reached clear across the country concerned a politician whose affair with his secretary was said to have induced his wife to slit her wrists. The first part was true; the second, false. But after I interviewed this man, everyone I met, from policemen to the corner butcher, would ask, "What's this about his wife trying to kill herself?"

Because of the fear of scandal, politicians who feel the need for feminine companionship outside home are likely to turn to their staff girls, who have proved their loyalty and trustworthiness. Because sex and power are intertwined, the men have a sexual advantage they would not possess if they did not hold power. The girls, even when there is no sexual relationship, can sublimate their sexual desires by working for and sharing in the politician's achievements and recognition. Jim Doyle, national correspondent for the Washington *Star*, says, "These girls make awfully good secretaries, because they have the same striving for power and ambition as the men they work for."

When a girl takes her first political job, she may have no strong commitments, but she quickly assumes the ideological coloration of her boss, with a passion that carries through life. Sylvia Neighbors, a shy, sugar-voiced woman of thirty, was secretary to a yarn broker in Spartanburg, South Carolina, when friends recommended her to craggy-faced Strom Thurmond, who was looking for a personal secretary. Sylvia says, "I was not that deeply interested in politics or issues. Of course, I had a conservative outlook on life, a Southern view of politics. Most people on the Senator's staff share his philosophy and have made the switch with him from the Democratic to the Republican Party. You have to have the same ideals as the Senator if you're going to give him so much of your time."

Due to President Nixon's Southern Strategy, in which Thurmond plays a key role, his office is very busy these days, and there is always a jam of people in the waiting room lined with rose-and-green blowups of South Carolina swamps. Sylvia juggles more than a hundred phone calls and visitors a day. She lives across the street from the Capitol and is always on call. "The Senator's hours are my hours," she says. "I came here to work, not to have a great social life. I never think about the future. As long as I serve him and my work pleases him, I'm happy."

On Sundays in the spring, Thurmond puts on Bermuda shorts over his spindly legs and takes his staff bike riding, then for a picnic of watermelon, lemonade, and cookies. He dresses up as Santa Claus at Christmas and arranges at least one party a month for "good fellowship with the staff." Sylvia says, "He's a fun person to work for. To me, he's the greatest American."

Girls with liberal viewpoints gravitate to figures on the left in each party. Edie Radley, who does scheduling for Mayor Lindsay, took her first political jobs with Nelson Rockefeller and another liberal Republican, Senator Kenneth Keating. She found that politics is "like a drug—once you get on it, you can't imagine going back to a normal life." In Washington, it is called "Potomac Fever" or "the power bug."

Edie says it was exciting to work for Rockefeller and Keating, but with Lindsay, she developed a feverish loyalty. "I could never work for Rockefeller now," she says. "I believe in John Lindsay. I think he's one of a kind. He really cares about improving the city, and I've got to do my part to help him."

Like most women who work for Lindsay, Edie was star struck and nervous at first. "I'd stand, fidgeting, outside his office and finally would take a deep breath and say to myself, 'Look, you're thirty-one years old, you're human and he's human, so just get in there and work.' After a while, you get very used to his good looks. You can go for weeks and not realize how handsome he is. Then one day he'll come in with a great-looking suit and his hair combed, and you say, 'My lord.' "

The girls who work for Spiro T. Agnew feel the same way about his looks. Michael Weiss, a reporter who covered Agnew while he was Governor of Maryland, recalls a conversation with Cynthia Rosenwald, a bouncy Baltimore housewife who followed Agnew to Washington and served as one of his speech writers until her recent resignation. According to Weiss, Cynthia said she finds Agnew's mind "phallic. The way he thinks is so sharp, so direct, that I react sexually."

Peggy Harlow, when told about this quote, said, "His being very direct and blunt is true." Peggy met Agnew at Christmas in 1968, when she was in Key Biscayne, Florida, with her father, Bryce Harlow, who had been designated Counselor to President Nixon. She was sitting with Defense Secretary Melvin Laird at dinner when Agnew came over to ask about people in the Senate. Peggy says, "I knew many of the Senators personally and others by rumor. We had this great, gossipy conversation, and a short time later, at a birthday party for Senator Everett Dirksen, Agnew walked over and blurted, 'I want you to work for me.' I was flabbergasted. I told him I was hoping to move out of the secretarial classification, and he assured me I would."

In Peggy's office in the Senate wing, there are a cartoon of Agnew with a dart board superimposed over his face, pictures of the Nixon family, Nixon with her father, and Agnew with an inscription "To Peggy—my senatorial right hand." On her desk is an orange sticker: "Agnews—Yes; TV News—No." While Peggy agrees in principle with Agnew's criticism of television commentators, when she heard his speech referring to East Coast intellectuals as "effete snobs," she went in the next day fuming. "I'll bet he doesn't know he's got one on his staff."

Peggy, who is twenty-seven, has worked in three Presidential campaigns, has been a volunteer for Everett Dirksen and Barry Goldwater and a press assistant for Colorado Senator Peter Dominick. Being a woman, she says, makes it difficult to advance to a higher position and salary. "Women who are hired as secretaries on Capitol Hill actually do anything from casework—solving problems and doing favors for voters—to writing speeches. It's a very fluid situation. Politicians are so busy that they're happy to have you perform to the maximum extent of your abilities. You do what's needed, not what your title is. But if you're a woman, you stay in a low classification at a lower salary than a man would. My position now is staff assistant. If I were a man, I would never be in this job." Peggy says that when she calls a man in government, "he immediately thinks it's a secretary. It's hard for Senators and Congressmen to think of a woman as anything but a secretary. And the women in high places in Washington are worse—they won't speak to another woman on the phone."

Despite evidence that they are discriminated against, women who work for politicians express hostility toward feminism and women's rights. Maxine Paul, who works in Rockefeller's New York office, where even switchboard operators have college degrees, says, "I'm antifeminist. I believe men should rule family and work situations. There are good reasons to pay men higher salaries."

Political girls dress in a conservative, well-tailored style, heavy on linen and knit dresses, with quiet gold jewelry. They are against Women's Liberation because the movement rejects the notion of gaining power through association and using so-called feminine wiles instead of direct action. Political girls compensate for the disadvantages they face because of sex by using prerogatives that are open only to women. Peggy Harlow says, "The exposure I get to Senators and Congressmen by taking them coffee or candy when they're in the chair, or walking their dogs, is something a man couldn't do, because it wouldn't be appropriate."

The most blatant exploitation of women occurs during political campaigns, when they are enlisted to perform the bulk of the dirty work at no pay. Ironically, it is in campaigns that true political groupies thrive. The high pressure, the crowds, the stimulants for emotionalism—bands, chanting, hoopla—create an adrenalin-charged atmosphere in which socializing is as intense as work. People who take staff jobs—in advance work, publicity, scheduling, research—realize that the campaign will be their life until election day.

Linda Lee, a Washington lawyer who has worked in campaigns for twelve years, says, "Out of every twenty-four hours, you work eighteen, and in the time left over, you can either sleep or eat, drink, and relax with other staff members. With everybody going at that pace, defenses come down, and you get to know each other pretty well. It's great fun, and there's always a good deal of fraternizing. I've noticed that many people in campaigns have recently had bad experiences with spouses or girl friends and wanted to plunge themselves into something that would thoroughly involve them. A campaign is very good therapy."

Political groupies set themselves apart in campaigns by focusing their attention on men at the top of the power pyramid. They often work for months without pay, trying to sleep their way closer to the candidate and competing for the plums of traveling jobs. One girl, on her first trip with a Presidential candidate's party, bribed a hotel clerk in Atlanta to give her the key to the suite of one of the candidate's closest aides. The aide, a balding, paunchy father of three, with an incipient ulcer, was delighted to find the young girl in his bed when he came in from a late meeting. The girl was bright, ambitious, and knew when to keep silent. She stayed in the traveling entourage through election eve.

Another girl, who was hired as assistant to a speech writer for one of the Democratic Presidential candidates in 1968, found on her first road trip that the speech writer did not book a separate hotel room for her. She was not particularly attracted to the man, but the affair was a boost to her ego and brought her that much closer to the candidate. She and the speech writer would work until three in the morning, she says, "and then the phones would start ringing. His wife would be on one line, a scout from the other camp on another, and on the third line would be the boss, wanting to add something to a speech. It was incredible to be involved on that level."

.   .   .

After an election upheaval, many girls find a spot with another politician or go into television or communications, where the pace, tension, and immediacy are the same as in a campaign. A few leave politics because they begin to feel stifled.

Linda Epstein, one of the few Senatorial secretaries who is married, has worked for Senator John Tower of Texas since 1961, except for a leave to have a baby. In the near future, she hopes to move back to Texas and start a ranch or small business. "When you work for a politician, you're always an appendage to another person," she says. "It's frustrating and destructive to the ego. Whenever people ask what you do, it's always 'I work for Senator Tower.' There's a temptation to rely on this for your identity. I want to have something more to contribute to my son than that I was the personal secretary to a United States Senator." Linda says she's learned firsthand how Congress works, but "I've become rather dull and haven't broadened my interests in other areas. With this life, there's no time to read or go to the theater or just be with yourself. You never have solitude."

Peggy Harlow has faced the same conflict and has decided that "if political work is worth that much, then other things are worth a lot, too. I'm making time for my own life—puttering around the house, taking care of my dog and cat, going to symphonies, playing tennis, and reading. I've stopped feeling like I'm in Limbo, wondering, 'Am I going to get married?' I'm committed to my own career now, with my own personal goals. This means that I'm concerned not only with the Vice-President's performance and reputation, but with my own. I want people to think well of what I do and give me more responsibility and authority."

On Lincoln's Birthday, Old Glory flies in triplicate from every lamppost along Pennsylvania Avenue. The red and blue interrupt the steady gray of the massive federal buildings. In the office of Senator Fred Harris of Oklahoma, who is away on a speaking trip, Margie Banner, his personal secretary, is showing a visitor the Senator's private office. "This is our view of the garden," she says proudly, "and these paintings were all made by Indians." When Harris is in the office, Margie does not leave her desk except to grab a quick sandwich in one of the Senate employees' cafeterias—small, steamy rooms with harsh fluorescent lights. Today, though, she can take off an hour to walk across the street from the Capitol to the Carroll Arms, with its dark-wood booths, red wall coverings, and place mats with drawings of all the Presidents surrounding a giant head of Nixon.

Margie went to Washington before World War II. She worked in the White House, then as secretary to Army General Royal B. Lord, fourteen years with Senator Robert Kerr of Oklahoma, and, after Kerr died, seven years with Senator Harris. She is a delicate, sunshine blond with the face of a young girl who has simply got older. She wears a bright-yellow dress, red scarf, a piece of colored yarn in her hair, and a gold bracelet with inaugural medals as charms. Because of her sweet, buoyant nature, Harris calls her "Margie-Belle," but she always calls him "Senator." Women who work for Congressmen call them by first name, but in the Upper House, it's strictly "Senator" or "the boss."

Margie says, "When I first came up to Washington from Roanoke, Virginia, I thought I'd probably get married. I didn't know how much I'd enjoy working. Then, when I went to work for Senator Kerr, I became totally committed, full of ambitions. I knocked myself out, working every Saturday and Sunday. I wanted to be as good as I could. Kerr had always had a male secretary, and when he made me his personal secretary, it was as if I'd been given a million dollars. He would say, 'Marjory, you're indispensable.' I'd say, 'Well, Senator, *you're* indispensable.' I'd never let him pay me a compliment without paying him one back."

It was a great shock, Margie says, when Kerr died of a heart attack in 1963. "I'd had visions of always being with him. I wanted him to be President. I knew he would always be a great man, and I would always have a spot with him even if he quit the Senate." After his death, the Senator's son, Robert Kerr, Jr., suggested that Margie "go help this young fellow Fred Harris," who was running for Kerr's seat. Margie says, "It's amazing the way I transferred my loyalty from Kerr to Harris. But the two men are like peas in a pod. Harris carried out Kerr's program."

Margie is a veteran of five national conventions and, in 1964, single-handedly organized a floor demonstration for Harris at Atlantic City. "It's great to be part of history," she says, "but most of the time you're so snowed under, working your little heart and soul out, that you don't see the total picture."

For years, she lived on a shady street of colonial houses in Georgetown, until her roommate bought a house and Margie moved to southwest Washington "to be closer to my work. I'm so wrapped up in my work that I could be living anywhere."

She started taking ballroom-dance lessons once a week and joined the Capitol Hill Tennis Club, "to keep myself sane. I wanted to have something else to do but work. Ballroom dancing is really my only relaxation."

I ask Margie if she would recommend a Washington political job to other women. She takes small sips of her bloody Mary. "If a girl is interested in serving her country, I'd tell her to come. It's exciting and demanding. My life has almost gone by now—I'm in my middle forties—and I've worked for one brilliant man after another. I seem to have a faculty for it. Bob Kerr became king of the Senate, and here I get with young Fred Harris, who is such a mover. It's just amazing to think about it: a small-town girl coming to Washington and winding up working for men who are geniuses, meeting people like Vice-Presidents and generals, Senators, kings and queens."

She looks around the room at the tables of women in twos and threes, nursing glasses of wine. She smiles and mouths, "Hi," to several. "I think the young girls here now are finding it very fascinating." She laughs, a light, tinkly sound, full of cheer. "Of course, all of them won't wind up staying as long as I did. I didn't plan to, either. It just came naturally."

16. The McCarthy Kids:
Campaign Workers

from *We Were the Campaign*
by BEN STAVIS

When Rosann and I took a bus to Concord, New Hampshire, in early February 1968, we saw no other way to help end the war in Vietnam. With countless other Americans we had watched in horror and frustration as our country unleashed an ever larger war on the people of Vietnam, rendering modernization of backward countries impossible and preventing racial progress at home. There seemed no way of stopping it. Newspaper advertisements, demonstrations, and protests were ineffective; even important senators were discovering powerlessness. The supposed safeguard of democracy, the presidential election, seemed irrelevant. Throughout 1967 it seemed that the choice would be between Lyndon Johnson and Richard Nixon, leaving no chance to vote for peace. We would not even be offered the choice of Establishment liberals: Kennedy, Fulbright, or Rockefeller.

Thus, when Senator Eugene McCarthy, Democrat of Minnesota, revealed interest in challenging the incumbent president for his party's nomination, I was encouraged. I felt that only a presidential campaign offered a vague hope of mobilizing the peace forces of the country in a politically relevant way. I knew of Senator McCarthy because I had met him about six years earlier and liked him. He had visited Haverford College when I was a student there, participated in classes, and informally chatted about American foreign and domestic policy with students for several hours over coffee. He impressed me as a man of decency and integrity. Then, when McCarthy came to New York City to explore potential support for a presidential bid, I happened to meet Paul O'Dwyer, who was eventually to become the McCarthy movement's senatorial candidate in New York. Thinking that McCarthy might check with this former city councilman, I said half-seriously, "If McCarthy asks you what support he will have, you can tell him I would like to work in his campaign." I hoped that if McCarthy were assured of enough envelope sealers he might be encouraged to take up the peace banner.

I did not mean this as an empty promise, although I certainly had no idea of devoting all the energy that I did to the campaign. A previous experience in an electoral campaign had taught me that I could probably be useful. During the Christmas vacation of 1965 Rosann and I had helped to organize a campaign for Robert Schwartz, a "peace candidate" seeking the Democratic nomination for the congressional seat vacated by John Lindsay when he became mayor of New York. The nominee was chosen by members of the New York County Committee of the Democratic party. They seemed more concerned with using the nomination to reward people than with ending the war. We lost badly. Although generating considerable public support, we could get only 10 percent of the County Committee votes. This experience did not make us experts at organizing political campaigns, but it did teach us that anyone, even ourselves, could be of use politically. It also showed us how losers can illuminate the issues. As a result of Schwartz's campaign, all the other candidates for the nomination suddenly came out against the war. For that reason the campaign was a mild success, and I was impressed with the potential of electoral politics.

During December and January after McCarthy announced, while I stayed at Columbia University and studied for oral examinations for my doctorate (I was a student of Chinese politics), I followed with some concern the debate about McCarthy's candidacy. There were serious questions about his precise position on the war and his suitability as an antiwar leader. McCarthy had not been a leader in the Senate against the war as Morse from Oregon and Gruening from Alaska had. He actually had not even matched Robert Kennedy's modest contribution to the peace movement. Even after the announcement of his candidacy McCarthy's position remained weak. At an early press conference he argued that America could leave Vietnam because she had great strength in military bases in Thailand. He implied that Vietnam was a foolish place to try to contain communism, but he was not disputing the imperialist world view that supported the containment policy.

Despite these misgivings, the logic of a presidential challenge remained. If it could prove that peace was politically viable, perhaps Kennedy or Rockefeller would enter the race. Neither could fundamentally change American institutions, but either could introduce flexibility and unknowns into the political situation. Of course there were legitimate objections to McCarthy's leadership, but no one else had volunteered to carry the flag of peace into the contest.

Then, at the beginning of February, Rosann and I had a block of free time. I had just passed my oral examinations and could leave campus and studies for a while. Rosann was working on her dissertation in home economics education at New York University and could also leave New York. So on February 14, St. Valentine's Day, we took a bus to Boston and, next morning, another one to Concord, New Hampshire—almost four weeks before the New Hampshire primary. We walked into the headquarters about 10:30 a.m., suitcases in hand. Headquarters was an old electrical appliance store and, although it bore a sign **McCarthy for President,** it was not yet functioning.

We were quickly put to work. We shoveled rubbish from a side room, taped extension cords to the ceilings to support light bulbs, and carried pails of water to the basement to serve as fire extinguishers. A large wooden spool that had once held heavy wire was set on end to become a table for a borrowed coffee maker. Posters were put up to cover holes in the walls. Tables were placed over holes in the floors. We then began to stack cartons of literature and sort piles of posters. The campaign existed in the national press and on television, but it had barely begun in New Hampshire.

Rosann and I thought we might be able to coordinate some of the office work, do some of the envelope stuffing—that sort of thing. We expected to stay for a week or two, on the assumption that the campaign would have many effective workers from the Senator's staff and from New Hampshire. An assignment the next afternoon forced me to reassess drastically. I accompanied two other students to Rochester, New Hampshire, about an hour's drive from Concord. We were to annotate voting lists with party affiliation, so as to avoid canvassing or sending mail to Republicans. The people of New Hampshire, seemingly not trusting any centralized bureaucracy, had no single location for party registration records; each ward official kept his own lists in his own way. At Rochester the records for one ward were at the police station; for the second ward, in the official's isolated farmhouse; for the third, posted on the outside of a school. I volunteered to transpose party information from the latter list. For about two hours I stood outside in 15-degree weather shivering, carefully noting who was a Democrat and who was an Independent. I wondered whether my time was being properly used. I wondered why the local committee had not already done this.

While we were driving back to Concord, I began to understand that the McCarthy campaign was not the property of Senator McCarthy or the people of New Hampshire. If I was willing to stand in the cold, freezing wind and take down information, it was my campaign. The campaign was no more than the people who worked in it. With this realization, we decided to stay, at least until the New Hampshire election. Beyond that we made no plans. Maybe McCarthy would withdraw if he got very few votes. We were only peripherally aware that Wisconsin was the next state to have a primary. So with this decision the staff acquired two more graduate students, one in home economics, the other a sinologist.

I should clarify what the word "staff" meant at that time in New Hampshire. A staff member was essentially anyone who worked during the week. He prepared materials to be used on weekends, then supervised the people who came on weekends. To be on the staff one only had to come to the office during the week, even part of the week. If he arrived on Thursday, he would know enough about procedures on Friday to supervise people on the weekend, so he was a staff member. The concept of staff involved no financial distinction. The full-time workers thought it likely that if the campaign got money they would be fed; but that would come only when the wallets grew thin and the stomachs empty.

The original staff was composed almost entirely of graduate students. There were a few undergraduates, but generally their class schedules prevented them from spending great amounts of time with the campaign.

The office was headed by Sam Brown, a former National Student Association official, who knew a great number of students. He was registered at Harvard Divinity School to keep his student standing. He kept his hair at a perfect length: long enough so that he could pass as a student radical but not so long that he would be mistaken for a hippy. He had a myriad of problems to solve—an interesting and frustrating one being that he was apparently too young (twenty-four years old) to rent cars from hesitant New Hampshire businessmen.

John Barbieri, a recent Peace Corps returnee, was Sam's assistant. The Peace Corps had given him considerable experience in organizing and leading people. John was under substantial personal pressure during the New Hampshire campaign. He was scheduled for induction into the army the day after the election. For him the campaign was a brief attempt to stop the carnage in Vietnam before he had to join it. Fortunately for him and his country, he failed his physical and he remained a crucial worker throughout the campaign. John had originally gone to New Hampshire to help Romney, but the Republicans did not have a job for him, seeing no place for student-oriented workers in political campaigns. Students were thought, in January and February of 1968, to be indifferent, incapable, and ineffective in "constructive" politics. The Romney campaign was doubly uninterested in him because of his neatly trimmed goatee, even though it was not accompanied by an unusually long haircut. Romney probably never learned that he lost a top-rate political organizer. (Some of the secretaries and receptionists in Romney's headquarters dated McCarthy workers. When Romney dropped out, they too joined us.)

Our staff included Dianne Dumonofsky, an attractive blonde graduate student in English from Yale. She telephoned New England colleges to recruit volunteers and found people in Concord to supply housing for the full-time workers. She had never before done this kind of organizational work and was occasionally flustered by the rapidity of the campaign's growth. When I rather casually urged a friend to come to Concord and assured him we would house him, she was terrified; not only were we out of beds, but some of the hosts were leaving for vacations, so there were fewer beds than usual. She quickly learned, of course, that the expansion of the campaign could not be limited by the number of beds we could find.

Another crucial member of the staff at that time was Joel Feigonbaum, a graduate student at Cornell. He too had never been involved in campaigning, but he had a clear idea of how to canvass, how to prepare for canvassing, and what it all meant. He recruited many of his friends from Cornell to come to New Hampshire and later organized canvassing in Hartford, Connecticut, and Portland, Oregon. His wife, a social worker, had experience in working with people and helped make the office run smoothly.

From Yale University's Law School came several full-time workers. There was a program called "Yalie of the Week," in which a different student came up on Monday and worked for a whole week. This supplemented the full-time staff during the week and was a tremendous help. One of these Yalies was Mike Rice, who with his wife Kate had canvassed in Lowndes County, Alabama. Another staff worker was a graduate student in philosophy at MIT. Large and handsome, he looked like either a football player or a rising TV executive, not a philosopher.

He worked quietly and diligently with rare interruptions for food or sleep. But after the New Hampshire campaign, he left. He feared that electoral politics simply could not achieve the radical changes he believed America needed.

There were a few staff members who were not graduate students. A beautiful and dedicated Wellesley College contingent included Belle Huang, a stunning girl of Chinese descent, who coordinated volunteer workers in the office. The press, always looking for a gimmick, was disappointed to learn she was not Vietnamese; I, wanting to practice my Mandarin conversation, was disappointed that she could not speak Chinese. She was president of the student council at Wellesley and felt obligated to return to school during the Indiana campaign. Also, she wanted to graduate so she could go to Harvard Medical School in the fall. Another gem from Wellesley was Bobbie Kramer. She went back occasionally to take exams, but campaigned full time through the California effort. To make up incompletes, she went to summer school and then joined us in Chicago to help for the last week. Katie Odin was another member of the full-time office staff. She came all the way from Portland, Oregon, to work in the New Hampshire primary. A Berkeley graduate and a social worker, she would not admit for a week that she was not a graduate student. Her job was to find church basements and other places around the state to house students who arrived to help. We got Katie on television as much as possible as a spokesman for the young staff. She was so beautiful, so charming, and so exuberant, we felt conservative America could never reject her.

For an advance staff there was one Yale law student, Eric Schnapper. At that time we didn't realize that politicians needed lots of people to precede their visits to make sure all the arrangements were perfect. Actually, there was no press to interest in McCarthy's trip and there were not too many arrangements to make. Schnapper did, however, try to get maps of the areas beforehand so the Senator would not get lost driving around the back roads of New Hampshire. Schnapper was one of the few McCarthy workers to go to the Kennedy campaign.

The counterpart to staff was volunteer. Of course everyone was a volunteer in the strict sense, but in New Hampshire volunteer meant part-time worker. Volunteers were the college students who came to work for the weekend. On weekends, the office quickly became cluttered with sleeping bags, portable typewriters, textbooks, and term papers in various stages of completion. The most important item of logistical support was a record player and hard-rock records. Each weekend meant a new set of records. After a week of the Beatles, Country Joe and the Fish came as a welcome change in office environment. By the next weekend, everyone was overjoyed at having The Grateful Dead for a week.

At that time there were two major projects for volunteers. The first was to put out a mailing to all Democrats and Independents in New Hampshire. During the week, we philosophers, theologists, sinologists, economists, lawyers, and a few people with only bachelor's degrees all tore mailing labels, pasted them on envelopes, stuffed, sealed, stamped, and sorted by zip code. When masses of volunteers came for the weekend, we learned how to supervise. We did appropriate time and motion studies, developed executive training programs, analyzed the relationship between endurance and commitment, and moved cartons, tables, and chairs. We had seminars in folding, advanced stuffing, elementary sealing, and interdisciplinary stamping. All this work was geared to the throbbing rhythm of the hard-rock records. Unfortunately the professors devoted too much energy to the development of student-faculty relationships and ignored analysis of the final product. A butcher's scale revealed that it was slightly overweight, and the post office would not accept that extra fraction of an ounce without extra postage. Not being able to afford that, we developed new courses in advanced unstuffing, resealing, and stamp saving.

We also sent some of the mailing materials to Boston for assembly. A Yale law student, one of the original Yalies of the Week who would come to Concord for a whole week, became a truck driver and took material to the intellectual center of New England, Harvard University. Dozens of students who could not come to New Hampshire for an entire weekend did similar work.

At the same time a small group of weekend volunteers experimented with another method of getting votes. We tried to canvass. Rosann and I went out with an experimental canvassing group to talk with the people of New Hampshire on the weekends of February 17 and 24. It was a chilling experience in many ways. First, it was cold and windy. This problem was partly overcome with long underwear, heavy clothing, and boots. Sunglasses helped reduce the intense glare from the snow. Second, people often had huge dogs near their houses, whose barks replaced doorbells in alerting the household to the approach of a visitor. Only courage and careful checking of the length of tethers helped here. The reception by the voters was also chilly. There were numberless excuses for not talking with us. The people had guests, were eating, were getting ready for a funeral, or had sickness in the house. This kind of coldness could not be combated with gloves; it needed quick response. One man would not let me in his house because he was hanging wallpaper and his house was a mess. He immediately agreed with me when I observed that the country was in a mess also. I didn't get in the house but did give him McCarthy literature and a smile. The voters with whom we did speak in Hudson, New Hampshire, were aware of McCarthy's candidacy and knew that there would be a primary. They were frustrated by the trends of the country and wanted change. They knew they wanted new leadership and an end to the Vietnam war but could not make up their minds whether they wanted immediate withdrawal or military victory. The means did not matter as much as the immediacy of the exit. Thus several voters were carefully weighing McCarthy and Wallace, considering them to be similar, not at opposite ends of a political spectrum.

During the first attempts at canvassing the only adult interested in hearing about it was a stocky bald man who said he was a motivational analyst hired by the campaign. He carefully discussed with us our encounters with the voters and explained why the voter could see McCarthy as similar to Wallace. He suggested ways of explaining to the voter how the war was related to tax increases and inflation. He urged us to try conversing with the voter instead of merely offering literature.

I was thankful for his help at the time, but later he tried to take over operational control of the Manchester, New Hampshire, campaign, putting out literature, issuing press releases, and commandeering manpower, all without checking with anyone. This was too much, and finally he was actually shadowed by staff members to make sure he would not further harm the campaign. He showed up in Indiana working for Kennedy, to the relief (and joy) of some of the staff.

Despite the weather and the dogs, canvassing was fun. I enjoyed meeting the voters and the local McCarthy supporters in Hudson. Dorothy Spaulding, our local contact, insisted on feeding a group of fifteen canvassers. Eight of us stayed at her house one Saturday night so we could get an early start Sunday morning. Such enthusiastic assistance assured us that Mc-Carthy had some support beyond the campuses. There was, of course, no way of precisely measuring the impact of the canvass, but it seemed better than doing nothing, so canvassing emerged as a major part of the campaign. When over three hundred students came all the way from Washington D.C. by bus for the four-day Washington's Birthday holiday, it was clear that manpower would be available for mass canvassing on a scale never previously imagined. We could canvass the whole state.

Not only were there many canvassers; they were unbelievably enthusiastic. They would stay up all night preparing maps and then canvass the next day. Not even sub-zero temperatures or snow storms could keep them from voters' doors.

I was concerned that the time of people coming such long distances be used most efficiently and so assumed responsibility for making the technical preparations for canvassing. I developed a technique for routing canvassers by making file cards for all Democratic and Independent voters, alphabetizing them by street, grouping them into geographically compact units The cards were accompanied by a map of streets in the neighborhood. My nickname became "map man" because I made maps. I kept this job for the entire New Hampshire campaign. It was not an exciting one, but it was necessary in the same way that the Department of Sanitation must plan routes for its trucks.

I was also in charge of procuring maps from the state highway department. To avoid alienating the man in the state office building who supplied the maps, I carefully sent over different attractive girls to ask for them. They wore no buttons, but the map reproduction room soon knew that only we (not LBJ, Romney, or Nixon) were planning a large-scale grass-roots organizing effort. The man was proud of his efficient blueprint copying machine on which the maps were made, so the girls were briefed to ask questions about how the machine worked. Their job was to get maps, not to radicalize him. He and I developed a relationship of mutual respect, based on our knowledge and use of the state highway department maps. We discussed the fine points of scaling, lettering, dating, and filing. He dropped in at our headquarters one evening as a visiting professional to see my workshop and discover how we cut up the maps, duplicated them, and marked out routes.

I and my helpers worked in the basement of the headquarters. It was dark but warm because the furnace heated it directly and there were no windows. We had no telephone, no noisy meetings, and no shouting (which was the only intra-office memo we knew of). For furniture, we built tables out of old doors and scraps of plywood. To cover the stone walls, I hung maps of various cities of New Hampshire we were canvassing. A flashlight was near the stairs for use when the fuses blew. Newsmen coming from the quiet carpeted offices of Nixon were unprepared to believe that we too had a political campaign.

I quickly became a specialist, concerned only with maps and not with other preparations for canvassing. My interest in the problems of literature was marginal. The canvassers were to go out with packets of several flyers enclosed in a tabloid-size newspaper-style circular that had press reprints. Careful prepackaging was necessary; the cold wind, numbed fingers, and clumsy gloves made it impossible for a canvasser to carry and assemble different pieces of literature at each door. We wanted these packets made up before the canvassers came, but somehow the components were never available until about 3:00 a.m., Saturday, just a few hours before they would be distributed. So usually a crew of volunteers who arrived early Friday evening went to bed early, to arise in the predawn when the truck brought the literature. Sam Brown and John Barbieri both wanted to be present when any work was done. The result was that neither slept during the weekends. I saw no sense in this form of masochism, purging, masculinity proof, or whatever it was and simply ignored the making of literature packets.

.   .   .

.... Throughout the campaign we found that the young people were much happier working in other states than in their home communities. Exceptional staff members in several states would not function at home. College students who would never canvass near the campus would charter buses for hundreds of miles. Several factors contributed to this phenomenon. At home people have friends and social obligations that interfere with political work. Campaigning, all friends are doing the same thing. Totally dedicated, diligent work was the normal way of relating to friends. Doing a good job was a social obligation, not a bothersome chore. More important, the young people working in other states were never considered children. They went into the field and were treated as adults, not as Mr. So-and-So's little girl or boy. They usually had political and financial resources from the campaign to back up this standing. They could produce canvassers as promised; they could obtain literature; they could influence the activities of the Senator on a visit. They could often get money from the national campaign.

These full-time volunteers were a source of great strength to us. One of the most dedicated people to hitchhike west* was Pat Jenkins, who wore a leg brace. In Los Angeles she answered telephones and took messages for Curt Gans and Sam Brown. She did this work politely and accurately for about sixteen hours a day, never leaving her assignment. Her dedication enabled Gans and Brown to function much more efficiently, and they were extremely thankful to her for making it to California, not accepting our decision.

*Ed. note: To California for the primary there.

17. Robert S. Moga:
A Voice from
Middle America

"Voices from the Silent Majority"
by JOSEPH C. GOULDEN

*And so—to you, the great silent majority of my fellow Americans—
I ask for your support. Let us be united for peace. Let us also be
united against defeat. Because let us understand: North Vietnam
cannot defeat or humiliate the United States. Only Americans
can do that.*
—President Nixon to the nation, Nov. 3, 1969

We were riding through downtown Aurora, Illinois, in William G. Mitchler The Real Estate Man's brand-new Cadillac automobile. "Damn it, Mitchler," said Bobby Moga The Township Supervisor, "if you ever get into politics you're going to have to sell this thing. Who'd vote for a man who rides around in a car this big?" "I earned this car," replied William G. Mitchler, whose shoulders filled about half the front seat. "Give me a choice between the office and the car, and I think I'll keep on driving around."

Moga twisted sidewise in the seat to talk to me, the visiting journalist, in Aurora in quest of Mr. Nixon's Silent Majoritarians. Over the phone a few nights earlier I had explained to Moga that I had obtained, from Herb Klein's office in the White House, a sampling of letters written to the President after the November 3 speech, that I intended to do an article on some of the persons who wrote them, and that I would like to visit him.

The attention pleased Moga, a stocky fellow of thirty-seven with thinning hair, a firm grip, and a metal American flag in his lapel. "You mean that Mr. Nixon The President actually sat down and read my letter?" he asked when I arrived in his office. That I did not know, I said, only that the White House bureaucracy, upon request, disgorged his letter as "representative" of the 400,000-odd received the week following the address. "Think of that," Bobby Moga said. "You write the President, and they listen to you."

Now we were driving through Aurora, and talking about its attitude toward the war. Aurora is forty miles and two counties due west of Chicago, originally farming, now light industrial; population (Chamber of Commerce estimate) 100,000; but still far enough from The City to avoid what Moga called "the kooky stuff." "Most patriotic place in the whole country," Bobby Moga said. He pointed to a hardware store that rambled most the length of a city block. "Fellow there, on patriotic occasions, he furnishes flags for this entire section of the street. Good people here, none of that mess you have in Chicago or New York.

"This is a cute little incident that happened during the Moratorium. We have some of those damned people here, even in a decent town like Aurora. Some get out here from Chicago, some of them are homegrown, those damned hippies. But nobody pays much attention to them.

"Anyway, this guy with greasy long hair and those granny glasses—a ridiculous-looking creep, I get mad just looking at them—anyway, he came into the township building and he started setting up a card table and some signs.

"I got red. God but I got mad. I walked over to him and I didn't even read his sign. I knew what the hell he was all about. I said to him, What's your problem, pal? What's with you, pal? I kept calling him pal every second breath, that's the way to keep those bastards off balance.

"I said to him, You ain't setting up nothin' like that in here, pal, let's get movin', pal.

"Oh, hell yes, he started protesting, he was saying Nazi Germany and civil rights and freedom of speech and how I was no better than a German storm trooper, and I started getting madder.

"I reached out and grabbed him under my left arm—got a good hold on him, just like this"—and Moga turned in the seat and gripped himself under the arm to demonstrate his hold—"and I was holding him real tight, and he was hollering. And with my other arm—my right one, I'm right-handed, too, you know—I picked up his lousy stinking card table and his goddamned sign and I pulled the whole mess right through the door and pitched his ass out on Water Street. Don't bring that sort of crap into this building, pal, and don't make me mad, I told him. That's the only way to handle jerks like that—hustle'm right on outside. I'm not letting any goddamned hippie jerk of a demonstrator use my office for that sort of thing."

·   ·   ·

Bobby Moga was especially pleased that I had come to Aurora on December 8, a Monday. "The combined service clubs are having a luncheon over at the YMCA today commemorating the Jap attack on Pearl Harbor. Let's go over there—it will give you an idea of what a helluva town this is, and how we get together behind the right ideas." Soon I found myself standing in line with several score Aurorans on a basketball court, awaiting a paper plate of fried chicken and stuffed cabbage. Bobby Moga's brother, John, shook my hand and gave me a red plastic comb embossed: **Make Johnny Moga the Plumber Your Plumber.**

Moga tugged at my arm. "Come on. We're putting you at the head table." I insisted I'd just as soon sit among the citizens at the long common tables. "No, no," Moga said, propelling me to the platform and a wooden folding chair next to a Marine major general. "Let's make sure I got your name right from Moga," said the toastmaster. He handed me a slip of paper on which was printed: **Mr. Golden, Representing the White House.**

My first horrified impulse was to snatch away the paper and swallow it. Posing as Captain John Golden, head of the Philadelphia Police Department's homicide squad, and as Joe Dealey, publisher of the *Dallas News,* are stunts I have performed under the impulsiveness of reportorial license, each time capitalizing upon someone's misintroduction. But as an agent of the Nixon Administration—"God no," I said. "I'm just a writer, here to do a story." "But Moga said Herb Klein sent you." "No, no, I got Moga's *letter* from Klein's office. I don't work for Klein." This intelligence disappointed the man, and I thought for a moment I would be sent to the kitchen to eat with the help. A few minutes later he said to four hundred assembled Aurorans: "And also with us at the head table today is Mr. Gordon from Herb Klein's office in the White House." I said something *sotto voce* that brought an alarmed glance from the Marine general, and I continued eating my fried chicken.

The luncheon was the idea of Dr. Stanley Parks, a dentist who is president of the Aurora Navy League, a quasi-official organization which lobbies for bigger Navy appropriations and warns the public against the Soviet naval menace. Parks said he had been questioned "as to why we would want to remember this day; are we trying to open up old wounds?" Something more was involved than honoring 2,400 Americans who died at Pearl Harbor: "We remember that Americans reacted to the shocking attack with a unity that has never been expressed in the history of our country. . . . Americans weren't ashamed to profess their loyalty and their patriotism. . . . *Yes, patriotism stood at a high ebb.*" Now, Parks lamented, "loyalty and patriotism are regarded cynically as being left to the squares, and it is really something 'cool' to criticize and protest. The Constitutional right of dissent has degenerated to an excuse to undermine. From the Senate floor, the college campus, sensationalist picture magazines, and other such media, sanctimonious hypocrites would castigate the men who loyally serve our country. . . ." Rising applause. ("Damnit, let's make sure Senator Percy gets a copy of Doc's speech," I heard a man say later. "Or better yet, let's send Doc to Washington and bring Percy home for a rest.")

Nine Pearl Harbor survivors from Aurora and the vicinity sat at round tables-of-honor with their wives—self-consciously excited about an event almost three decades distant, now revived to bring them unaccustomed attention. Police Captain Alex Puscas spoke for them. How sad it was, Puscas said, to hear taps sounded over soldiers' graves. "Will taps ever be sounded for the last time? Will America ever die? Not so long as its people do as we are doing at this moment—*Remember Pearl Harbor!*"

A local music teacher closed the proceedings with "The Battle Hymn of the Republic," truly a song for all seasons— Andy Williams sang it, agonizingly low and slow, the sad June morning when Bobby Kennedy's body was borne from the heavy gloom of St. Patrick's Cathedral; the Republicans sang it in Miami Beach two months later, then nominated Richard Nixon for the Presidency; now the Silent Majoritarians sang it in anthem rhythm, finding in Mr. Lincoln's song a soulful bond to the American tradition: quasi-religious verses that bring tears to the eyes and send them back to their insurance offices and grain stores and drug counters with the satisfied feeling one gets from a good Methodist sermon or a close football victory.

"These are real people," Bobby Moga said as we left the YMCA. "Did you ever see anything like this in Washington?"

.　　.　　.

Robert R. Moga is classifiable as a Silent Majoritarian solely because until November 1969 he had never undertaken to tell a President of the United States what he thought about a subject. But he has long been an activist. As a Jaycee he originated Keep Illinois Beautiful, a statewide cleanup campaign. But Moga didn't share the chronic Jaycee proclivity for foolishness. At a state convention he was reading a report on his beautification work when Jaycees from East St. Louis trooped in with a giant Budweiser can, hoping their town's famed beer would attract next year's meeting. "I got disgusted. The chairman rapped for order, but nobody would listen. They all stood up and yelled about the beer can. I walked off the platform. That ended it with me and the Jaycees." Aurorans knew Moga as the sometime basketball announcer for a local radio station

—and he says unabashedly he was a good one. Moga dropped into his broadcaster's voice to demonstrate his technique, telling how he described "a scuffle between two colored boys" at a tourney. "Come on, Peaches, give 'em some skin and let's get this show on the road." Moga laughed. "I didn't have to say they were colored . . . everybody knew it when I said it that way . . . folks here were laughing about it for days."

Moga entered politics almost by impulse. Five years ago he was working for an Aurora trucking firm. One morning factory workers were slow unloading one of his trucks, and he went over to speed them along. Moga gave the men cigars and joshed to a bystander that he hoped "the hillbillies"—an Aurora term for Southern immigrants—would work faster. The shop steward, who was also a local elected official, objected to the term and ordered the men off the truck. When Moga returned there was a bitter confrontation. The steward accused Moga of prejudice and called him "a hunky bastard from Pigeon Hill," referring to Moga's Romanian ancestry and the East Aurora neighborhood where he was born. There were no fisticuffs. But Moga made an instant decision: "I'm going into politics, I said. Here was a man whose family had run a goddamned whorehouse—that's where all his money came from—here was this kind of man representing the people of Aurora. The only way to get his kind out of office was for people like me to run for office. So I did." Moga didn't challenge the shop steward directly; what he did was run for County Board, and win handily. (Johnny Moga The Plumber met the steward later at a wedding reception on Pigeon Hill and told him he didn't like the term "hunky bastard." The conversation continued: "You going to leave, and you going to leave now—by the door or through the wall. Now which do you prefer?")

After four years on the County Board—a part-time job—Moga bucked the Republican organization to become Township Supervisor. His principal duty is administering the welfare program, in some of which he takes a personal interest because, as he says, "I'm one of the biggest homeowning taxpayers in East Aurora," paying $1,200 per year on his house. "Animals," Moga calls his welfare clients. "They breed like animals, live like animals; they do things your wife, my wife, wouldn't do." He gave me examples: A caseworker visited a welfare recipient just released from the hospital. "She had to go through this living room where three or four big colored bucks were sitting drinking. I told her never to go in a house like that again. Now there's a case for you—a $360 hospital bill. They ain't a-never gonna pay that—the taxpayers are going to pay it. . . . All they do is take—they never put."

Moga chuckled at his ingenuity in disposing of cases. "We had a woman come in here who had family in Peoria. She wanted money. I asked if the family would take care of her if she got to Peoria, and she said yeah. So I called a gas station and said give her a tank so she could get out of town. That's one we don't worry about no more."

We switched suddenly to the war, for Moga's opinions on proper family conditions, which make welfare anathema, are in large part responsible for his views on Vietnam. Indeed, Moga asserted, the fact that Aurora is heavily Romanian and Hungarian is responsible for the town's militancy. He lowered his voice, as if he didn't want to appear to be indulging in ethnic boasting. "Certain kinds of boys from certain backgrounds are more patriotic than others. They learn to jump at the sound of an order. Discipline. There's discipline in these homes. Percentagewise, of all the Aurora boys in the war, the highest number was from the Hungarian and Romanian communities, Pigeon Hill, where I was raised. The same for the dead—go over to the cemetery, look at the tombstones. Most of the names, Hungarian, Romanian. When a guy is in the trench and the lieutenant blows the whistle and says, Let's go, there's always a percentage that stays behind. Boys with *background* are the ones who go."

We crossed the street to the Woolworth store for coffee. School had ended, and teen-agers crammed the lunch counter. We found stools in the corner.

"Look." Bobby Moga muttered. "Just look at them. You ever see anything like that in your life?"

Pea jackets. A few peace medallions. Natural hairdos on several of the black girls, no bras on several of the white ones. The boys' hair appreciably longer than Moga's thinning locks.

While driving into Aurora that morning from Chicago I listened to a radio station in Gary, Indiana, and jotted down a line from the midmorning commodities report, not knowing how or when I would ever use it: "Slaughter sheep plentiful, pork bellies firm."

. . .

Home. A brick rancher, the driveway curving through the snow to a three-car parking area, basketball goal, and the ice-crusted tracks of a snowplow. "They don't work as good as a shovel, do they?" Moga said. A 36-foot flagpole on the front lawn. "Didn't cost me a thing. I welded it myself, even got the ball and the eagle at the top." Moga stopped. "I hope I'm never in the vicinity of a crowd where somebody burns an American flag." Why? "I don't think I could control myself. I think I'd do something awful to the people—kick the hell out of them, even kill them. I don't think anybody could hold me back."

Joyce Moga, a pretty brunette who smiles and blushes easily, was ironing in the kitchen. We joke about husbands who don't warn they are bringing company home, and about wives who don't like to be caught wearing curlers while they are ironing.

The living room. Family history. Bobby Moga's Uncle Jack was a city policeman whose ferocity alarmed even his colleagues, inclined to end tavern quarrels by banging the relevant heads until the noise ended. "In the old days there were no squad cars. At the end of a shift each officer walked his prisoners to the station house. One snowy morning Uncle Jack was check-ing doors in an alley when he saw an officer with a prisoner fall. Uncle Jack started after the prisoner, and the officer yelled, 'No, Jack, no, he didn't do anything; I slipped and fell.' " Moga smiled. "The policeman knew good and well that Uncle Jack would have killed that prisoner with his bare hands for hitting an officer."

Many of Moga's stories had this undercurrent of violence. The Romanian community once played the Aurora Swedes in baseball, a social event replete with cheering women and kegs of beer behind the screen, and gradually escalating enthusiasm for victory. There was an argument at home plate while Uncle Sam Moga was batting, and he turned and lifted the mask from the Swede catcher. "They had to call an ambulance to haul the

Swede away when Sam finished him," Bobby Moga laughed, as did his eight-year-old son, sitting with us.

Moga's brother Romulus. "Rome, we call him, he was the fifth in a row to have the name." Rome was killed in the Battle of Java Sea in 1942, and a boy brought the telegram on Sunday morning. "We decided to keep the word from Mom until we knew for sure. We did this for two weeks. She heard. There were four Aurora boys on the USS *Houston,* and two of them were killed. She heard from a reporter."

A TV news show from Chicago. Bert Quint of CBS narrates a film of a South Vietnamese soldier putting cigarettes into the mouth of a dead North Vietnamese, clowning and smiling for onlookers and the camera. "That's the sort of thing that shouldn't be shown," Moga said. "It depresses you."

Sources of information on the war? "I read books, magazines, everything, I can't sit down without reading, even on the throne. The car radio, television. No, no books. I don't have time, no. See, I get calls out of the house all the time—people in trouble, that sort of thing. I'm a very busy man, a public official. Why the other night, I got a call from a guy who had been in a stabbing at a club. A Republican committeeman, and I had to take care of it, get him out on recognizance. All sorts of things like that. . . ."

The newspaper in which Bobby Moga and other Aurorans read about the war and Nixon policies is the Aurora Beacon-News, *owned by the Copley Press, Inc., chain. Although the* Beacon *was the first Copley newspaper (Ira C. Copley, sometime colonel, natural-gas entrepreneur and Aurora resident, bought it in 1905) the editorial tone of the fiercely conservative chain is set by the flagship paper, the* San Diego Union, *which Herb Klein edited for ten years. During my visit the* Beacon *was publishing a series on the Moratorium by Francis J. McNamara, longtime staff director of the House Un-American Activities Committee. "The most important fact about the demonstrations," McNamara wrote for the 26 Copley papers and the 340 newspaper clients of the Copley news service, "was the revelation of a weakness in U.S. ability to deal effectively with internal Communist subversion."*

.   .   .

Aurora Downs, a trotting track, celebrated its grand opening that night, and as a township official Bobby Moga had gratis clubhouse tickets—gold cardboard affairs entitling the bearer to free admission, free dinner, free drinks, and free access to pari-mutuel lines where he could bet the contents of his wallet on the horses puffing clouds of steam during warm-ups. Joyce Moga bright-eyed and smiling in a new dress, excited about a night out. Hard-frozen snow pushed into the infield, mid-20s temperatures. "This was a drafty old barn last year," Moga said. "But Johnny my brother put in a new heating system. Feels pretty good, eh? Johnny has it heated up real nice."

Aisle table. Bobby did some politicking. "Hi-ya Hallie boy, any of these horses been telling you how fast they can run?" He bounced around the chair, looking into the stands and behind us for friends and acquaintances and for people who should see him in the honored guest area.

Bobby was serious about the trotters, and after we ordered prime ribs he excused himself for the first of many whispered consultations with assorted insiders. His brother-in-law, a track faithful, had talked to a trainer who knew a jockey and who knew something special about a race. (The horse lost.) "I think all of this is silly," Joyce Moga said. We bet—and lost—the first three races, following faithfully Ambassador Annenberg's form sheets. "Let's use my system," Joyce Moga said, "It makes as much sense." She held her pencil at arm's length above the table and dropped it on the program. "Number Six. Hit it right on the nose. That's our horse." We split a $2 bet. And glorious joy Number Six took a quick lead, led by three lengths at the halfway mark, by four at the three-quarters post, and by five no less than fifty yards from the finish—saliva-blowing, snorting ferocity, but we aurally antiseptic behind the plate glass that kept us snug in the clubhouse. One glimpsed, but could not hear (and thus emphatically feel) the wrrrHACK-kkkkkkk of the crop; muscles and neck veins pulsating in glistening ridges.

Number Six stumbled in the stretch, broke stride, and went from first to seventh quicker than we could moan our disappointment. "Horses," said Joyce Moga. Bobby Moga threw a pile of pari-mutuel slips on the table and we went home.

After midnight I tried to find something to read before going to sleep. The bookcase in the Mogas' guest room contained William Shirer's *Berlin Diary,* a world atlas, a collected works of Shakespeare, the *Dell Crossword Dictionary, The Day Christ Died* by Jim Bishop, *The Exciting Story of the White Sox* (about their pennant year), and the *Handbook of Beauty.* I sat down on the bed and read Bobby Moga's letter again.

> We watched you on television, address the Nation on the Viet-Nam situation. We wholeheartedly support your position, and think that ninety per cent of Americans do too.
>
> Funny thing, I've always considered our young educated people to be the strength of our Nation. Much to everyone's surprise the so called intellectuals strangely enough are a weakness. They can not see the students in Czechoslovakia, trying to tell the world about Russia, and Communism.
>
> I honestly, think that what some of these younger people need, is a callused hand, wheeled by a strict father, or a boot camp Master Sergeant, to bring a full appreciation of our beautiful Country.
>
> Both of my parents, were born in Romania, and when I asked my Dad recently, whether he would like to visit his birth place he said, and I quote "what for, sixty-seven years ago I ran away from that place."
>
> Also, I want to tell you that our family supports you even though, we lost our older brother, in World War II in the Battle of the Java Sea, in 1942. In 1945 another brother was wounded on Okinawa. I myself, served in 1950 to 1952 in the Korean War.
>
> I can guarantee you that our family is ready, and will always be ready to fight for our beautiful Flag.
>
> > Yours very truly,
> > Robert R. Moga
> > Township Supervisor